WESTWARD HOES

I0550492

EDITED BY
RICH BOTTLES JR.
GARY LEE VINCENT

Burning Bulb
PUBLISHING

Westward Hoes
Edited By **Rich Bottles Jr.** and **Gary Lee Vincent**

Burning Bulb Publishing
P.O. Box 4721
Bridgeport, WV 26330-4721
www.BurningBulbPublishing.com

First printing.

Edition ISBN

Paperback 978-0-61575-958-6

First edition.
Printed in the United States of America.

Library of Congress Control Number: 2013932696

CONTENTS

i

FOREWORD

"I love it! It is wild with adventure!"

Those were the final words of outlaw Henry Starr, who is said to have robbed more banks than the James-Younger Gang and the Doolin-Dalton Gang combined, as he described life in the Old West (shortly before he was shot to death in a gunfight in Arkansas).

People from across the world have always been fascinated by the Old West, especially people who have never had to endure the lawless, isolated, unsanitary, territorialistic conditions of the true American Frontier. From 19th Century dime novels to today's Hollywood blockbuster movies, writers and artists have expressed their personal visions of how the West was won, lost or drawn. And sometimes those visions got weird.

According to our friends at Wikipedia, "Weird West is a literary sub-genre that combines elements of the Western with another literary genre, usually horror, occult, or fantasy." Pulp magazines and comic books, such as DC's "Weird Western Tales," helped popularize the concept of the genre, while more contemporary examples include writers, such as, Joe R. Lansdale (Dead in the West), William S. Burroughs (The Place of Dead Roads) and Stephen King (Dark Tower), and recent films like "Jonah Hex" and "Cowboys and Aliens."

But if you're looking for the unintentionally weird or the inadvertently bizarre fictionalization of the Old West, you have to look to the proverbial Spaghetti Western. With the help of Spanish technical advisors, Italian filmmakers in the mid-1960's decided to produce their own interpretations of the iconic Hollywood Western movie. And once director Sergio Leone made a fistful of dollars with his first production, he went on to make a few dollars more with his second film. These movies weren't just popular in Europe, they were widely popular in the west, and as a result, hundreds of so-called Spaghetti Westerns were made before the Italians finally moved on to a better-suited film genre, affectionately named "Trash Films," in the 1980's.

The basic plot line of the most familiar Spaghetti Westerns is as follows: Mysterious stranger rides into town; townsfolk mistrust the stranger, especially the outlaws in town; stranger tries to ingratiate himself with the locals, although his motives are suspect; stranger is mistreated; stranger seeks vengeance.

You'll see many of these Spaghetti Western plot devices in the book you now hold in your hands, but there is an even more common theme present in iconic Western fiction, which we've decided to shamelessly capitalize on: The independent, feisty, extroverted, back-stabbing, heart-of-gold prostitute (e.g., sporting woman, soiled dove, fallen angel, scarlet lady, painted cat, nymph du prairie, whore).

This "Westward Hoes" anthology was conceived after the publication of "The Big Book of Bizarro" (heretofore known as the BBoB). The BBoB was a gargantuan undertaking, selecting and editing 57 strange stories into a 538-page, two-pound tome. The BBoB was well-received and many of the readers and contributors asked if Burning Bulb Publishing was going to do a sequel.

Considering the time and financial resources exhausted by producing the BBoB, Burning Bulb Publishing was reluctant to repeat the effort, at least on the same scale. Thankfully, the fruity contacts we established via the BBoB within the tri-state loop of West Virginia, Ohio and Pennsylvania helped bring our Western Bizarro project to fruition.

The Pittsburgh area authors represented in the BBoB have been our strongest supporters and it's hard to turn down such folks when they say they want to work with us again. Thus, this Western

Bizarro anthology was an invitation-only collaboration. No offense is intended to the other great international authors involved with the BBoB, but Burning Bulb Publishing wanted to try to keep this current anthology "not so big" (but still plenty bizarre none-the-less).

So why is Wol-vriey included in this more localized Bizarro anthology? Well, because he's one of those Nigerian pirates you've been hearing so much about on TV, and his crew would not release a cargo ship commissioned by Amazon until he had assurances that his work would be included in this Western anthology. Besides, Wol-vriey is one of our favorite bizarro authors.

Enjoy.

Rich Bottles Jr.
April 1st, 2013

"They saw me, those reckless seekers of beauty and in a night I was famous." – Lillie Langtry

DEMONEYE
BY DAVID J. FAIRHEAD

*David J. Fairhead was first published in **The Big Book of Bizarro** with his apocalyptic tale **The Fall**. Also the writer of the comic book series **WZWA** (World Zombie Wrestling Association) in association with Jon Towers and Stigmata Studios (www.jonnyaxx.com). David is host of the Radio Podcast show **Kettle Whistle Radio**, working with co-host Heather Taddy of A&E's **Paranormal State** fame, where they talk Horror, Comics, Music and interview writers, directors, actors and musicians. Check them out at **RedHorseRadio.com**. David is currently completing his second novel, **CHARLIE: A Child's Tale of Terror** and another novel, the Demon Epic **In the Dark**. You can also look up David Fairhead and/or Kettle Whistle Radio on Facebook. He grew up on Long Island and currently resides with his wife Denise and dog Teddy in Pittsburgh.*

When people ask me if I know fear, or whether or not I am scared at our current state in this damn sandy abyss they call Texas, I have to say no. I'm the alpha male; I'm the one to fear. But I had to learn that. My hair shot gray at the early age of twenty five, and it tends to hang low on the shoulder below my sombrero... can't hide it... it shields the back of the neck when the sun is beating down. In some towns I've come across, they pick up on the fact rather quick-like: that I'm quicker with my Colt than most riders can pull their dick out for a piss after a long stretch of sand. This is true. Ha-ha… Not saying much really.

But over in Caravass Pass, that town that you may or may not have come across in your travels, there was a little tavern called Paven Stone, coincidentally where I did some residency, and where I came across some thick-headed wrangler type who just did not see fit to leave me the hell alone.

I had been in the town for two weeks, but seldom could I stand more than one swig of their rotgut whiskey. Town was full, mostly of passers-by. But along the walls of the cavernous rocky shale stone was this slit of a town. Hot times during the gold rush, but now sex and drunkards make me envious of the hard-asses that made their cash and got the hell out.

Then this dolt walks up to me after my first sip of that foggy glass of swill, knocks my sombrero off, mistaking me for a Mexican. Mistake either way, mind you! Those bucks can fight! But old drunken puss, with his flab and limp jab (he swung and missed me), had true gray in his beard and not much else.

But my hat came off… and the gray hair fell to my shoulders, and then the giveaway… My shock of black hair on top that fell over my left ear showed itself. You see, this may appear as a weakness to blokes like this old fart pick'n a fight with me.

"WHO'RE you… looks like you got some yellow-belly in you…" he muttered, grabbing the attention of all those around. Even the teenager playing the piano stopped his jovial tune. The bordello girls that had swooned about the young piano player, well, quit their swooning. The bartender walked somewhere I couldn't see. Card players turned… eh… you get the damn picture!

I stood taller than the old drunken coot. He was new in town, and apparently still human, if he did not know who Dekker Collins, the Dead Shot, was. "No qualms with you sir, but that black streak I got on top is the only part of me that ain't scared no more. Now, can we finish our drinks?" I said calmly, looking down on the shaggy fellow.

2

I never had to touch the Colts at my sides, 'cause when he went to swing again, I had him by the elbow and broke it the way that elbows don't bend. There was the usual shout and fall to the ground. Bobby Kin, last of the deputies in town, came over to attempt carrying the man out of the Paven Stone Tavern. He struggled at his job, not fit to be a deputy or any law enforcement for any town. But this was Caravass Pass, and trouble came here 'cause trouble wanted to make a name for itself and strip me of my insidious reputation: Dead Shot Dekker.

"Come on Dekker, did-ja have to break it?... Doc is still sewing up the Brewster kid. He doesn't have time..." Skinny Bobby Kin whined as usual, helping the old angry coot out the door.

I could have said something typical like..."And that's what you get...." or "maybe next time he'll think twice..." Ugh... makes my stomach twitch at such bravado when things are creeping out of the earth and nipping up settlers like... Oh, dammit... "fish in a barrel..." There I said it!

Deborah came up to me after flirting with the teenage piano kid. She thought she had her money for the night, like I had a swig in a jar. She didn't. The kid with the braids through his long brown hair, and suspenders, I think they called Weaver, was half Injun and completely not interested in the beauty that is Deborah. She was clean too. Not all the girls that worked upstairs of Paven Stone kept themselves as well. You could not blame them when you considered the clientele. I monopolized on that situation.

You see, all it would take is one time for you, one chance to see what they are capable of, and you too would be as calloused as those that lived in Caravass Pass. Most locals stay because of me. Those that leave, we don't usually hear hide of again.

"New one came in yesterday, Dekker. A pretty one. Tall like you but blond. He's upstairs with Loreen right now." Deborah's dark brown hair was up in a bun on the back of her head, and curly up top and front. She seldom let it down, always ready for a brawl.

3

I liked her. She wore a pink puffy skirt with a tight white top to it that held her bosom at bay. Oh hell, they all did! God, how I love them whores!!

She sat down next to me, smelling of powder and some soap that the Injun kid Weaver had sold her. It was nice, compared to the whiskey before me. "Guess I need to turn off the house whiskey for a bit, huh?" I said knowingly, placing my hat back on my head. GOD, I could feel the new wrinkles on my own dry skin. Skin stretched tight on my face, but not as tight as our friends that rolled into town smelling like burnt chili and molten flesh.

"Did he turn into town looking for me? Make any mention?"

"Not yet. His eyes are wild though. Looks right through me and poor Loreen. Hope he doesn't go for the full blown ending with her. I've grown attached," Deborah said, motioning for Ole Clacky to bring down my private stock. Bald, long-eyed, sad and not much for conversation, we referred to the old man behind the bar as Ole Clacky because the bad smelling evil ones had torn his right leg off at the knee a couple of years before I even knew this half-assed town existed. His peg leg made a clackity clack sound. Funny…

Ole Clacky brought me my jar. I poured the whiskey into my now empty glass, fogged with resin, and downed it quick, warming my belly and my smile for the lovely Deborah.

What a good girl. GOOD GIRL. She slipped me a rolled up piece of paper, immediately getting my gratitude with a kiss on her upper cheek. She works fast! It's always good to be ready.

***

So, let me explain something. And I'll keep it current. No use for back story. Like I said, I ain't scared, now; I was scared THEN, when I watched my family die… HELLS, I went gray overnight!!! So when I first rolled into town with my black and white Shetland (good story where I acquired that ride, but little Stoney only carried my gear. I was too kind to ride him), it was goin' on dusk. I could see the cavern that sheltered Caravass Pass from the glassy dunes where I was traveling, for quite a ways, even with the glare. The desert cool was setting in, and I had come from just more of the same trouble elsewhere. Bored with it now, but when I saw those damn X's in the dark standing upright I knew it was time that I stop. You see, when you learn the things I did, early in the game, you feel responsible to do what you can... as much as possible.

I pulled Stoney over another hill, which may have been a mile from the town itself. The sun was on its way to its desert pillow, yet shimmered just enough so that I could see the dozen or so bodies (some fresh) hanging on the wooden planks shaped in "X" fashion. This was their way of showing off, and an attempt to keep the likes of me out.

I stepped forward.

So the land had cracked and given way to evil, like a boil popping and spreading its fine wine, staining the sand with blood. Funny to say, the tide was turning. Maybe starting out in the plains, where everyone was armed comfortably, was a poor choice!! Ha-ha... But not so easy mind you, they are cunning and merciless. Standing there looking at their methodology will remind a man what needs to be done. And what they have done to my own family.

The human casing that houses the demons becomes bonier, harder, like an exoskeleton, and bones poke through like weapons. Most have yellow eyes, long and moonlike, only shining at night while in a feeding frenzy. Their teeth get sharp, growing out the old human teeth only when need be. As I have witnessed, it takes a long time for their teeth to look human-like again. And as I said, their numbers are diminishing, so they like to stay incognito as long as possible.

So, the day I arrived at Caravass Pass, it just so happens that one young boy, who was posted on those "X"s that day, was Deborah's young brother Harris. He was only fourteen. They enjoy

5

using the hard shell of their nails like claws to poke into the temples and pull out the arteries and veiny stuff, the way bird beaks nab grub worms. All the while, the poor slobs are kept alive, and one or more of these possessed human carcasses peel the straws of life free from the skin and suck down the life fluid that God gave us all. The screams go all night usually, so the town can hear their beloved's final throes.

AND they look like you and me… for the most part.

Hideous.

If you talk to the Indian tribes, they will tell you that they saw the spirits come through the larger canyon cracks in the earth, those holes in the Earth that seem to have the most exposed surface area out West. The Indians know to stay away, so the pickins were weak. Human bodies don't hold up too well with all that malicious intent and physical ability that the demons have.

So I'm here to trim the numbers down a piece even more-like.

Sometimes it feels like peeling briars from a bush. However, I have an edge now.

***

"Loreen's screaming…. Ms. Deborah!!" that Injun Weaver kid yelled as he came running up to us. I could hear Ole Clacky grab his rifle from under the bar. "UPSTAIRS!!!"

Deborah ran behind the bar to the staircase as I got my boots upright.

"NO…Dekker. Stay. Let's keep the game rolling," she said, pointing at me before disappearing up the staircase behind the bar.

I had to respect her business. She was in charge of twenty odd women, and most were still alive, so breaking the chain would lead to... Well, I always said, "STICK WITH THE ORIGINAL PLAN," so I do.

There was some thumping upstairs, I heard a woman or two gasp, and then someone was "thunking" rider boots rather hard,

6

down the stairs. Hand's ready, I could smell him before he rounded the bottom of the staircase… burnt chili and molten flesh.

He was taller than me, thin wisps of blond hair to his chest, face long with the skull peeking through. Those blue eyes were big rounded almonds, which I knew would turn that lantern light yellow in the moon light. Luckily, I had dispatched with the contents of the roll of paper that Deborah had given me before she ran up to check on Loreen.

Ugh… there was a smear of blood on the right corner of his mouth matching his right palm. I had hoped he had not killed Loreen. These beasts like to torture more than kill. Killing is not their only game. To simply kill would provide no satisfaction, and one less shell to crawl up into, ya' know? They do have a penchant for the blood and flesh, a lust that cannot be harnessed with the strongest of mesh.

Oh damn, the smell of his dark brown long coat was that of a cattle carcass that was pecked by carrion crawlers for a week. The inside of the tavern was dense with the scent of this lanky bitch of a man while he seated himself next to me! He put his rifle on the bar.

"Dekker Collins? Dead Shot Dekker?" he smiled through human teeth shaped like horses' teeth, square and ready to fall out when he needed to show some real choppers.

"Dirty Smoked Chili man?" I harassed, smirking wildly.

He smiled back, tipping his brown hat. They love a challenge. That's all they got for their little time they have in the plain of the living. "Game time. Smoking too many of my friends. You good? You that good?" its voice rattled like gravel down a washboard.

I swigged down my second glass of my own hooch. It eased me into good spirits. "Good enough for you, and whoever you got, stinky."

"Marvelous."

His thin gray lips showed his horse grin of teeth as he got up from the stool. I smiled back over my shoulder while he walked away. Sure he could have whirled around and tried to smoke me then and there, but I knew already that he would not.

Everyone was already outside the Paven Stone when I set foot on the gravelly sand. I nodded to old Stoney across the way, tied to his post at the Sheepskin trader shop. (Did we really need that? I never got so cold that I had to wear that shit). Poor pony sort of knew about what was to follow, though I doubt he had any hearing left after the last two towns we had wandered to. Lots of rifle fire power on those goes! But not a one had my edge.

The whiskey hit me harder than usual… worried me for a bit. Maybe three large glasses was too much? Yep. The demon posse always thinks you're too drunk to fight, and even will tell you on occasion that their boss downstairs supplies such spirits to make us weak. Gift of tolerance may or may not help the old gunfighter.

It did me good.

Just like their tolerance for blood, violent sex and ripping flesh know no bounds, but fills them with pleasure.

So, Mr. Tall-and-Smokey-Stench was there on the other end of town, and approaching. Only I could see the bright yellow of his eyes, like pools of gold; and with that, my focus carried on, breaking through thin dead mucousy cornea. Thwap... thwap... the sound it made in my mind's eye, while I poked into the gray matter being puppeteered by evil. That was when I could really see. NOW, I was in his gray matter, the fool. Another dead eye fool! He had others with him. Five of them lay in wait. The closest were behind a wagon to my left about eight paces.

"I BELIEVE IN A FAIR FIGHT, SMOKED CHILI MAN! NOW, GET YOUR BUDS OUT FROM HIDING BEHIND THAT…" I motioned to the wagon. The demon's credibility was shot, and he stopped walking. Pride makes up for their lack of hygiene.

He snarled, glanced to the two henchmen with rifles to emerge. And they did, and down they went, in two shots from one of my colt's chambers. Two men with beards, dressed in black, snarling

8

through their demon teeth, had just received brand new orifices in their skulls.

My smelly lanky friend at the other end was in disbelief that I had drawn and downed them. The edge... I knew he had no plan to draw at that moment. Back to focus.

"THREE PACES DEKKER COLLINS... and..." it snarled, already its human teeth were dripping down its chin, while steel needles poked their way through. Eyes, yellow.

"OK... back to basics... I'm good on three..."

I knew when he would move, I knew the angle, I knew to inch one step to the right, and I also knew that when we drew, this creature would have a colt drilled fresh through his noggin. Done.

Made a nice sound though! This bud had a thick skull!

There were cheers, but I was already blowing four more shots above the other Saloon, down the way where two more of his cronies had rifles at the ready pointing over the fenced-in porch. Got 'em. One fell to the sand, bones broken. I had missed his head, so he was lurching on one leg, dragging toward me. BLAMO! His head went backward and flying hunks of hair went out the back! That one felt good. Now, earlier, old Stinky Chili man's gray matter had also informed me there was one more outside the bank, in the dark behind some crates by the door. Oh Lucifer in the grass!! He had drawn on me before I could turn. Lost track of him... dead Dekker!

But no sir! Bobby Kin, that skinny bastard, had come up behind him and blew his head to shards of chalk and hair.

"How'd you know, Bobby?" I asked him, turning around.

"I grabbed a shot of your hooch on the way out. I'm the law..." he smiled riley. "Got to do my bit for the team now and then."

I nodded, thankful, but not terribly happy. I mean, yeah, Bobby Kin stole my thunder a bit, but there was more to it than that.

I ran back into the Paven Stone and up the stairs. It smelled of sex, musty wood and dead flesh... demon flesh. Deborah was outside of Loreen's room. The pretty little dark-skinned lady was dead on her bed, blue dress soaked with her own fluid; that which the creature had not finished apparently. He had pulled the veins from her right wrist, underneath, where it is soft, straight out about a foot, and sucked her like a straw in a child's malt.

"I should have known... I should have known..." Deborah cried in my arms while a dozen or so other girls gathered in the hallway to see. "Loreen gave me the roll of paper after their second... go around town earlier..."

What Deborah told me was that this bloke I killed outside was a repeat performer today - and Loreen managed to dig some of his skin under her fingernails for me. A good bit actually, and these things enjoy pain as much as they like to give it. He went for the happy ending with Loreen. Not good. But she did her part.

***

I remember how Weaver cried that night. The kid had a crush on Loreen, like I did for Deborah. That's tough on a kid. Dunno if we'd hear much piano after that.

You want to know how I came to "see" things as I do? My edge? You guessed by now, silly, I'm sure you did.

As I write this down for you, I had just had some of my hooch. Demoneye we call it. Weaver, Bobby Kin and even Ole' Clacky call it that, but only in certain circles.

I'm gonna label it Dekker Collins. But we'll see.

There was this horrible incident a while back, before Caravass Pass, when I called on my first lady of the night. Some place in Rushdale, Arizona. It was quite the digs! Beautiful girls everywhere! Some clothed, some not... some on tables, while a crazed group of band mates strummed multiple banjos, a piano and some washboard device... it made a ruckus and the place was packed. FOUR BARTENDERS!!! Now that's some drinking! My family had been gone for a while, and other than my Stoney, I traveled with this Cedric Bodnatsen guy. Tall and lanky, like that demon you just heard of. They shared the same long blond hair (that's what made me think of my old riding pal, Cedric!), but this guy was deadly with just about any weapon you gave him… and funny as all hell! He had campfire stories that made your skin crawl and your guts burst with laughter. Just don't get too personal, or out-do him in any way, 'cause then you'd lose your traveling buddy. We found each other in a tavern like this, months before; got drunk, had laughs and stuck together. He knew a lot about the demon epidemic and did not blame the Indians as some had, with their magic. He joked sometimes and said his own evil ways may have conjured up the depths of hell!! Oh that Cedric… killer of comedy sometimes. Miss him.

Anyways… we were eyeing up our own women that night. He picked some scrawny blonde thing with scraggly hair and smelled like yesterday's rotten potatoes. Dunno what that was about, but Cedric had said she reminded him of someone a lifetime ago. So upstairs they went after the money was exchanged. I followed a red-headed harpy up the stairs. These were big stairs, with flocks of cowpokes and busty young ladies goin' to and fro. So she did not see me follow her. Young, in her twenties, this one I stalked, with her long red hair to her waist, dark brown eyes, and a maroon skirt, with white underall leggings. A bit shorter than me, I took to liking her immediately. She had clothes on the whole time, so the mystery was the GET!

She turned and smiled, stopping short in front of a door, which led, more than likely, to her temporary quarters. Along the hall there were broken bottles of whiskey on the floor, and a sticky substance I did not care to identify. "Oh, Hunny Bunn, you have to wait, I have a man waiting for me inside… Wait your turn cutey, I'll come hollerin'!" Her smile was amazing, her eyes dazzling. My mind, drunk. This could work fine.

I saw what waited for her behind the door as she opened it. A most unpleasant, pock-faced lug of a wrangler with skin browned from hard work, and eyes… well, the eyes locked onto mine before the door shut.

Desperate as I was, I watched Cedric leave a room with a girl in tow, nodding to me with his hat on his back and a shit-eating grin. One of us was having fun. The blonde girl he was with had looked exhausted. OK, two of us were having fun.

Then the door opened, and the red head came out, grinning with her mouth closed tight. All I could think about was the heap of a man in there and how I could take her away from all this. Whiskey talking, of course. Without any concern of those party folks surrounding the hallway, and the man still in the room, I planted my lips on hers and forced my tongue in her mouth to kiss her… She struggled a bit, and fought me off, shaking her head and her hand out, as if to say… "no no… not yet…"

That's when I tasted the copper in my mouth and saw the bit of red fluid drip from her mouth. I gagged. Their transaction was not quite complete yet. I am so stupid!

I spit out the brackish fluid to the ground, gagging and hating myself for my desperate ploy for affection. Then, her customer, thick brown mustache surrounding an angry jaw, emerged from the room and entered the hall, while I wiped my mouth with my sleeve.

"Enjoy that?" he rasped, a bit of blood coming from his mouth. "She's a biter, if you pay enough. Ha-ha-ha-ha."

With that I turned back down the stairs to where we had left our glasses. They were gone… I threw some coins on the counter and downed whiskey to clear my mouth. The salty taste of the blood, and whatever else had been happening on the other side of that door, washed down my throat…

The dark-skinned man, now wearing his black hat and vest was coming down the stairs, smiling at me, but then turned away. That was the moment…

Cedric, with his handsome, yet sturdy features, barreled into me, mocking me. "So… don't cha know to let bordello girls clean up before you try to..." he made a kissing gesture. "Ha-ha-ha-ha-HAH!" He punched my shoulder. Disgusted as I was, something new had happened. I saw the rugged man's yellow demon eyes from the stairs. More to it, I saw inside his head. He was a demon, all right, but he also had planned on shooting my friend Cedric and stealing his horse when we left. I HEARD his mind say so! "Damn long-haired fool took my favorite bitch... I'll take his..." referring to the young blonde attached to Cedric's hip.

"Stay here, Seed..." I said to him. I called him that 'cause it was easy.

"WHY... Dekker what the f..."

"That man wants to kill you... You got his girl tonight... and... he's one of THEM! Don't think he's alone either..." The man's voice in his own head said something about telling Gordy... There's another man out there!

Cedric knew what I was saying, but there was some disbelief, so the fool followed me out the door, young blonde girl in tow.

The man was there, just untying Cedric's black stallion, so we had the surprise on our side. Before he could whirl, I shot him dead in the back of the head, as his gun was being pulled from its holster. The man called for Gordy. This partner I did not see had already shot at Cedric, missing him, but taking the young blonde wench out with a shot to her throat. She held herself, gurgling with futility and gobs of blood. Poor thing.

Cedric shot him full of holes in the chest. "WANTED ANOTHER ROUND WITH HER...!!! PAID FOR IT!!" seething, my blue-eyed friend shouted, at the fallen man named Gordy.

"Calm down, Seed... but put one in his head... his eyes are yellow to me..." I told my friend. Cedric was a little angered with me - and envious that he could not see the demons for what they were.

As soon as Cedric turned his back, the man (that was not a man at all) named Gordy sat up, and reached for his gun on the ground. I had already triggered the shot to his head.

13

My friend turned around, thankful, but angry too… leery of me perhaps.

We parted ways that next morning. I lost a friend to trust, and my taste for red heads, forever.

***

Deborah came over to me and handed me a small roll of paper. She sat next to me, smiling but sadder than when we met weeks ago. We had buried Loreen two days ago, and that's all that it took for more scum to roll into Caravass Pass. Sadly enough, she was not the first of the bordello girls to hand me a roll of paper with some bits of flesh that day. I was handed a small vile of some fluid, which I preferred to not identify, from a young girl earlier in the day. I had poured the fluid into my jar, mixed it, poured a shot, and promptly went upstairs and shot a horny demon that waited for her to return. It's funny, I do not always have to look them in the eye, depending on how much of their body fluids, flesh or otherwise, I consume. This bloke I shot right through the door: I knew he was flanking the left side, waiting to jump the young lady as she returned. One shot, through the door on an angle, and his head was all over the girl's (was her name Tiffany?) bed.

She had thanked me.

As did Deborah now.

"This one is smart. I had to scrape dander from his hat while he relieved himself. He never let me touch him."

I took the paper from Deborah, opening the wrapped scroll. I began sprinkling the tiny pips of scalp flesh into my jar of whiskey that Ole Clacky had put in front of me, right on cue. You'd be amazed how much skin falls free of these stinky beasties.

"Two in one day, Deborah, I dunno… it's taking a toll on my soul I think."

She kissed me. "You're doing God's work…"

14

So she said, but for how long?... You see, I told you, I ain't scared no more, because I'm the alpha. But for how long? She removed my hat, pushed the gray silver hairs from my face to kiss me and noticed the black shock of hair was gone to gray. She blinked, after another hug. "This one is already outside waiting for you," she said as she stepped back and went up the stairs.

"Out in the daylight...?? Cocky..." I said to Weaver and Bobby Kin to my right. They looked to each other, like frightened squirrels, and they nodded.

"DOWN we go..!" I downed the big glass of Demoneye, the whiskey hiding the rank taste of the dead skin mask. "Showtime." My confidence waned, my stride slowed. This sumbitch wanted a gunfight in the daylight?!

The town was outside, lining the sandy road that led to and from Caravass Pass. Folks I had never seen outside their own windows lined the street. All the girls followed Deborah outside the Tavern, as did Deputy Bobby Kin and Injun Weaver. I noticed Weaver had Stoney by the reigns. "I'll take care of him for you Dekker Collins. I promise." He looked sad.

Cedric Bodnasten waited on the other end of the street.

I could not see into his eyes. They were not yellow, but still diamond blue. No demon sense about him. Or had he learned to hide it?

So as I write this, Deborah is by my side, crying. We are in her room. My old long-haired, blue-eyed friend by her side... gun drawn on me. DAMN! ONE OF MY GUNS!! Cedric had handed me a scroll and ink to get this down. There is a bullet hole on my left shoulder. Yeah, that hurts. Guess I lost that fight. How about that! Dead Shot Dekker lost... to a demon?? Or just an old jealous friend that used new friends to thwart me, because I had become...

"You did good my dear, you really did... for as long as you could," Deborah said.

I could smell her powder fresh skin, and the blood pulsing in her veins, and... Cedric is wanting me to log as much of this

15

treasure trove of information that I can, so I am; but that damn long itchy finger of his on that trigger tells me I will not have to fear what I will become much longer.

"I'm not afraid. I never liked long lasting acts." – Lillie Langtry

THE UNDESIRABLE
BY JESSE J. SAXON

Jesse Saxon lives and works in the zombie capital of the world, Pittsburgh, PA with his wife, daughter, and their cat. He has written various macabre short stories ranging from zombie fiction to dust bowl horror, and a full-length zombie novel. His short story **Karnivali** *was published in* **The Big Book of Bizarro**. *Jesse graduated from California University of Pennsylvania in 2006 and has been writing semi-professionally ever since. Look for Jesse on Twitter @jessejsaxon.*

"Then there I was, upon the highest hills. There before me the lands where we hunted. Where we shared the same breath with the birds and the beasts, where we were one; where we were only identifiable by the tracks that we left behind." – Chief Kapawanee, the Battle of Burning Hawk, 1889.

The blood was still wet on the fresh snow. Some coagulated clumps clung to tufts of blonde hair as first winds of the morning swept through the plains. A small blood trail led off to the west; to the Black Canyons, where only the three tribes of the Lakainaw lived. Bits of torn clothes were intermingled with trampled down snow and hunks of skin like some gory collage. The house was still intact, though; the belongings inside were completely destroyed.

17

The front door was off its hinges and an unreasonable amount of blood looked like it had exploded out of the house covering the door frame and the ground outside in front of it.

Inside, Randall Wade and his family were killed and cut to ribbons by their assailant. Most of Randall was left, but there was no sign of any of his children. The torso and upper portions of Randall's wife, Holly, was found a few yards away from the home, her fingers were broken—trying to dig in to the ground to hold on; though there was no sign of the rest of her. The family's horses had all gone missing, and their tracks led south through the snow, toward Sheridan City.

January was a harsh month in the Dakota territories. The weather alone was more than most people could handle, but the allure of a working farm on a land claim with potential of gold in the hills was enticing enough for folks to make a run at it. But a vicious murder scene on a farm just outside of town was only making the unforgiving winter worse on Samuel MacArthur, the sheriff of Sheridan City. Sam MacArthur was as honest as anyone could be out there. That didn't mean he was squeaky clean, it just meant that he did what he thought was right without anyone's outside influence; and that's why he was made sheriff. Now though, citizens around the city were being brutally killed and when the news of the Wade family's slaying hit the town's frozen streets, Sam knew he better have answers.

Billy, the Wade family's farmhand, came to Sam at first light after he arrived to find the scene. He told Sam that he had too many drinks the night before and retired to the upstairs of the saloon with Rae Anne, a fact Sam knew to be true from seeing it himself.

Billy led Sam and his deputy, Jacob Smith, back to the Wade's farm. When they arrived, Sam shouted for survivors. No one answered — not that he expected anyone to anyway. He nudged his horse to walk forward to the house, but the horse understandably refused. Sam dismounted and walked closer to the home until he got close enough to see into the door. Directly through the door, against the rear wall, was the body of his friend Randall Wade — chest cavity ripped apart and hollow, no legs or right arm, and his jaw was partially missing. "God in Heaven," Sam said.

"Holly's over there," Billy said.

"And the children?" Jacob said. Billy puffed his cheeks and shook his head 'no.'

Sam took a deep breath. He knew that both Billy and Jacob were waiting for him to make a move, to take some sort of charge over the situation. He puffed his cheeks and watched his breath vaporize in front of him in the cold as he exhaled and said, "Burn it; burn it all."

***

Sam and Jacob took up two stools in Sheridan's Saloon. Sam did his best thinking at the saloon; plus it was an easy out if someone wanted to bother him. The saloon in Sheridan was equal parts saloon, hotel, and brothel on three floors, respectively. Sam had never taken much interest in the latter, but since the passing of his wife two years ago, Sam had become quite familiar with drowning sorrows in the bottoms of whiskey bottles on the first floor. His wife never bore him any children. When she died, Sam immersed himself in his work. Being sheriff was all that he had left. He worked diligently at keeping Sheridan City's streets respectable. They were by no means the shining picture of perfection, but with the help of Jacob, Sheridan City garnered a reputation of not being vile, which was more than the majority of settlements in the territories could boast.

It seemed now though that that reputation was in trouble. The Wade murders would cause an understandable uneasiness in the city. There were not going to be bodies, there was not going to be a funeral, and now the last farm that stood between Sheridan City and the frontier was a mass of blood and fire with no explanation ready. When Sam and Jacob got within the streets of Sheridan City, they could see people glancing at them and whispering. It was clear that the news about Randall Wade wasn't a secret, though secrets don't stay secret in Sheridan City very long; and the black smoke pillar rising behind them wasn't helping their case. Not that Sam expected to hide a murder for very long, but he had hoped he'd be able to stall long enough to find an excuse to how he was going to keep everyone safe. He knew that it was only going to be a matter of time before he needed to start giving answers and he needed time to think. The saloon was the obvious choice for Sam.

"Do you think some shithead Lakainaw done it?" Jacob said.

"I suppose that is a possibility; but I ain't never see one get away without leaving footprints in the snow," Sam said.

"Then who else?" Jacob said.

"Not who, but what," Sam said.

"Sam, come on," Jacob said.

"I'm serious, Jacob. What happened inside that house wasn't done by no man. Not even a Lakainaw would do that. Five or more maybe could'a, but five or more would'a left footprints," Sam said.

"Maybe they took the horses into the city?" Jacob said.

"Did you see a pack of natives ride through here in the wee hours of the morning covered in Randall Wade's blood?" Sam said.

"No," Jacob said.

"DID ANYBODY SEE A PACK OF NATIVES COVERED IN RANDALL WADE'S BLOOD COME RIDING THROUGH TOWN THIS MORNING?" Sam said, screaming to the entire saloon.

"Christ's sake, Sam. Calm down. These people are bound to be shook up by noon if everyone knows that you're all up in a fuss and full as a tick," Jacob said.

Before Sam could muster a defense, his jaw fell slack as he smelled the aroma of honeysuckle and verbena, the same perfume his wife used to wear. Except, of course, this wasn't his wife he was smelling. In between him and Jacob now was a fair-skinned blonde. Sam immediately recognized that she was new in town. She was fit and had green eyes and a pinch of red in her cheek bones. She wore her hair down in curls that made her look more ornery than playful. She carried herself confidently, which impressed Sam rather quickly, and she was without argument a beautiful woman. In a German accent, she introduced herself to Sam and Jacob as "Gisella."

"Now which one of you fine gentlemen want to spend the rest of your morning with me?" Gisella said.

Sam was still too taken back to answer.

"No thank you, ma'am; we're a little busy today," Jacob said.

"Well maybe you two boys just need to relax. How's about, say, I show you my new room and we get to relaxing?" Gisella said.

"I said no, thank you," Jacob said, pushing Gisella away.

Gisella didn't take kindly to the shove, but restrained herself from getting out of line. She had contempt in her steps as she walked away. Gisella had never been refused before and she didn't like the feeling. Sam detected the anger in her short, purposeful walk. "You didn't have to be so mean to her, Jacob," Sam said.

"You know how these new girls are, Sam. If you don't let them know you mean business up front, then they just walk all over you and take all of your money every chance they get," Jacob said.

"Can't say that I knew that, Jacob. She seemed nice enough, though," Sam said.

"They all do," Jacob said.

Sam followed Gisella with his eyes as she crossed the room. If he tried hard enough, Sam could still smell her perfume. It comforted him the way a warm bed does on a cold morning when you have no place you need to be. "You say she's new, huh?" Sam said.

"Must be, I'd never seen her before — must be fillin' in for Abigail. She's filling in her dresses at least. Nobody's really got a story on her yet, though; I think it's because her accent's scaring everyone off," Jacob said.

Sam watched Gisella make her way to the end of the bar and nod to the bartender. He poured her a glass of whiskey and as she was bringing the glass up to her mouth, her eyes locked with Sam's and she responded with a slight smile as she took a swig of the honey-brown liquid. She put her glass back down onto the bar and bashfully smiled at Sam, a move Sam fell for entirely. "I think I'm going to go talk to her," Sam said.

"Don't be foolish, whatever it was that killed the Wades is still out there and we have work to do," Jacob said.

Sam nodded in agreement and finished his drink in one gulp. "Blood trail went west; I suppose we should start there," Sam said.

Two Nights Ago

The village of the third tribe of the Lakainaw was devoid of any women; so Gisella knew what kind of shit she was in for when she arrived there after her wagon train was ambushed by the Lakainaw on her way west. She wasn't scared, but more upset at the inconvenience. As a large native was tying her up along the midsection with rope, she thought about the process of having to find new clothes, transportation, and all of the comforts she had brought with her on her journey from the mountains of Germany that were now lost in some fire somewhere on the road. Most importantly, out of all of her possessions, was her prized silver-lined trunk. It had been passed down to her from her mother. Her brother made sure that she was safely asleep inside of it every night; but he was dead now and the trunk was gone. She didn't put up much of a fight when the Lakainaw raid took place. She saw no point in it; they were too many to fight off. Instead, she waited

22

inside of her carriage patiently until someone decided to kidnap her.

Initially, they yelled at her in words she did not know, nor care to understand. She knew what they meant, though. When men speak like that, when they use that sort of tone, in short sentences, with their brows furrowed together, she didn't need to know the Lakainaw language to understand they were calling her things like "white bitch" or "invader," or spouting out their intentions for her. Gisella remained silent as they tied her. She was upset, though, as any normal woman would be, but she wasn't scared.

Gisella was laid on her belly across one of the natives' lap, on horseback. From behind her, she could hear two members of her party, both males, whimpering for their lives. When they arrived in the Lakainaw village, there were no women or children to greet them. Teepees dotted the foreground and a handful of old men poked their heads out of them to see their warriors returning home. The village looked normal enough until the horse she was on passed through the designated gate, and she was able to see that it was constructed out of human bones and horse skulls. It looked carefully constructed, and was clearly more than a bone heap to them. Next to the gate were the dismembered bodies of other unlucky travelers whose drained bodies communicated that they had died of blood loss. The bodies also communicated that they were harvested for their meat — a suspicion confirmed when the two males from Gisella's party were strung up beside the others.

She felt her rider's hand grab her hair by the back of her head to steady her as he dismounted and brought her down with him. She landed on her feet, but awkwardly, causing her to slump over and her hair to be pulled even more. The native yelled something at her that she took as an insult to being a clumsy white woman who was going to be raped, murdered, and made part of the gate by the end of the week. She figured at least a third of that might be true.

She was taken into a teepee where nothing but a bison pelt rug decorated the room. "Romantic of you," Gisella said. The Lakainaw man violently pushed her down onto the rug. The sudden impact of the shove, combined with her hitting the ground, was the first time in the entire experience that Gisella felt anger. She rolled over to snap at the man, but before she got to her knees, his hand was in her dress and feeling between her knees. She squirmed in her rope cocoon to get a hand free to push him off. She pinched her knees and pushed her calves together. She tried to use the heel of her boot to dig into any part of the man that she could find with it, but it was all of no use. She submitted to the man, and the next one. It continued like that the rest of the day.

When all of the able-bodied men had left her alone, she realized she hadn't felt anything at all, but rather stewed in hatred after the last man had finished with her and left. She nearly shuddered at the sound of the teepee's door flap opening, but her contempt grasped her, and held her firm from showing any fear as the footsteps approached her. A hunk of smoked meat fell by her face and the man spouted some boorish Lakainaw at her. She asked to be untied but the man said nothing as he exited the tent. Gisella wormed her way upright and sat in the middle of the teepee to wait till the time was right for her to mount her offensive and make an escape.

Hours passed and no one came in to bother with her. She could hear the shuffle of feet outside of the teepee and the ground was uneven enough in some areas to see the shadows of the passing men as they moved past. She listened to them talking outside, all the while collecting her anger and resentment, biding her time. Soon enough, she felt her stomach begin to ache, and her forehead became moist with a sheen of sweat. Normally, Gisella hated this time of the month. She made sure to avoid all human contact for fear of killing someone she loved for the next five days. It wasn't her fault that she would hate everyone that she saw, or that she felt her existence was dependent upon killing everyone that crossed her path. That was just how she was; she knew it, she hated it, but she knew it was unavoidable — it's nature taking its course. The beast inside of her needed to be let out.

Gisella felt her heart rate pick up, and her lungs demanded more oxygen. She was breathing in through her nose and her mouth heavily now and she knew it wouldn't be long until her monthly visitor made an appearance. Soon, she knew, she would have no control over herself, her emotions or anything she did. Gisella smiled to herself and laid back down on her side, on the floor, and let nature take over. Her toes curled inside of her boots and she was beginning to hate the feeling of wearing clothes. She looked at her hand and pulled the rings off with her teeth and spit them out onto the ground. She could smell the Lakainaw men in the village and hated that their stink filled her nose and throat. The fact of just being in the teepee now was enraging. She hated all things human and anything to do with people. She couldn't stop stretching out her hands and fingers as big and as wide as they could go. She needed to be unbound and free. She was struggling with maintaining rational thought, and just as the sun recessed behind the hills of the Dakota plains, Gisella's hands popped at the joints and began to grow thicker.

Her mouth opened wide as her jaw muscles pulsed, growing in size and forming a snout. Her teeth had fallen out and been replaced by the sizable canines behind them. Her body grew in size, easily tearing through the clothes she had on and the rope that had once bound her. The muscles that she had grew in size and the muscles she didn't have before were now present. A thick coat of gray fur now covered the entirety of her body and a now present tail. Her former tiny figure was now gone and replaced by a beast; a monster that hated humans and all human things. Once her transformation from human to werewolf was complete, without hesitation, she tore off through the door flap on the teepee and into the first man outside of it.

He was about six paces away and barely saw the wolf coming for him. He reacted fast enough to make a move for his tomahawk at his side, but before he could get a grip on it, the wolf made a leap and wrapped its jaws over the Lakainaw man's mouth and nose. The wolf bit down, crushing the man's face in her jaws. Blood gushed through her mouth and she loved it. When the man's skull gave her jaw a moment of resistance, she shook the man's whole body violently, separating it from the head and sending the body through the air until it crashed into the pile of human bones that served as the gate. She dropped the man's head and sprinted to another man that she saw patrolling the perimeter of the village. The man was startled by the noise of crashing bones, but didn't fully react as if it was anything more than normal. Like the first man, this one noticed the sound of the wolf's running paws too late. She approached him from the rear as he was walking away from her, and when he turned to investigate the approaching noise, she was on his back. Her size was bigger than his and her weight alone was enough to topple the man over. Her claws dug into his back as her teeth tore through his neck, spraying blood wide around her latest kill. Still though, she smelled more. Her contempt for humans took control as she tore through the entire village.

She was too fast for arrows. Anyone who got close enough for blades died before they could use them. Rifles and pistols were too inaccurate for her speed. The entire tribe didn't stand a chance.

When the third tribe of the Lakainaw had been utterly slaughtered, the wolf was far from satisfied. For an entire month it sat inside Gisella's body. She controlled her emotions enough during that time that the wolf inside of her was able to be kept at bay. During that time, it saw humans and smelled their stink. Through her, it felt humans and their human objects. It tasted humans and their food. It hated humans every moment of every day; and most of all, it hated being a human for those twenty-eight days that it was not allowed out. There was one time of the month, though, that Gisella could not control her body, or her emotions.

26

She was weak then, and the wolf took over. It never wanted to go back. It wanted to kill every human it saw, hoping to kill the one that it had to go back inside of; but not knowing the changing process, nor how it worked when the sun's rays touched it and transformed it back into the cursed German girl on her quest for freedom. The tribe would not do in terms of satisfaction. It wasn't enough for the wolf and the wolf knew there were more.

She howled at the moon the first moment she got to see it. It was loud; and powerful. The vibration from the howl resonated through her whole body; and she would have continued, had she not run out of air. Her mouth dripped with blood and she felt it drip down her neck, along her coat; and she listened to it hit the ground. She loved every second of it. Like a drunken lust, the wolf instantly recovered and needed more.

The wolf took off from the village at full sprint. The wet snow and grass on her paws felt wonderful as her claws dug into the ground and kicked up dirt as she ran. Her olfactory system was operating on high-alert now. The smells of burrowed rabbit and bison were pouring into her nose. Those types of prey wouldn't do, though. That was human food; and humans were wolf food. Her rage blinded her back at the village. She never even noticed her hunger. The need to destroy humans was all that mattered, and now that she had killed everything in sight, she wanted to hunt.

She concentrated on her sense of smell and picked up the scent of human to the east. Instantly, her body kicked into a high gear of blood thirst and hate. Without command, her hind legs pushed off of the ground so hard that she was almost leaping rather than running. Her large body moved along the plains effortlessly at full speed. She cut through the snow like an attacking shark cuts through water. Her heart was pounding, her lungs swelled, her muscles clinched and exerted. If she concentrated on one isolated part of her body, she could feel it working at its maximum potential. Everything was performing in unison and she felt it — she was the perfect killing machine in the flesh.

Soon, she picked up the smell of smoke; the smell of burning wood. Only humans burn wood, and she knew that; and she hated that. As she got closer, the human scent became stronger. The scent became all she could concentrate on until she reached a small ridge, just beyond Randall Wade's pastures.

***

Sheriff Samuel MacArthur and his deputy Jacob Smith arrived at what used to be the settlement of the Lakainaw people's third tribe. Neither Sam nor Jacob had actually been to the location before, but it was clear that the scene before them was not the normal state of operation. Each of them had anticipated approaching the village hesitantly, but neither of them had expected to see the level of poignant carnage that unfolded as they crested the rim of the low hills that lay just beyond the destroyed gate of the Lakainaw village. They looked out over a landscape littered with gore. Various body parts were intermingled with the pulled innards of the inhabitants.

"Fuck all," Jacob said.

"Guns up," Sam said. "What's been done here might not yet be over."

Sam encouraged his horse forward. Reluctantly, the horse pressed forward and into the battered wasteland. Human skulls and femurs littered the ground on the beaten path that led into the village. Sam and Jacob held their pistols up alongside their heads as their horses trotted into the blood-soaked land.

"What the hell is going on, Sam?" Jacob said.

"I wish I knew," Sam said.

The eerie silence of the scene was only equaled by the amount of butchery. Bodies, body parts, spears, blood and arrows were all laid across the field in front of them like a blanket of war's afterbirth. Their horses carried them into the village, and blood splashed with every step made by the hooves. Hands, attached to dismembered arms, still clutched knives that couldn't stop their demise. Armless bodies, with their innards spilled, laid dejectedly in the red snow like dead meat islands. Teepees were knocked over and some were halfway burnt from the fires intended to keep the inside warm in the cold winter night.

"Lower your gun, Jacob," Sam said. He shouted for survivors, but no one answered.

"I don't like this, Sam," Jacob said.

"Shit, Jacob, me either," Sam said.

"Something's fucked here. Something's not right. Whole villages don't die, Sam. Someone survives. First Randall's, then this, what's next?" Jacob said.

"No footprints," Sam said.

"What?" Jacob said.

"There were no footprints or horse tracks on the way up here; nothing going either way. Nothing leading out of here," Sam said.

"You sayin' a ghost did this, Sam?" Jacob said.

Sam spit on the ground out of habit, and the impact created a dripping noise when it made contact with the blood pool below his feet. "I don't know what I'm sayin', Jacob," Sam said. "I guess what I'm sayin' is that we can rule out these Lakainaw as our murderers."

"Maybe one of the other two tribes?" Jacob said.

"Maybe; doubt it though," Sam said.

"Well, it sure wasn't the entire city of Sheridan that come out here and slaughtered a whole Indian village, and then went on to kill the Wades just for fun," Jacob said. Sam nudged his horse to turn around to head out of the village. "All's I'm sayin' is, maybe this tribe of Lakainaw had words with one or both of the other tribes and Randall got in the middle of it somehow."

Sam looked at Jacob as calmly as he could. "If something to this scale were about to go down, one of those tribe would've told us. We would've had warning. At the very least, they'd have sent a representative to Sheridan this morning to bring us to speed on what unfolded," Sam said.

"Maybe we missed them? Maybe they just got there after we left?" Jacob said.

"My thoughts exactly," Sam said as his horse led them all out of the massacred village and back to the main road to Sheridan—leaving bloody tracks behind them.

***

The streets of Sheridan City were hard with frozen mud. Busily, citizens walked the wooden sidewalks that ran alongside of the storefronts. Fresh snow was starting to fall as the day began to cool off in its final hours of light. Sam made it a point to keep his head down and avoid eye contact with anyone as he and Jacob rode to the saloon. The people of Sheridan City seemed normal enough that Sam suspected no random Lakainaw had shown up to cause a mild ruckus.

Inside of the saloon, everything was just as normal as it was on the outside. The bartender welcomed Sam and Jacob with a smile, and the piano was alive with a simple, but upbeat song. Patrons seemed to be none the wiser about the slaughter at the Lakainaw village, let alone at Randall Wade's place. Sam ordered two glasses of whiskey; the first of which he drank all in one gulp.

"That sort of day, eh?" the bartender said to Sam.

"Yeah, you can say that," Sam said.

"Well what would you say it was, Sam?" the bartender said.

"Something awful happened to Randall Wade and his family. A pack of wild animals or something must've gotten to them in their sleep," Sam said.

The bartender shook his head in a mournful contempt and muttered about the winter being sparse times for creatures. Sam was barely into his second glass of whiskey when he saw Gisella at the opposite end of the bar, whispering into a man's ear but making eye contact with Sam. She playfully smiled at him through her talking, and Sam caught himself smiling back.

"Gisella's been acquiring a lot of new fans today," the bartender said. Sam glared at him scornfully. "Oh, no, no, not that way, Sam; I just mean that everyone is really taking notice to how pretty she is, was all I meant." Sam snickered at his brief lapse in character. Gisella's eyes called to him through her blonde locks, enough to make him forget about a number of butchered bodies that all lay within a day's ride of the town that he swore to protect.

He hit the rim of the glass off of the bridge of his nose as he took a swig from his second glass. He thought to himself, "Nothing I can do, except just keep a diligent eye on things, I suppose. No sense in making a big deal out of what might be nothing."

"Hey, uh, Sam; if it's alright with you, I think I'm going to call it a day," Jacob said. Sam nodded, and Jacob finished a mug of beer and gave Sam a firm pat on the back. "We'll get'er figured out soon enough, Sam. Best'ta rest your eyes and your mind now, come back fresh tomorrow."

"Yeah; yeah, okay," Sam said and held up a hand to signal he'd be right along, just as soon as he finished his drink. Jacob reassured him that they'll start putting the pieces together first thing in the morning. Sam wasn't ready to call it a night just yet though. After what he'd seen earlier in the day, it was going to take a good, hard state of drunk to get him to sleep. Otherwise, he'd be up all night thinking about poor Holly Wade's torn-in-half body, the missing children, and how something horrible enough to destroy an entire village of native warriors, happened inside of that small house.

Grisly murders were commonplace in the expanding west. It's something Sam had grown used to. Occasionally, a mutilated body of some trailblazer, who had a run-in with a pack of pissed-off natives, needed to be cut down from some tree, or given a proper Christian burial. But what he saw today was altogether different. The Lakainaw village at least looked like it had a fighting chance,

31

but the Wade family didn't stand any chance. Something took them by surprise, and judging from the connecting lines that flowed from the village, through the Wade's farm, and into Sheridan City, the problem was either coming to Sam or going away. He didn't want to take any chances.

Sam stepped outside of the saloon and into the winter air. The sun was starting its descent and soon enough it would be dark. Sam pulled a cigar out from the interior pocket of his leather duster and held it in his mouth as he fumbled for matches. He heard them rattle in a box in his pocket and got them out with enough effort to make him consider whether another drink was going to be necessary or not. He struck the match and steadied himself to light the cigar between his teeth. He puffed on his end hard, as the match's flame licked the other end. Sam exhaled a puff of smoke that soon enough faded away and revealed Gisella's face.

"Awfully cold out tonight," Gisella said.

"There are worse things out there than the cold," Sam said.

"What sorts of things?" Gisella said.

"All sorts; I suppose," Sam said.

"I bet you've seen all kinds, being sheriff and all," Gisella said.

"Yeah, I have," Sam said. "I've seen some pretty nice things, too."

"Oh, like what?" Gisella said.

"You, for starters," Sam said.

Gisella smiled and slid her small hand inside of his. "I'd love to hear more of your stories," she said.

Sam thought for a moment before he answered. He considered his life in Sheridan, and the Wades. He thought about how they had all been ambushed and how a third floor room might not be such a bad idea with something lurking just beyond the city. He said, "Tell ya what, I'll agree to a night with you and to share some of my stories, if you agree to get out of here with me first thing in the morning. Deal?"

"Oh, you wouldn't want that," Gisella said.

Sam looked at her again. He smelled the perfume on her again. He really thought she was pretty, and for him, right now, that was enough. "Of course I would. I'm growing tired of this place and this life. I'd like to get to somewhere warm, somewhere where life moves slow. Somewhere where you and I could make a nice little life for ourselves before we're too old to get married."

"That's really sweet and all, but I don't think that's really a possibility," Gisella said.

"And why's that?" Sam said.

"I'm just another undesirable and the beast inside of me would just get ya," Gisella said.

Sam chuckled, "How about we start with just one night then?"

Gisella smiled and agreed. "Let's get back inside with everyone else and let me show you my room before the sun goes down. It's getting deadly cold out here enough as it is."

"A pair of six-shooters beats a pair of sixes." - Belle Starr

THE TAILSMAN
BY GARY LEE VINCENT

Gary Lee Vincent (born 1974) is an American author and musician. As a fiction writer, his credits include **Passageway** and the West Virginia Vampire Series: **DARKENED** (featuring the standalone novels **Darkened Hills** – winner of Foreword Reviews Magazine's 2010 Book of the Year Award for Best Horror Novel**, Darkened Hollows** (2011), and **Darkened Waters** (2012). A fourth novel in the Darkened series – **Darkened Souls** – is planned for 2013. For more information, visit **www.DarkenedHills.com**.

For Burning Bulb Publishing, he served as Contributing Editor to **The Big Book of Bizarro** and **Westward Hoes** anthologies.

As a musician, his albums include **100 Percent, Passion, Pleasure, & Pain**, and **Somewhere Down The Road**. For more information, visit **www.GaryVincent.com**.

INTRODUCTION

He's hot on the trail, looking for some tail…

Sly Franko was a man of the West, a forger of the wild frontier. Like the Country Western song that would be written years after he died, the words, "Faster horses, younger women, and more money," seemed to be the anthem of this horn dog cowboy.

Franko would ride into town on a blazing saddle, find the closest saloon to wet the whistle, belly up to a good card game, and find him a hot-loving hussy to get his cowpoke on with.

He would never stay in any one town too long, always mindful not to wear out his welcome and also mindful to glance over his shoulder from time to time just in case his 'lady of the night' from the night before happened to be married. The last thing Sly Franko needed was an angry husband hot on the trail of "The Tailsman."

Yes, Franko quickly earned the nickname of The Tailsman and it would be an accurate statement to say he always seemed to find some tail on the trail wherever he would roam…

THE SIOUX CITY SHITHOUSE MONSTER

The rolling hills of western Iowa – Summer 1859
where a visit to bathroom leads to
terror and death

CHAPTER 1

The old bartender of the Rolling Hills Saloon and Inn quickly spotted Sly Franko as he entered the establishment. He had been riding on his trusted steed for nearly a week and wanted to wash the grime from his crust-coated body before heading over to "The Parlor of Pleasure," a mansion on the edge of Sioux City that was known for its annual poker tournament and lovely ladies of the night.

The mansion tournament was an invitation only event and because he was good buddies with Denver Ratcliff, a poker friend from way back and the event's organizer, he got invited to partake in the festivities.

If it's anything like last year, he thought, *I might not be able to ride Bessie for a couple days!* A small grin crossed his face as he remembered a romping good time he had with two ladies in particular that left him quite sore, but in a good way.

The saloon seemed especially busy today. *There can't be more than a couple hundred people in this entire town and it looks like half of them are here at the bar!* he observed, noticing that it was three deep and elbow-to-elbow.

Franko pushed his way through the crowd and yelled at the bartender to give him a bottle of anything wet. After getting the beverage, Franko quickly pulled back from the thirsty patrons and made his way to a small corner of the establishment that looked to be the least crowded so that he could enjoy his drink in semi-peace.

The bartender called for one of the wait staff to attend to the bar and made a beeline to where Franko was sitting.

"Sly Franko!" he exclaimed! "If it isn't the old Tailsman himself."

Franko nodded. "Nice seeing you, Bucky."

"I thought it was you when you came in," the bartender said, "but with it being so crowded and loud over there" – he motioned at the bar – "I couldn't be sure.

"Hey, are you here for Denver's poker and 'poke *her*' party?"

"That'd be a fair assessment," Franko replied.

"Well, I need to give you a 'heads up' before you go over there."

Franko raised an eyebrow at the barkeep.

"One of the reasons we are so crowded is that the people are scared."

"Scared of who?" Franko asked.

"Not who, but *what*," the bartender replied. He looked around and lowered his voice just above a whisper. "People 'round these parts have been disappearing."

Franko looked at his now-empty bottle of beer. "Buddy, I want to hear more about your situation, but first I need to drain the old lizard. That beer went right through me. Where's the outhouse?"

"Hold your horses pilgrim," the bartender replied. "That's what I was getting around to. There's only two or three outhouses in this town. One of them's 'round back. The other's over at the mansion – Denver's place. There might be one behind the bank, but I've never had to go find out."

"So what, you want me to hold my piss in and wait until I get to the mansion party tonight? Hell, I'll piss myself before then!" Franko replied.

"That's just it," the bartender said, "if you go to *any* of the outhouses, you might not make it out."

"What do you mean, I might not make it out?"

"What I mean is that those people who have been disappearing have one thing in common: the last time any of them were seen was when they were going to the outhouse. They go in, but they don't come out."

"What are you saying – they're falling in the hole or something?" Franko asked.

"No," replied the barkeep. "There is *something* else in the hole."

"Take no offense, but that sounds like a crock of bullshit to me." Frank stated matter-of-factly. "I've been all over the West and I ain't never heard tale of a Sioux City Shithouse Monster – or a shithouse monster from any other town come to think of it."

"Well, you just be careful, never-the-less," the bartender replied.

Franko thumbed at the colt revolver strapped to his hip. "I'll be vigilant," he replied. "Thanks for the advice."

He stood from the table and made his way outside of the saloon. His horse Bessie made a noise in recognition from the post she was tied to as her master came outside.

"Not ready to leave quite yet," he told her. "Need to go take a leak."

Much to his surprise, Franko saw quite a few of the bar's patrons standing up against the side of the building relieving themselves. There were about five people whom he passed along the way and not one of them was using the outhouse.

Maybe there's something to the old coot's rambling, Franko thought to himself.

As he approached the door to the outhouse, he had every intention of just opening it up and stepping on in, but at the last moment thought better of it.

"Ah, hell!" he said out loud to no one in particular. "Might as well just piss on the outside walls like the rest of the townsfolk."

As Franko began peeing on the outside back of the outhouse wall, he wondered just what he would do when it came time to

39

have a bowel movement. *I guess that's when I'll encounter the Shithouse Monster.* He began laughing uncontrollably at the thought, but no one else who was peeing outside that night was as lighthearted.

CHAPTER 2

After bathing, Sly Franko hopped back onto Bessie and rode the four miles or so to the Parlor of Pleasure. It was a trail he knew well and he always tried to pay his friends a visit when he was in this neck of the woods.

Denver Ratcliff was one of the wealthiest men west of the Mississippi River and although most of the people believed his riches were from cattle, Sly need only look at the pretty lasses that frequented his parties to know the real reason behind his riches.

Ratcliff reminded Franko of Santa Claus. It wasn't that he had a beard, but he was round like Santa and had white curly hair. Maybe it was because Franko always liked opening the presents over at Santa Ratcliff's house when the women would ask his help in untying their corsets.

"Sly Franko, you old dickmaster! How the hell ya been?!" Denver exclaimed as he came down the beautiful entry staircase to greet him. "We have a few new additions since the last time you were here."

"Fair to midling, I suppose." Franko said, grinning in his usual ornery way and made his way through the door.

Even though he was from Iowa, Ratcliff spoke with a distinctive southern drawl. "I'm glad you could join us for a little Texas Stud. I never really know from time to time whether you'll make these little shindigs of mine."

"It would be a cold day in hell before I miss one of your parties, Denver." Franko replied.

Ratcliff's parties were so much more than poker games. They were a weeklong hedonistic fest of whiskey, cards, and wanton women; and in Sly Franko's mind, what more could you ask for?

"Let's get you settled in with some drinks in ya," Ratcliff jovially offered.

"Hey, before I get started," Franko said, "there's this bartender down in Sioux City that was warning the town not to use the outhouse. Some kind of shithouse monster or something. Crazy-ass talk if you ask me, but if I go to your shitter is it safe?"

Denver Ratcliff chuckled a bit nervously. "Yeah, I suppose it is, boy. Go check it out and when you get back here, you can tell me if you met him."

Had Denver just laughed outright, Franko would have been okay. However the slight nervousness in his laugh made him think that there may be something more to the mystery than the host was letting on.

Sly Franko stepped back out into the cool night air and barely heard Denver's words, "Don't forget to wipe," coming from behind him.

"I'll try not to!" he replied.

The bowel movement went off without a hitch and Sly Franko was relieved in more ways than one not to have encountered the infamous shithouse monster, which he now believed to be some kind of sick joke that the old bartender back in town was playing.

Going back inside the mansion, the parlor was every bit as opulent as Franko remembered. In one corner was an overstuffed, embroidered couch where two women sat playing with each other's hair. In the middle of the great hall was a grand piano. A cherry fireplace was behind it and even though it was a summer night, there was still a fire burning in the depths of the hearth to add to the ambience. A crystal chandelier sparkled overhead.

Several people standing around took notice as Sly Franko entered the room.

"Now look what the cat drug in and forget to bury! Looks like The Tailsman has made it to the party after all!"

"Nice to see you again, Gilbert." Franko greeted.

"Actually, I was hoping you'd skip the festivities this year so I'd have a chance at winning."

"I think everybody wins at this party, if you know what I mean," Franko said as he winked at the two ladies on the couch.

"I heard that!" Gilbert replied. "It would just be nice to leave the party with more money than I came here with, that's all."

"Well, I am sorry to disappoint you, old friend."

"Old, am I?" Gilbert said, pretending to be offended. "How old do you think I am?"

"I don't know, probably old enough to be my dad?" Franko laughed in reply.

"I'm only forty-two, thank-you-very-much."

"Well, that's still ten years older than me, so I'll ask the ladies to take it easy on you after I'm done."

"I'll have you know that I can fuck with the best of them! Besides, what makes you think I want your sloppy seconds?"

Franko laughed and said, "I just thought you wanted me to get the women all filled up with spunk – lubrication, if you will – and broken in, that's all. But maybe we'll have a contest later on who can last the longest in the whorehouse rodeo."

"Now, that's a bet I'll take you up on!" Gilbert said.

Both men were laughing.

"I see you boys know each other," Denver Ratcliff said, now joining the conversation.

"Yep." Gilbert replied. "Franko and I go way back, don't we, Ann?"

Beside Franko, a woman mumbled, "Mmmmm."

Sly Franko turned to see a gorgeous blonde with a very well-endowed chest – it was Gilbert's 'girlfriend' from back in El Paso. From her long, flowing locks to her beautiful high heel shoes, she was just as sexy as he remembered her. Yes, it was another whorehouse in another town, but Franko still remembered the fun threesome that he and Gilbert had with Ms. Ann."

"Madam," Franko said, blushing slightly. "I see you made it all the way from Texas."

She stroked his arm. Franko always liked Ann. Her touch still electrified him and he felt a warmth begin to form in his manhood as blood was being redistributed. She always had that effect on him.

"I'm looking forward to you spending some money on me," Ann said.

Franko grimaced. Last year, he had spent nearly eighty silver dollars over the couple times he was with Ann and it was hard to tell how much Gilbert had given her. No matter how much you won at the card table, Ann could suck a cowboy dry in more ways than one.

"Aaah, shit!" Franko exclaimed. "I better pack up right now or Ms. Ann here is going to take all my dough."

"Gee, Sly, don't be such a sourpuss," Ann replied. "Stay around a while and let a girl relieve your tension. Besides, I'm wearing my most expensive perfume just for you!"

"Yeah," Franko replied. "There's something about your perfume that is like a siren to a sailor, and you're whittling down my will, woman."

Ann reached down to his crotch. "That's the spirit!"

Denver kindly chided, "Now Ann, how about you give Sly and I a couple minutes to gets ourselves a drink before you distract this young man."

Ann put on a puppy dog face and faked a pout. "If I must. But don't get him too drunk or he'll simply pass out when we go upstairs."

"You have my word," Denver replied.

Gilbert raised a glass of whiskey he was holding. "You go ahead and help yourselves. I'm good."

The two other men nodded and Denver led the way to a small room off the main one where the liquor cabinet was situated. "Help yourself, Franko," Denver announced as he motioned to the inventory.

"Now those are words I like to hear!" Sly replied as he grabbed a glass from the shelf and poured himself some bourbon.

"Hey, while I got you alone, I wanted to talk to you about a couple things."

"What's that?"

"First off, I hear the Springer boys are heading into town."

"Excellent," replied Sly Franko. "I guess they didn't lose enough last year and are looking for a rematch at the tables."

"Well, that's just it," Denver replied. "I heard rumors that they have a beef to settle with you after you cleaned them for over two hundred dollars. Consequently, I didn't invite them back to this year's party because I don't want that kind of trouble in my house."

"And so they're hell-bent on some hell raising then?" Franko deduced.

"That would be a fair assessment. May nothing come of it, but we'll want to keep an eye out, nevertheless."

"Got ya." Franko took another sip of his beverage. "And the other thing you wanted to talk about?"

"That shithouse monster thing," Denver replied.

"Oh, no. Tell me it's not real," Franko replied. "I did make it out of your hut unscathed."

"True," Denver said. "I didn't have any doubt that my outbuilding was safe. It's just... hell I don't know. It's just that there may be something to the Sioux City ones."

Franko had quickly finished up his first glass of liquid velvet and proceeded to pour him another. He was about to hear about shithouse monsters whether he wanted to or not.

"That town has a bunch of underground caves under it. The Indians used to use the system to store food and things in during the warmer months because of the cool temperatures.

"Something happened as the town became settled and the tribe that used the caves was driven from them.

"The entrances to the caves were sealed up and none of the new folk coming to town knew about them.

"There's a chance that the caves were sealed because of something else that was inside and my bet is those outhouses were built over the natural holes of the cave."

Franko interjected, "In other words, when you take a dump over at the Rolling Hills Saloon your shit isn't going just a couple feet down, it's landing in some pile deep in a cave?"

"That would be a fair assumption," Denver Ratcliff replied.

"That still doesn't answer what is going on," Franko replied, taking another swallow of the liquor. "This is good stuff!" he commented about the beverage.

"Like I said, help yourself," replied the host. "I've got an entire case of it for this week's cards and fucking party."

Both men laughed.

About that time there was a pounding on the front door.

"Let's see who that may be," Denver said as he left the little room to answer it.

A gaunt man standing roughly six foot tall was standing on the porch. He was sweating profusely from underneath a large cowboy hat and looked like he had just finished running a long distance cow drive in the warm summer heat.

"Roy!" the host began. "What brings you out to— "

"Denver, it got Toehead!"

CHAPTER 3

Roy was blabbering on and on like an idiot when Sly Franko approached the two men talking at the front door. Sly, who was on his third glass of bourbon, thought for a moment that this newcomer might have been drinking a fair bit more than he had this evening.

"Toehead Walkins…YOUR cowhand. IT got him! TOEHEAD, holy hell, Denver!"

"It got what?" Denver asked. "Get your foot out of your mouth and get a fucking grip, boy. Come in here and sit down on the couch. Get a hold of yourself and tell me what happened."

The man known as Roy staggered into the parlor. Denver showed him to the couch where the two ladies were still frolicking and motioned for them to move their play somewhere else.

They didn't protest but left the staggering cowboy to have a rest at the sofa.

"I'd offer you a drink," Denver began, "but from the looks of things, I'm thinking you had one too many." He shot a glance over to Franko, who simply nodded in agreement.

Gilbert, who had been feeling up Ann over by the fireplace, thought it best to pull up a chair by the other men and see what all the commotion was about.

Roy looked around, rubbed his hands on the tops of his legs, took his cowboy hat off, and wiped his sweaty brow. "It's not good, Denver. It's not good at all."

"Go ahead, boy, tell us what happened," Denver urged.

"Me, Ronnie Holmes, and Toehead were down at Bucky's place seeing who could drink the most and still stand. Anyway, Toehead had to take a shit and went around back.

"Bucky warned all of us not to use the outhouse, but it was so crowded outside and Toehead didn't want anyone seeing his business. You can't blame a man for wanting some privacy, you know?

"Anyway, I thought it might be a good idea to relieve myself as well and stood outside the shack and waited my turn.

"Suddenly, I heard Toehead scream! I yanked the door open just long enough to see this large beetle-like thing eating into his torso and dragging him back down into the shithole. I tried to pull my pistol on it, but there was no way to see it in the dark and all."

Roy sat back in the couch, closed his eyes as if trying to hide himself from the memory, and said, "All at once, Toehead stopped screaming. It was only silence and nothing more."

"Holy mother of God!" Gilbert exclaimed. "That's the strangest story I ever heard!"

Gilbert looked over at Denver. "Damn! It looks like a big fucking dung beetle ate your man, Watkins. Heck, I just saw him earlier when I was coming over to your place."

Denver asked the obvious question, "So, Roy, what's the town doing about it?"

"Everybody's scared," Roy replied. "Jimmy Smith is trying to round up men with guns to see if we can take it out. I came out here to let you know about what happened and to see if you would like to join us."

"I suppose we better postpone our little shindig here, gentlemen, and head downtown to see what's going on," Denver proposed.

Gilbert and Sly nodded in agreement.

Within the hour, the four men were back in downtown Sioux City. As they approached Main Street, they were instantly aware that something wasn't right.

"The town's too quiet," Franko remarked.

Gilbert nonchalantly maneuvered his .44 Henry Repeating Rifle to his front. "For the house or sporting arm, it has no equal," Gilbert boasted. "At least that was what was on the advertisement when I bought it."

"Nice rifle," Franko commented. "When we get back to Denver's, I'd like to play you a round of cards for it."

"Like hell you will!" Gilbert replied. "You're too damn lucky. Thanks, but no thanks. Besides, this is a pre-production model and if it weren't for my connections with the cavalry, I might not have scored one of these puppies until next year."

"Where do you suppose everyone's at?" Denver asked to no one in particular."

"They's probably scared," Roy said from somewhere behind the three. "Everyone saw it. They're probably inside."

When they finally made it to the Rolling Hills Saloon, they noticed that the place was empty.

"That's not good," Franko said. "I haven't even got checked into my room yet!"

Denver called out, "Roy – go inside and see if you can find Bucky. We need to find out what in the hell is going on."

"Sure thing," Roy said as he dismounted his horse and scrambled inside the establishment.

"Boys, let's go see the shithouse," Franko suggested. "If we see anything, I'm sure Gilbert can take care of it with the Henry."

The men tied up the horses and walked around to the back of the saloon.

As soon as they rounded the corner, the stench was overwhelming. The area reeked of summer-baked urine and feces.

But no matter how bad the area smelled, it was what they *saw* that was even more disturbing. Where the outhouse once stood was a large sinkhole. Even the outer frame of the building was gone.

"Guys, look at this," Franko said as he pointed to some damp red marks in the dirt.

"It looks like blood – and lots of it!" Denver observed.

"Right!" Franko replied. "That thing came to the surface and took several people with it."

"Bodies and all were dragged down into that!" Gilbert added, pointing to the sinkhole.

"Guys – Bucky's gone!" Roy said as he rounded the building and joined the others. "It looks like he – Holy shit and shinola! I swear it wasn't like that when I left!"

"Gentlemen, I have a theory," Franko said, as he cautiously approached the edge of the crater. "If this thing was some sort of dung beetle, then perhaps it was lured to the surface with all of

48

these people having bowel movements outside of the shithouse. I'm just saying – and take it for what it's worth – maybe they caused the problem."

"So, if what you're saying is true," Gilbert extrapolated, "then maybe we can use that to our advantage."

"Exactly!" Sly Franko replied. "I'm thinking that if we place some shit near the edge of the hole we can pick it off with your rifle when he comes up to retrieve it."

"I'm following you boys and all," Denver replied. "I'm just wondering where we are going to get the shit at for this 'experiment'."

"I don't think we have to worry about that!" Franko said as he pointed to Roy, who appeared to have just lost his bowels at the sight of it all.

CHAPTER 4

After making quite a fuss, the armed gentlemen were finally able to 'persuade' Roy to take off his pants, strip buck naked, and place them on the edge of the hole. Within a few minutes, a large, tail-like tentacle began feeling around the edge of the crater, snatching up the garments, and bringing them down into the blackness below.

"Shit!" Roy exclaimed as he witnessed his pants disappearing. "What am I going to do now?" He crept over next to where his pile of soiled garments used to be.

"What the hell you up to, Roy?" Denver asked from a safe distance away.

"I'm trying to see where my clothes are," he replied.

"Don't get too close to the edge," Sly observed. "That thing can probably smell you."

He no sooner got the words out of his mouth when one of the tentacles wrapped around one of Roy's legs.

Gilbert was quick to fire off a shot with the Henry rifle, but the bullet hit just in front of the tentacle, spraying rock and dirt. He cocked the firearm very quickly, but the tentacle had already retreated back inside the hole, dragging the naked Roy with it.

Sly Franko had his colt revolver drawn, and he and Gilbert ran over to the hole.

"Damn – too dark to see anything!" Gilbert observed.

"Let's see if we can get a torch or something and throw it down in there," Franko replied.

Denver was right on it and made a makeshift torch from a stick and Roy's shirt, which had luckily been preserved from the creature's earlier attack on the pants. Denver took some oil from a lantern, which the men had used to light their way on the horseback ride over, and used it as fuel for the torch.

The torch did help to illuminate the hole a bit better and they were able to see the creature deep below.

Much to their surprise, the creature paid them no mind, but instead appeared to be eating on the rectal cavity of the now-dead Roy. In the dim light of the torch, the creature appeared to have the upper body of a beetle and really long tentacles for legs. The legs were used to probe the orifices of its victims and scrape out fecal matter which it used for food.

As Denver held the torch steady, Gilbert and Sly began firing off rounds at the creature until they ran out of ammunition.

The shithouse monster emerged from the hole and faced the three remaining men, completely unfazed from the assault.

Each opponent held his ground.

Suddenly, Sly, Denver and Gilbert were hit with a telepathic blast, and found that they could hear the creature's thoughts and they in turn could hear it.

"I am very hungry," it seemed to say matter-of-factly. "And I am running out of food in the caves. It is not my intention to harm you, but I need food. If you can bring me food, I will not be your adversary."

Considering that the men had run out of rounds, Sly quickly offered a truce by thinking in his mind, "Sure. I'll have you as a pet and can feed you if you leave us alone."

Both Denver and Gilbert looked at Sly, as it appeared they heard the conversation and could not believe their ears.

The shithouse monster conveyed that the arrangement was agreeable to it, and walked/slithered over to stand next to Sly Franko.

The other men backed quickly away and all parties were a bit confused how bizarre the situation had become and what anyone's next move might be.

Sly reached over and patted the creature's head as if it was a dog, and it seemed to be fine with that.

"Now here's the ground rules," Sly said out loud, not remembering the telepathic link. "We'll shit and give it to you and you promise not to eat us when we are making the shit."

"That is acceptable," it replied telepathically.

All of the sudden, a large gunshot rang out. Gilbert collapsed, holding his stomach. "What the –," he almost got out, but the pain was too unbearable.

"There you are motherfuckers!" The words came from three men on horses.

"The Springer brothers!" Denver gasped.

"You thought you could have your little fuckfest without us, did you?" the front man announced.

"Thought you could get away with our money, didn't ya?" the second one said.

"We're going to kill you where you stand," replied the third.

They all drew a bead on Sly Franko and he was one hundred percent sure he would be meeting his maker that very night.

In their bloodlust for revenge on Sly, they never thought to notice what the men were doing in the tiny back area behind the local saloon. From their vantage point, they had not realized that there were not only men on the scene that night.

51

With incomparable speed, the shithouse monster seemed to sense the distress of its new 'master' and launched a vicious attack on the Springer clan.

Just as they started to fire, the creature put its body in front of Sly and took the first round of bullets. It quickly brushed Denver aside and crossed the distance between the Springers and the two remaining heroes.

The shithouse monster reared up on its tentacles, exposing its front side to the Springers and they were able to get off another round.

This time, the bullets hit their mark and knocked the creature backward.

The shithouse monster returned the attack by grabbing each of their legs with its tentacles and bringing them into its pinchers with lightning-fast speed.

The men screamed in terror. One of the men's legs came clean off and his blood began squirting uncontrollably in the air.

Even in their distress, they fired off another round of bullets. The creature hissed in pain and aggression.

It began eating at the men and probing for shit with its tentacles.

They eventually stopped screaming, like all of the others who had entered the shithouse earlier that night, and the creature fell on top of them to finish them off.

Something, however, was wrong.

After five minutes or so, the creature had not moved and the men were still lying in the dirt beneath it.

Denver and Sly carefully approached to see what the matter was.

A pool of green 'blood' was beneath the creature and covered the dead Springer brothers below it.

Apparently, the bullets had mortally wounded the creature, but not before it could take them out.

Gilbert had also given up the ghost and was lying dead on the other side of the lot.

"What a fucking shame!" Denver exclaimed.

Sly walked over to where Gilbert had succumbed and picked up the Henry rifle. "At least I got me a gun out of the deal."

"Is that all you can think about, Franko?" Denver asked.

"Not really," Sly said as he began dragging Gilbert's body toward the edge of the giant hole where the shithouse once stood. "Don't just stand there playing with your pecker, help me get rid of the bodies!"

"You can't be serious, Franko?" Denver asked, almost in shock at what the man proposed. "You're really wanting to dump everything down in the hole?"

"You're damn right I do. Now give me a hand."

Denver walked over to where Gilbert's body was.

Franko continued, "Look, this shit is not going to appear in any history books and when the town of Sioux City wakes up tomorrow morning, they are just going to have to move on. We can't have a panic and we sure as hell don't want to be around to answer questions, especially if the Marshall shows up. So, are you going to help me or not?"

"Looks like I don't have much of a choice," Denver replied.

As the men moved Gilbert to the edge of the crater, Sly looked up at the heavy man who was helping him, with a twinkle in his eye. "Now if we hurry up, hopefully we can get back to your place in time for me to eat Ann's sweet-smelling pussy."

With a big heave, the men threw Gilbert's body over the edge.

They repeated the process with the other three men, although it was a good struggle when they got to the shithouse monster, because it was so heavy.

"No one's ever going to believe this, Denver, and I'd appreciate it greatly if we never have to tell anyone any of this."

"Sounds fair to me," Denver replied as he gathered up the Springer brothers' firearms for his own collection. "At least we got some guns out of the deal."

"Time to hit the trail," Sly Franko announced as he inspected his work and was content that the area was clear.

As the men rode back to the mansion, Denver asked in the cool night air, "So, you really going to tap Ann tonight?"

"Yes, but I might have to skip the cards."

"You have more stamina than I do," the older man replied. "Gilbert called you something when you stopped by this evening. What was it? The Trailsman?"

"No. I believe it was The Tailsman!" replied Sly Franko. "And Ann will be the tail I ride tonight!"

The men had a good laugh.

"I never killed unless
I was compelled to." - Belle Starr

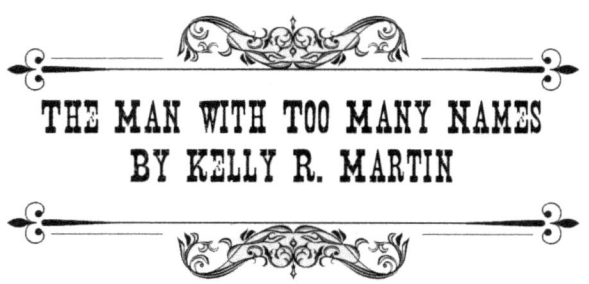

THE MAN WITH TOO MANY NAMES
BY KELLY R. MARTIN

*Kelly R. Martin lives and works a day job for the US Government in West Virginia, USA. His night job is as the owner (and sole employee) of Myth/Logic Press (www.mythlogicpress.com). His published works at the time of this writing are **The Lucky Cricket Tales from the Reading Dragon Inn Book 1** and **Thomas the Poisoner Tales from the Reading Dragon Inn Book 2**. He is working on the third book of this series – **Triskaidekaphilia**. His short story **Nothing Really Satisfies** was published in **The Big Book of Bizarro**.*

August 23, 1893 Iron County, Missouri

The golden colored grasslands stretched toward the big sky horizon in the hot August sun of a midafternoon. A single tree stood alongside the still newly gleaming train tracks. A man dressed in a black preacher's jacket wearing a black narrow brimmed hat stood under the tree in the shade beside a dappled mare. The mare grazed slowly under the spreading branches of the tree as the man inattentively held its reins in his right hand.

The man's eyes were partially closed with his irises rolled up underneath his barely open lids. A slim black mustache spread upon his slightly sweaty upper lip. The lips quivered as he imperceptibly whispered a message meant not for mortal ears.

A faint whistle sounded in the long distance along the rails. The man's eyes snapped sharply open as he turned toward the sound. A distant cloud of steam and smoke could be seen a long way off to the south. The horse chomped grass as the man gave a faint smile. "Your blessings are bountiful Lord. Thank you for answering my prayers. Amen in the name of our Savior. Amen in the names of the Prophets Smith and Young."

The man picked up the saddlebags at the base of the tree and placed them back upon the horse. The man then checked his brand new Saint John Browning designed Winchester Model 92 in the holster on his saddle. At his hip in a holster was one of Saint John's newest prototype innovations. A pistol which used a sliding block of metal to cycle rounds from a magazine, instead of rotating them within a cylinder typical for a Colt pistol. It used a .38 caliber brass cased round, also developed by Saint John specifically for this weapon.

The man opened up the saddlebag on the left side of the horse. It barely shifted as he pulled out two metal magazines and slowly thumbed rounds into each of them. Twenty rounds later, his magazines were ready and he placed one in each front pocket of his black preacher's jacket. The man looked up into the bright blue sky at the circling vultures. It wouldn't be much longer before they landed to begin their meal.

The man looked back at the hastily dug shallow graves among the tall waving grass with short stick crosses over them. There were five shallow graves for five shallow men. Men condemned by their own impure nature. Men full of lust, hatred and intolerance, and most importantly, bathed in their own sin. The man has purified them, baptized them in their own blood through the providence of Saint John Browning, as he called his benefactor. They were now free of their sin, and the Prophets would see them into the next life.

Nauvoo, Illinois, was a long way behind the man. Yet it was still not nearly long or far enough for his comfort. The man closed his eyes briefly again, smiling unconsciously as he remembered his last benediction. He remembered the expressions of religious ecstasy on the faces of the men as he gave them each the blessing which freed them from their sins. The red flower of their blood, spreading upon their chests, as their hearts burst with joy at their salvation.

Then he recalled the lamentations of the women with their silken petticoats, as they cried out in terror and fear. A slight frown crossed his features. They were such fallen creatures. They were unfit for his benedictions. Bathed in original sin, no mere benediction from the tool of Saint John could purify their fallen spirits. Only a lifetime of repentance could save such wretched creatures as they.

"You rotten son of a bitch. You murderin' bastard! They didn't do you no harm. Why'd you have to go an' kill 'em all?"

The man turned at the sound of the voice calling at him from a distant hill, where he had dug the graves of the five men. Standing upon the top of the low rise was one of the soiled doves from the saloon in Pilot Knob, Missouri. She was old, maybe as old as the man standing next to his horse under the tree. Her brunette hair had strands of gray, and she wore a look of proud defiance as she stood there in her blue gingham dress.

The man spoke, "The name is Deacon Mike Hawk, Madam. I saw those men needed to be brought over to the side of righteousness. Now they reside with our Lord Savior. May the Prophets Smith and Young guide their souls."

The woman shook her fist. "You done ruined the livelihood of those girls in the saloon. How they gone to make a livin' now with no menfolk to bed down with, you killer? You don't have no right to kill like that you small pizzeled whoreson."

The man replied, "You should redeem your wicked soul. I bid you to head west across the great rocky mountains. Go to the Great

58

Salt Lake, and prostrate your body before the temple, begging your Savior for forgiveness. Find a godly man willing to take you as his third or fourth wife and do honest labor for him."

The woman screamed out, "You're a gutless coward. The law will get you for gunnin' down innocent payin' customers."

The whistle of the approaching train blew closer and louder than before. The man tipped his hat forward with a grimace as he placed his left foot in the stirrup and threw his right leg over the dappled mare. The horse nickered briefly as he put a light spur to its side. It began trotting alongside the tracks heading toward the west.

The man called back, "Tell any law that Deacon Mike Hawk isn't frightened of them. I'm a righteous man doing the work of our Savior. His law is more important than theirs. Hi-yah!"

The horse began galloping faster as the woman called out, running down the hill, toward the departing back of the man, "Bear? Is it you, Bear?!"

September 11, 1859 Mountain Meadows, Utah

The young man was dressed in Indian style buckskins and war paint as he fumbled with the hammer on his Enfield Pattern 1853 rifle. He looked over at the older man beside him as he nervously placed the hammer at half cock, and put a primer cap upon the nipple under the hammer. The older man looked at him with a smile.

The younger man cleared his throat before speaking, "Major Lee what are we going to do? Are we sure this is the right thing still?"

The older man spoke, "It is God's work we do. These invaders must be taught a lesson or they will never respect our territory. They've spotted some of us not dressed as Paiute Indians. None of them can be permitted to escape this place now. Remember we must kill everyone except the youths. Don't forget, my name is

John Runningwater once we get started. It isn't safe to use your real name when engaged against the forces of the Devil. Don't forget we are supposed to be Paiutes. That way if the cavalry comes sniffing around afterward, they will go after the Indians like the British did following the Boston Tea Party."

The young man swallowed. "Major Lee I don't think I can shoot a woman. My momma wouldn't approve of that."

The older man replied with a pat on his shoulder, "You needn't be so formal. You can call me John. How old are you son?"

The young man looked serious. "I'm fifteen now, and old enough to shoot this rifle to defend our land."

The older man nodded. "I'll make sure you're assigned to the party which is supposed to separate and shoot the menfolk. There are those of us who don't mind taking care of the womenfolk. We'll make sure they never speak of this. Don't forget that they are all sinners; come to bring their brothels and ungodly ways to us. They mean to corrupt our pure nature, and to rob and steal our lands. Their heathen and heretic ways shall be punished. That is our mission here, to protect our people from their blasphemy. That's why we're dressed as heathens, so they don't come hunting for our godly womenfolk and children afterward."

The young man nodded. "Thanks a whole bunch, John."

The older man briefly smiled. "You're still looking a bit constipated. Are you certain you don't want to take a crap before we move out?"

The young man shook his head. "I just can't do it ever since I read that paper story about the Sioux City Shit Monster last month. Outhouses make me oh so nervous now."

The older man chuckled. "I just thought of your Indian name. We'll call you, Bear Crapsinwoods."

The young man frowned. "Let's just go shoot these Arkansas yokels already."

The young man looked down the barrel of his rifle, keeping the chest of the man in his sights, who was walking two paces behind the armed "Indian" leading the line of surrendered men. At the sound of the shrill whistle, he popped up from behind the rock, steadied the rifle upon its top, and pulled the trigger. A blossom of beautiful red spread from the hole in the man's chest as an expression of divine ecstasy seemed to appear upon his face.

The young man quickly began to reload his rifle as the other "Indians" began firing their rifles as well. Some of them missed, while others hit arms and legs. A head exploded in a mist of blood and fragments of bone. The young man brought his rifle to bear again and took another shot at one of the still standing settlers. Once more a perfect shot to the heart, along with an expression of ecstasy on the face of the man.

The young man began to grin as he realized the teachings were true after all. The baptism of blood freed a man's soul. If a bullet cleansed the man of sin before going to stand before their Savior, then they were doing God's work, and it was good. He imagined the reek of gunpowder and the loud bangs of the guns were the sounds and smells of salvation. No mere earthly choir singing in the temple could be as beautiful as this moment.

The young man braced his loaded rifle once more and saw one lone settler left running in the distance. Several other "Indians" shot in the settler's direction, but the shots went wide. The young man closed his eyes briefly, whispering a prayer heard only to him and his Savior. He opened his eyes with a snap and squeezed the trigger looking at the distant settler. A red spray of blood poured from the back of the settler as he went down face first. The young man already knew the expression of the dead settler was one of rapture.

Another man in buckskins came over patting him on the back. "Good shooting, Bear. That will teach those white men invading our Indian territory. You stay here and collect the items off these bodies here. Start digging some graves as well. Me and the others have got to go help take care of those womenfolk."

The young man pushed the last shovel full of dry dusty soil over the shallow grave in front of him. Already wolves were sniffing around the fringes of the burial grounds as he kept a wary eye on the setting sun. The smell of blood and meat had drawn them down from the mountains. He didn't think it would be long before the wolves would set to digging up the bodies he had just buried. Like most flesh, even a grave was a transient thing he figured.

The young man placed his loaded rifle over his right shoulder, and then lifted the shovel over his left shoulder. He started walking toward the last direction where he had heard gunfire earlier. He imagined that he would need to help finish the burying of the womenfolk. Killing women he couldn't abide, but he'd operated a shovel on the farm since he was old enough to pick one up.

The young man topped the rise and saw the remains of the covered wagon caravan. A few arrows littered their duck canvas covered tops, and even more bullet holes had pierced their sides. A hasty low earthworks berm, fortified with the bodies of dead oxen and horses, had held off the initial raid. Across the far side of the encampment the young man heard an agonized high pitched scream followed by lower rough laughter.

The young man ran toward the sounds of the cries of pain and the low grunting and laughing. He circled around the back of one of the prairie schooners, which was mostly still intact. The rough laughter and cries of pain were coming from inside. He slowed his approach and carefully peered over the rear gate of the covered wagon.

The vision was one similar to the twisted view of hell as painted by the perverse Hieronymous Bosch. Two of his former fellows were bent over beneath the canvas cover. Their throbbing manhoods were clutched in hand as they vigorously stroked their engorged venous members. Their faces were twisted by the devil-bestowed lust, as their ropey seed spewed forth upon the pale naked back of a fragile brunette girl.

The girl was held down upon a large burlap sack of flour on the wagon's floor by a third man, kneeling between her spread legs. The girl's pale blue gingham dress had been roughly torn from her shoulders and, worse yet, moved up to her waist to reveal her shapely young legs, brown peach fuzz covered quim and her pink star asshole. The girl cried out again in pain as the third man thrust his throbbing rod of deviltry into her tight asshole.

The young man knew a group of men besotted by the deviltry of witchcraft when he saw it. Only the purification of blood would erase this stain from them. He crept back from the wagon and used the setting sun to line up the silhouettes of the two devil-besotted men, standing and stroking their hard cocks even more furiously. A moment of closed-eyed prayer for their souls and the young man snapped open his eyes releasing the bullet to perform its divine duty.

A spray of bright red arterial blood, along with the red setting sun, preceded an even more terrified scream, followed by a furious voice, "What the bloody fucking hell is going on here?!"

The young man dropped the rifle moving forward rapidly with his shovel in hand. The last man stumbled from the back of the wagon with his face covered in blood and his limp member covered in shit and dripping his seed upon the ground. The man looked at the rapidly approaching young man with confusion in his eyes.

The man spoke loudly, "Look out, Bear! Someone is shooting out here! Get down while I try to find my rifle."

The man turned back toward the wagon, tugging up his buckskin pants from his ankles with one hand. The young man thrust the sharpened edge of his shovel into the back of the man's neck. He was surprised by how easily it sliced through, cleanly removing the head, now wearing an expression of rapture. A brief fountain of blood came from the severed neck, back lit by the last of the setting sun, before the body collapsed to the ground.

The young man dropped his shovel and looked inside the covered wagon again. The upper body of the girl was pinned beneath the two dead bodies of the men he had just shot. He could hear her sobs and see her furiously wriggling to free herself, while clamping her legs tightly shut. The young man paused in thought, and then closed his eyes briefly as his lips moved in silent prayer.

The young man opened his eyes again and steeled himself to climb into the wagon. He started by shoving the bodies of the two dead men off the back of the girl, then he helped to turn her front over toward him. Her heaving bosom was barely covered by her clutching arms across the blue gingham dress in the front, and the lower skirts had thankfully dropped down to cover her legs once more.

The young man looked at her and noticed her hands had been tied together by a piece of rawhide cord. The skin near the cord was raw and chaffed. He pulled out his Indian knife and the girl's eyes widened in fear once more.

The young man glared. "It is to cut those cords, girl. I'll need you to cover up your sinful flesh once more so that others are not tempted into evil by you."

The girl looked back at him. "I'm no older than you, Mister. You can't be more 'en fifteen I recon, same as me. September nine being my birthday an' all. Just two days ago innit? Been holed up in this hell hole all this time, and now I've done been corn-holed by those whoreson bastards. God's judgment has been passed upon them by your hand I reckon."

The young man motioned for her to bring her hands forward. "Let me cut those bindings, and then cover your shame girl."

The girl returned a firm glare as he cut her bonds. "It taint my shame here. They's a pack of degenerate rapists they is. They don't even like it proper and godly neither, takin' a young girl in her tender arsehole. Watching each other's pizzels more than my own flesh, I reckon as well. Sickness is what that is. I was lucky you done come along to save me then."

The young man picked up the loaded rifle from the bed of the wagon and turned away from her. "I didn't do this to save your whorish sin-ridden self. I did this to save them from the deviltry of your flesh, which allowed Satan entry into their souls."

The girl huffed as she grabbed a piece of cloth to wipe the blood and semen from her back. "I was a virgin before today. I still am technically, since they seemed to prefer my arsehole, like the degenerates they were."

The young man turned to glare at her suddenly. "It is talk like that which bewitches a man with deviltry. Don't mention your waterworks or shit hole any more or there will be another reckoning here today. Cover up your naked skin and flee this place before the others come back. Take what supplies you can and go."

The girl shook her head. "If you were going to shoot me, you would'a done it by now. I'll go from here, but you did save me. Those others are just dead meat now, and dead by your doing. Why aren't you killin' an' rapin' like the rest of those Mormon bastards?"

The young man flushed. "My mother wouldn't want me raising a hand to no woman. She was a proper disciple of the Prophet, and a true follower of the Savior. We aren't no Mormons neither. The proper name is the Church of Jesus Christ of Latter-day Saints."

The girl laughed bitterly. "An' here I was supposed to think you were a bunch of proper English speaking Injuns. That was the reason for all the deer hides and war paint, innit? You all aren't the first to try the old Boston Tea Party trick, ya know? The only reason the cavalry pretends to fall for it is 'cause they hate Injuns more than most other folks. They know they are savages, and to them, that is a worse offense than being murdering rapist whoresons."

The young man took a couple of steps from the back of the wagon before speaking to the girl behind him. "My name is Bear

65

Crapsinwoods, understand? That is all you can tell anyone: that it was Indians. If this gets out, then the Utah wars will start right back up again after just quieting down last year. Those Republicans are trying to dismantle slavery and polygamy, always pushing their noses into other people's business."

The girl nodded sadly. "That's what my dad would say. It's why we joined the trail from Arkansas, innit? To get away from the war what everyone knows is coming soon. Too bad we done got killed here anyway. Wolves howling already, diggin' up the bodies of those you Mormon bastards has murdered."

The young man nodded in recognition of the truth of her remarks. "I guess you're right. I didn't want to be killing your people, but we have to protect our own, don't we? More and more of you coming our way, robbing our towns, assaulting our women, killing our men as well. Bringing your sinful behavior into our lands to corrupt our young men. Better to discourage others from coming, because of the savage Indians, rather than to get pushed off our own property."

The girl asked, "You goin' to leave me a gun fer the wolves?"

The young man sighed, "I'm going to gather up our weapons, we can't leave any behind for the cavalry to find. I'd look for a loaded cap and ball pistol left over from your people around here. I'll watch from that hill over there with a rifle to keep the wolves off just till you find one. Then pick a wagon away from the bodies and stay up high and quiet on it. They should leave you alone through the night with all this meat lying around. Start out at first light before dawn, and head back to the southeast. You should be able to trade some of the gear here for a ride on another wagon train. I've got to get back to the others. Promise me, by the Lord's name, you'll just tell anyone it was an Indian attack."

The girl nodded. "In the name of Jesus Christ, I'll only say it was a bunch of savages."

The young man watched from the hill as the girl found a wagon and clutched a six shooter to her covered bosom. Once she was wrapped in blankets for warmth, he gave her a wave before setting off toward his own home. It would be dark by the time he arrived, but his ma would be proud of him following orders so well.

March 15, 1883 Dodge City, Kansas

The middle-aged man walked down the street as the sky turned toward twilight. He was wearing a double breasted woolen greatcoat. His warm breath chilled into a fog as he stepped briskly toward the office of the Dodge City Times. He tightly clutched a piece of heavy parchment, with carefully written text, within his hand.

The middle-aged man opened the door of the office, to be greeted by an overweight, short, bearded man wearing a printer's apron. The middle-aged man approached the desk and placed the piece of paper upon the desktop in front of the newspaper man.

The newspaper man looked at it briefly before asking, "What's this about then?"

The middle-aged man cleared his throat. "You'll want to be printing that then. It is the new proposed ordinance being put before the community."

The newspaper man read the first part of the paper out loud: "Section 1: Any person or persons who shall keep or maintain in this city a brothel, bawdy house, house of ill fame, or of assignation, shall upon conviction thereof be fined in a sum not less than Ten nor more than One Hundred Dollars."

The middle-aged man nodded curtly. "The Dodge City Vigilantes are forming up again. There will be law in Dodge City. This sin and corruption shall not be permitted to stand. This is the last chance to put a stop to it before someone comes along to do something more permanent."

The newspaper man frowned. "Now see here, what do you mean by more permanent? What is your name, after all?"

The middle-aged man turned to look out the front window. "My name is Bob Sherman. By something permanent, I mean a purification through blood. I must be going. Don't forget to publish that as soon as possible."

The newspaper man sighed, "Are you a relative of Tom Sherman then? You know they arrested him back in seventy-three for this Dodge City Vigilante business before."

The middle-aged man walked toward the doorway. "I have places to be. A reckoning is coming unless this sinful behavior in Dodge City comes to an end."

June 8, 1883 Dodge City, Kansas

The middle-aged man walked through the swinging doors of the Long Branch Saloon. He was wearing a long duster and a large cowboy hat, unremarkable in the infamous cow town. Several eyes glanced briefly in his direction, taking his measure, and then returning to their business at hand. The middle-aged man witnessed the drinking and the gambling. Yet it was the soiled doves near the back of the saloon, pretending to be singers after the new ordnance number seventy, which drew his attention.

The middle-aged man turned away from the supposed singers and walked toward the bar. He approached the bartender wearing a striped vest and waxed mustache. The man took off his hat, and waved to the bartender.

The bartender walked over to the man. "What can I get you then? Our beer is a fresh batch, and we have some fine whiskey all the way from Tennessee."

The middle-aged man briefly shook his head. "No, thank you. I was wanting to talk to Mr. Luke Short. Is he available this evening?"

The bartender shook his head. "I'm afraid not. He's gone over to the fort yesterday with Bat Masterson, Charlie Bassett and Doc Holiday. Left him in a foul mood I hear, so he hasn't come in today. I heard they were expecting more trouble from those reformed Vigilantes. There ain't no Vigilantes who can out shoot that bunch though. They're a cold-blooded bunch of gun slingers."

The middle-aged man nodded in understanding. "Are any of them in this evening?"

The bartender shook his head. "They are all out with Mr. Short. Kind of his insurance, seeing how the Vigilantes want him run out of town."

The middle-aged man looked over toward the back of the saloon. "Are any of the soiled doves working?"

The bartender spoke quietly, "Not here, but arrangements can be made. There is a house a ways behind the saloon, where special customers can be accommodated, if you take my meaning. Just pick out a girl you like now, and pay me the delivery fee. Then you go to the house and pay the doorman's fee. Then you pay the girl's fee."

The middle-aged man sighed, "Sounds expensive with all these fees. How do I know I will be delivered the service I pay to get?"

The bartender smiled. "Why, I put your name down in the ledger under the bar, along with the name of the girl you pick. She sees you paid Mr. Short's fee, and knows you are good for her share. You'll have to wait an hour so no one sees you walking together."

The middle-aged man looked back at the stage. "What about that Sioux girl over there? Is she one of yours?"

The bartender nodded. "A bit of an alcoholic that one. Bring a bottle with you, and she'll cut her fee. We call her Pokeherhotass, since she ain't none too particular about how you do her. She prefers a whiskey enema before butt sex though. That is what the bottle is for, of course."

The middle-aged man shudders a moment before pointing at a middle-aged red head. "What about her? Is she more normal?"

The bartender smiled. "Ole Firecrotch is one of our more experienced girls. She'll treat you nice, and is not getting as much business as she used to. Getting on in years, but older is wiser they say."

The middle-aged man looked back at the bartender. "Very well, send her in about an hour. I'll go now and meet her there. Which house is it?"

The bartender put out his palm. "Cross my hand with silver first. Two dollars is the delivery fee. Two dollars at the door for room rental. Ole Fire Crotch charges a buck for an hour, or three bucks for all night."

The middle-aged man reached into his coat pocket, and after a quick shuffle, he placed two silver dollar coins in the bartender's hand. The bartender looked at the coins closely before being satisfied they were legitimate. Then he pulled out a heavy ledger book from under the counter.

The bartender carefully wrote out the number Two in one box on the page, and in the next space wrote out Fire Crotch.

The middle-aged man asked, "Where do I go now?"

The bartender replied, "Your name, good sir?"

The middle-aged man hesitated before answering, "I. P. Freely."

The bartender chuckled. "I'm sure you do, but what is your name?"

The middle-aged man frowned briefly. "Ignatious Percival Freely."

The bartender replied, "We'll just go with I. P. then, I think. Too long otherwise, Mr. Freely. You'll go two blocks south and one block west. Look for the house with the green gables. Knock on the door, and give them the pass phrase 'Purple Parakeet.' They'll know we sent you then."

An hour later, the middle-aged man approached the house with the green gables. He knocked on the door and waited for a moment until a man opened the little mail slot in the middle of the door.

The man asked, "What do you want?

The middle-aged man replied, "I was told I could find a purple parakeet here."

The man spoke back, "We haven't got any purple parakeets, but you might want to look at our other fine birds."

The man opened the door for the middle-aged man. The middle-aged man stepped inside, looking at the doorman, and a burly bouncer sitting in the parlor behind him with a drink in hand. The middle-aged man swept open his long duster, even as he kicked the door shut behind him. The noise startled the doorman and the bouncer.

The bouncer stumbled to a standing position, as the middle-aged man drew a Colt Single Action Army .45 caliber revolver and placed it against the chest of the doorman. A loud chorus of angels sounded their trump as the revolver kicked in the hand of the middle-aged man. The doorman's expression was cleared of sin in holy grace, as the middle-aged man placed the second round into the heart of the bouncer.

The middle-aged man stalked down the hallway of the house and kicked open the doorway of the first room on his right. Inside was a small unoccupied dining room. The middle-aged man heard the faint sound of people moving ahead as he stepped back out into the hallway. He kicked open the door on the left to see a living room with two women cowering on a couch beside a man holding a drawn gun.

The middle-aged man fired his third shot into the heart of the man before he could aim the weapon. The women began screaming in panic. The middle-aged man smiled at the rapture of the man, and then looked at the woman on the left reaching for the dropped pistol. He quickly took aim at the pistol and fired his fourth round. The pistol went spinning out of sight underneath the divan, as the two women began shrieking even louder.

The middle-aged man stepped out into the hall again, and ducked back as a bullet went past his head barely missing his right ear. The middle-aged man dropped low and came around the

71

corner at a crouch firing his fifth round up into the heart of a naked man, clutching a pistol in one hand and a shirt over his crotch with his other hand.

The middle-aged man kept to the side of the hallway, as he peeked with his head around the doorway of the room behind the naked man. Peering over the edge of the bed was a blonde-haired girl. She was pretty with freckles lightly dusting her face.

The middle-aged man spoke to her, "Stay put whore. You're not worth shooting."

The middle-aged man quickly pressed against the opposite wall of the hallway as he heard the sound of a hammer cocking behind the last doorway. A sudden blast of buckshot tore a wide hole in the door, but it ended up in the wall, where the middle-aged man had been standing when he spoke to the prostitute. The middle-aged man dropped down onto the floor and dove in front of the door, shooting his sixth round into the naked chest of the man holding the shotgun.

The divine voice spoke in the middle-aged man's mind, "Two more men to go. That revolver is out of bullets. Switch to your other revolver. There is one man entering from the side door of the dining room. One more is approaching from the rear of the house. You'll have ten seconds to make it to the front door. Break left. Turn around the side of the house five seconds after. Go behind the house as they go in. Catch the one in back from the rear. Now go."

June 9, 1883 Dodge City, Kansas

The well-dressed man held the heavy tome of the ledger in his hands trembling with anger. "Are you meaning to say this feller's name is supposed to be I. P. Freely? Is this some kind of prank? He shoots up my doorman, my bouncer, two paying customers, my cook, and the neighbor of the green gables, and he also has this juvenile sense of humor? Did any of the whores get a look at the man at least?"

The calm sharp-eyed man answered, "We've heard his description before."

The well-dressed man asked, "Well, who the hell is this bastard? How do we find him to cut off his balls and stuff them in his mouth?!"

The calm sharp-eyed man replied, "You don't want to tangle with this one. Everyone who's tried to find him either fails to get onto his trail, or else they never come back to report what they find. No one has ever captured, cornered or killed him."

The well-dressed man sputtered, "Well, I'll see about that. A two-hundred-dollar bounty should get some results."

The calm sharp-eyed man looked over at another man behind him, who passed over a thick sheaf of papers. Bounty poster after bounty poster of various individuals, each individual dressed differently and each poster bearing a different name. Only two things were in common between every poster. First, the man was wanted for killing men engaged in having sex with prostitutes or for killing the men running houses of ill repute. Second, the drawing on each poster depicted the same penetrating fanatical gaze being worn by the man.

The well-dressed man looked at all of the names. "Bear Crapsinwoods, Harry Balzak, Harry Wiener, Dick Liquor, Ben Dover, Peter Gozinia, Drew Peacock, Clint Toris, Dick Zucker. What is wrong with this guy? Are these names serious?"

The calm sharp-eyed man nodded. "Those are some of the names he's used in an area before going on a killing spree. The rumor is that he never uses the same name on subsequent days. He changes his mode of dress frequently to suit his new personality. He often spouts fanatical chastisements at the prostitutes after shooting up the menfolk. Invokes the names of the Prophets Smith and Young at times."

The well-dressed man shook his head. "Those Mormon crazies, damn it. Something wrong with a man who won't drink or whore

73

around, let alone a whole society of them. Are they behind him then?"

The calm sharp-eyed man shook his head slightly. "Every inquiry down those lines comes back as him once being a part of their cult, but he's been declared an apostate by their faith now. They say he's excommunicated. He doesn't go near their folks, and they condemn his violent actions, at least in public. Speculation is that he's got a source of private funding for his arms and such."

The well-dressed man sat down and pondered, "How can a wild-eyed fanatic like this feller get someone to back him?"

The calm sharp-eyed man sighed, "The better question is how he manages to consistently get one shot kills on multiple targets. It doesn't matter which gun, he always kills a person with one bullet. Most usually straight to the heart. According to your soiled doves, he moved unnaturally fast, and shot a pistol on the floor away from one of them before she could grab it. Eight shots for seven men, with one to prevent a whore from arming herself."

The well-dressed man asked, "What do you suggest then?"

The calm sharp-eyed man pointed at the stack of papers. "Put out your bounty like the rest. I wouldn't count on having to pay out. Any experienced bounty hunter looks at his crime and knows it's him. They won't take the job, as they figure it is a waste of their time. Any inexperienced bounty hunter is going to either never find him, or never come back."

The well-dressed man rubbed his nose. "Then why put out another bounty at all?"

The calm sharp-eyed man smiled. "You never know, some dumb kid might just get lucky and shoot him anyway. Gunfights are like that, after all. Skill doesn't beat sheer dumb luck."

The well-dressed man looked at the posters again. "Any idea what his real name is?"

The calm sharp-eyed man shook his head. "Bear Crapsinwoods is the oldest, but it is also obviously a fake name. That one was from that Mormon massacre of settlers over in Utah back in fifty-nine. A survivor watched him kill three Mormons who were raping her. Some figure that might be why they excommunicated him, since he killed their Mormons instead of the woman. The bounty hunters all call him El Fanatico, the Fanatic. That's because he chastises the female prostitutes, yet he never hurts them. Just tells them to marry an honest Mormon and change their evil sinful ways."

November 12, 1893 El Paso County, Colorado

The woman looked at the man sitting on the train bench across the aisle from her. She was wearing a long-sleeved yellow cotton dress, which went down to her ankles. She wore a practical set of shoes, and a no-nonsense expression on her face. Her face was more wrinkled now than as a young girl in Arkansas, and her hair had streaks of gray through the brunette. She may have been pretty once as a younger woman, but now she was just plain and worn. No pretense to vanity remained to her.

The man she watched looked to be about her age of forty-nine. His features were weathered from many long years spent outdoors. The woman couldn't help but think that he looked better this way than he did as an angry youth. He looked at peace with himself, dozing lightly on the train bench. The man's eyes suddenly snapped open, looking intently in her direction. Then he closed them again as she resumed her needlework.

The woman reflected that he had alternately ignored and watched her since she had followed him onto the train in Iron County, Missouri. He had sold his horse and rifle in exchange for a dapper businessman's suit, complete with string tie and some cash. He traveled now with a valise, and his newfangled guns were always tucked neatly inside his inner coat pockets.

She also noticed that every time he was asked his name by someone different, he gave a new one. Very common names like Robert, Thomas or Michael. The last name was usually Smith or

Thompson, or sometimes White, Brown or Green. For the most part, as she followed him, he was shy of speaking unless he was buying something or getting directions to a shop or lodging.

The one time she had approached him directly in Kansas City he had simply said, "Good day, Madam."

The woman had looked him in the eyes and asked, "Don't you remember me, Bear? You saved my life back when we was just fifteen."

The man casually stepped around her saying, "You must be mistaking me for someone else, Madam."

Hours later the woman awoke from a light sleep as the train pulled into the Colorado Springs Station. She glanced at the bench across from her to find it unoccupied. A slight panic started up her heart as she hastily gathered up her traveling bag and her sewing. She looked down the aisle at several people moving off the train, and then took a quick glance out the window.

The man stood on the platform, lightly tapping the toe of his right shoe, looking impatiently back at her. As she moved toward the exit of the rail car, he leisurely walked along the platform to the train station. She gave a brief smile knowing that he deliberately waited for her to see him before departing.

The woman walked after the man and was close enough to hear him ask for directions to a full service clothing store for men and women at the station ticket window. He asked in particular for a place which sold riding clothes. She followed half a block behind him once he left the station.

The woman entered the store after the man, just in time to hear the man ask the proprietor for clothing fit for rough use and riding.

The man turned toward the woman as she entered and spoke, "There you are. Don't just stand there gawking, my dear. That dress won't be suitable for the trail. My good man, let us get a couple of sets of suitable riding clothes then. Do you have any jodhpurs for women?"

The woman rode beside the man on a matched set of appaloosa ponies. Smaller than thoroughbreds, they were well suited for the varying terrain of the eastern Rockies. She smiled as they coursed down the trail together with the rising sun at their backs. A sense of the younger woman she used to be came through with that smile.

The woman asked, "You said there'd be answers. I never did get your real name. I know it weren't really Bear."

The man cleared his throat in embarrassment before speaking, "It is a most unfortunate one. I was named after my mother's father Harold."

The woman nodded. "Not a bad name. Sounds a bit biblical even."

The man spoke again, "My father's last name was Busch."

The woman asked, "Any relation to Adolphus Busch that brewery feller?"

The man nodded. "His older brother Ulrich Busch, Jr. was my father according to my mother. He got my mother with child without the blessings of God. He later married one of Eberhard Anheuser's daughters for the money. My mother joined up with the Church of Latter-day Saints to find a husband to raise me. I kept the last name though. At least until I first met you."

The woman nodded. "I never did properly thank you for savin' me back then."

The man shrugged. "As I said then, it wasn't for you. You women can't help being the creatures you are. It was Satan who turned you into temptresses of men's will."

The woman laughed without humor. "I haven't gone an' tempted a man since that day. Still a spinster and a virgin in God's truth. I don't take any kind of comfort with men."

The man looked at her strangely. "Why were you at the saloon in Pilot Knob?"

The woman gave a coy smile. "I was a customer of the soiled doves there, not one of the workers. The bible only says a man shall not lie down with a man. It don't say much about what we women can do with each other."

The man contemplated this thought for a while before asking, "That was more information than I was asking, but it is understandable as to why you don't like men."

The woman's face twisted into a slight grimace. "The word is hate. I hate men for the pigs they are. You're the only decent one of the lot I've ever met, since we first met. You've never looked at me with lust in your eye, and I thank you for it."

The man nodded serenely. "My eye only sees the beauty of god's grace in his creation. Like these marvels of God's work you see here in this place called the Garden of the Gods. Women are just creatures upon God's creation like any other creature. Look, those up-thrust rocks there are called the Three Graces. That is our destination. That is where you'll find the answers you seek."

They dismounted and tied their horses' reigns to some of the low brush. The woman followed behind the man as he moved toward the narrow crack in the formation of rock. As he stepped toward it, she tapped him once on the back.

The woman spoke, "It's too narrow. We ain't gone ta fit."

The man turned his head and smiled. "Like the righteous toward heaven, even the narrowest path will open if you have enough faith."

The man stepped through and seemed to slip between the narrow crack, and disappear from her sight. The woman grasped her bosom briefly and stepped through to follow him. A sensation of greasy squeezing occurred and she became unconscious.

The woman's eyes opened and she found herself groggily lying upon a molded table made of a mysterious white material. Her arms and upper body were strapped down, and only a thin paper-like gown covered her upper torso. He legs were strapped into stirrups and her lower extremities felt a breeze as they were exposed to the gentle movement of the open air.

A voice sounded in her head and she looked over to her left: "Remove the rectal telepathic interface."

Laying face down on a white table beside her was Bear. His hairy ass was exposed, as the thin paper-like gown he wore only covered his upper torso. A line of drool came from his mouth as a long chrome metallic armature came down from the ceiling toward his buttocks. A set of intricate pincers gleamed at the end of the arm.

The woman looked on in horror as the gleaming arm reached between his cheeks and extracted a gleaming red tube from his tight-sphinctered anus. A spray of soupy shit came out shortly after, as Bear emitted a contented sounding sigh.

The voice spoke again in her mind: "Send in the fecal cleaning organisms."

A pair of foot-long chitinous bugs, with tentacles instead of legs, entered through a small doorway, and began joyously eating up the shit forcefully ejected from Bear's ass onto the floor. Once the shit monsters finished, the chrome armature returned from the ceiling, grasping a glowing blue tube glistening with lubricant.

The voice spoke again: "Insert the upgraded rectal telepathic interface."

Bear grunted as the blue tube was inserted into his rectum. A slight smile spread on his lips as a few drops of piss dripped from his limp penis. The woman looked over toward her right in revulsion. A long line of similar tables, covered with various people wearing robes, turbans, miters and clerical collars, was stretched out into the distance, getting tubes either inserted or removed from their rectums.

The voice spoke into her mind again: "All the intolerant assholes are here. They will all get a thought stick up their asses, and hear the words of Xenu. They will think the words of Xenu are the words of their gods. When they have finished riling up their followers and killing each other off in the name of their religions and hatreds, then the ones who are Thetan shall arise. Xenu will bring them back, and they will find paradise."

The woman screamed as a gleaming armature came down from the ceiling above her - a glowing blue tube in its grasp.

"Anyone who limits her vision to
memories of yesterday is already dead."
- Lillie Langtry

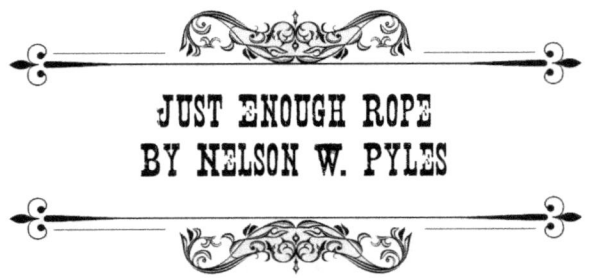

JUST ENOUGH ROPE
BY NELSON W. PYLES

*Nelson W. Pyles is an author of horror fiction. His latest work can be found in **Fear The Abyss** from Post Mortem Press and in the upcoming **From Beyond The Grave** from Grinning Skull Press. His short story, **Decorations**, was published in **The Big Book of Bizarro** by Burning Bulb Publishing and **Dark Doorways** by Post Mortem Press.*

*His work has appeared alongside F. Paul Wilson, Jack Ketchum, Jessica McHugh, John Russo and Harlan Ellison. He also hosts **The Wicked Library**, a weekly podcast featuring the work of up and coming horror writers.*

*He currently resides in Pittsburgh PA. Find out more by visiting **www.nelsonwpyles.com.***

CHAPTER 1

Clem smiled as the bullet slammed into his forehead and threw him backward onto the dusty street. When he hit the ground, the dirt and sand flew up around his body. There was a thud and then silence as the dust began to blow in the wind. Blood poured from the hole in Clem's forehead like a geyser. His body gave a small twitch in the bright Arizona sunlight.

Wall holstered his gun and walked toward Clem's body. The sound of his boots broke the silence, and the small crowd that had watched quietly began to scatter. It was the way of things; people gunned down in the street for money or justice or both. The show at this point was over and no one had seen anything worth waiting around for anymore.

Wall reached Clem's body and knelt down to look at him. Clem's eyes were still open and he still wore that damn smile. Wall reached over and closed the dead man's eye lids. He couldn't stand to have him looking up at the sky. He stood up and looked around. Of course, there was only the mortician, ready to claim his prize, and already moving to take the body with his huge assistant. They both dressed in black suits, covered in dust.

"That was a hell of a shot, Mr. Wall. Name's Dooley" the mortician said, sticking out his hand. Wall took it and shook quickly. "Yes sir, we heard you'd be looking for Clem and we heard you was a hell of a shot."

"More lucky than anything," Wall said. "How long you reckon you're gonna prop him up for, Mr. Dooley?"

The mortician shrugged.

"I guess a day or two, unless you need to leave in a hurry," Dooley replied. "We got a nice hotel right there across the street and some good eats right next to it."

Wall looked down at Clem. He would clear five hundred dollars after dragging Clem back to Texas. After tracking him for three months, it was over. Maybe he'd stay a day or two. Maybe he'd earned some sleep in a real bed.

He looked at Dooley, who seemed to be waiting for an answer.

"I reckon a day or two would be good. He's yours until I come for him."

Dooley beamed.

"Oh, thank you, Mr. Wall!" he said. He hit the large brute in the ill-fitting suit next to him. "Shake the shit out of your eyes and pick 'im up, Big Pink."

The man he called Big Pink walked over to Clem and grabbed him under his arms. He lifted the dead man easily and dragged him away, boots making two lines in the dirt. Dooley had started making light conversation about putting Clem's body on display and the money that would come in from "photo opportunities," but Wall had already tuned him out and looked at the hotel. He was suddenly very tired and wanted a drink and some sleep.

He walked away from Dooley, giving a small wave so as not to be rude. He walked slowly to the wooden steps and climbed them as if he had suddenly gained weight.

He opened the door and stepped into the lobby. There were scattered few people sitting, chatting up whores from the place next door, but he ignored them and walked to the front desk. A small burly man walked over to greet him, smiling.

"It's an honor to meet you, Mr. Wall," the man said. "I'm Stanley Bosen and I'm the manager here at the Bosen Hotel."

Bosen looked at him. Wall was a tired-looking man of about 30 and fairly average looking with black hair. But his eyes... ice green and cruel-looking.

"I'm sure once the whores next door find out you're staying here, they'll be all over you."

"If you could kind of keep that quiet, I'd be obliged," Wall said. "And you don't have to keep calling me mister. Tom or Wall will do just fine. How much for two nights?"

Bosen smiled.

"Our regular rooms are five a night Mister... I mean, Tom. The suites come with a full bath. Just filled them up about an hour ago. Those are seven-fifty. But..." Bosen stopped and grabbed his ledger. "I may be able to make a slight deal with you."

"What kind of 'slight deal?'" Wall asked.

"Well, it seems the object of your visit to our fine little town had stayed here and actually paid for a suite in advance. Three days left to go, seein' as he won't be coming back anytime soon." He gave Wall a wink. "It's all yours if you want it. It's a suite!"

Wall considered this. He wasn't broke, not even close, but if he could save a little on the trip... Well, maybe he could get a train ticket back to Texas, instead of hauling Clem around for weeks. And damn, he sure was tired.

"I couldn't just stay for free," Wall said. "But a discount would be awful nice."

Bosen smiled even bigger.

"Two dollars a night," Bosen said. "And a picture of you to hang up at my billiards room next door. It isn't often we get a genuine celebrity here."

Wall frowned.

"I ain't a celebrity," Wall said. "But I'll take the deal."

"Oh, but you are a celebrity, Tom. I can try to keep your presence here quiet as I can, but everyone knows who you are and this is the only hotel in town..." Bosen said. "And that'll be two dollars for the first night."

Wall reached into his pants and pulled out the money requested. Bosen took the money, put it in a drawer and filled out his ledger. He spun the big book around for Wall to sign.

"Just sign here, Tom," Bosen said. Tom grabbed a pen and signed his name. Bosen suddenly slammed the book closed and rang a bell. He pulled a key out from behind the counter and handed it to Wall.

"Your room is 311, top floor. If you wouldn't mind, we'd like to give the room a good once over before you go in and get settled. Take this over to the billiards room next door and have a drink on me."

Bosen handed Wall a round-looking coin that said "FREE DRINK TO THE BARER." He turned it over and it said the same thing.

"We'll let you know when your room is ready, Tom."

Wall nodded and said, "Much obliged again." He tipped his hat and walked out of the hotel. As he left, a young man ran over to Bosen at the front desk.

"Please prepare 311 for a new guest. Box up Mr. Clem's items and bring them to me in my office, okay?"

The young man grabbed a ring of keys and ran up the stairs in the center of the room to do as he had been told. Bosen watched Wall through the window slump over to the billiards room next door. He smiled.

CHAPTER 2

Wall knew the second he walked into the billiards room, it was a huge mistake. He didn't care though. A free drink was a free drink and he needed one badly.

He tried to keep his head down and walked to a dark corner of the bar. An old bartender came over with a slight limp and a mouth full of bad teeth.

"What can I do you for?" he asked, wiping the dusty bar in front of Wall with a filthy rag.

"You got beer?" Wall asked.

"Hell son, it's even cold," the bartender said, grinning. "That's a quarter if you want it."

Wall slapped the drink token on the bar and slid it to the bartender.

"Well then, a drink for our special guest," the bartender said. "On the house at that!" The bartender disappeared and returned with a foamy mug of beer. He set it in front of Wall, who grabbed it and downed about half of it before putting it down again.

"God damn, that's cold!" he said, laughing a little. He wiped his mouth off on his sleeve and smiled. How long had it been since he smiled? He couldn't recall. The bartender laughed with him.

"Told you son, we serve 'em cold here."

"Damned if you don't," Wall said. He reached into his pocket and pulled out some coins. He put four on the bar.

"That first one's on the house, but keep them coming, sir," Wall said, reaching for his beer.

"Call me Hank, and you got it. Don't drink 'em all that fast. Your head'll feel like old Clem's before too long if you do."

Wall laughed again and took a deep drink of the beer. He had always been amazed at how one small thing could turn you right around. He was ready to go lie down and he was still damn tired, but a cold beer was a rare thing even in the big cities. And just when he needed a cold drink, he found it in the tiny town of... of...

"Hank, what's the name of this town?" Wall asked, but Hank had gone on to help another customer.

Aw, hell with it. Who cares? Wall thought. Just enjoy your damn drink, dummy.

He adjusted how he was sitting and began to relax for the first time in weeks. He took a deep breath and let it out slowly. He closed his eyes for a minute and let the cold fire in his belly soothe him a little bit.

It didn't last long.

He felt a hand gently touch his shoulder. His nose was filled with flowers and almonds. The hand gently massaged his shoulder and moved down to his back.

A whore.

He opened his eyes and expected to see a large woman, rode hard for too many years and looking to make some money. What he saw was something he'd not expected.

She was beautiful. She couldn't have been more than twenty, if that. She had coral lips, gray eyes and a mop of long curly black hair that was tied in an unruly bun underneath a small hat. She was dressed like a fine lady. He knew damn well she wasn't, but she could pass for one to be sure. She saw him looking at her and she smiled.

"Hello, Mr. Wall. Buy a lady a drink?"

Wall honestly didn't know what to say, so he smiled. He brushed off the seat next to him and gestured for her to sit. He forgot his manners, but recovered enough to stand slightly until she sat. She winked at him.

"You are definitely not from anywhere near here, are you? Such courtesy," she said smiling. Wall blushed a little. Must be the beer, he thought. He slapped his hand on the bar and beckoned Hank over, who obliged.

"Drink for the lady and I'll take another beer please," Wall said. He looked at the girl, who gave a shy nod, still smiling.

"I'll get you and Veronique drinks right quick. And, good call, son!"

Hank went to get the drinks and Veronique turned to Wall.

"Thank you," she said. "And might I say, that was one hell of a shot you made on Mr. Jackson a little while ago. Hell of a shot."

"Thanks," was all Wall could think to say. He picked up the rest of his beer and downed it in one gulp. It felt good and he was feeling a little loose. He had to be careful not to get too loose. Veronique was a whore and, as pretty as she was, just a whore out for some of his money. He'd known enough whores who would slit your neck if you had enough money on you. She didn't seem the type, but he'd been wrong about women before.

"Where did you learn to shoot like that?" she asked.

"Ma'am, I was a Texas Ranger for about ten years. Learned real quick, you had better hit what you're shooting at, or you wouldn't last too long in the job."

Her eyes lit up.

"A real Texas Ranger? That's exciting!" Veronique pulled a little book out of the side of her dress. It was a 'penny dreadful' that had a picture of what was supposed to be Wall. She held it up.

"I must have read this about twenty times and it didn't say anything about you being a Texas Ranger," she said. Wall frowned and took the little book.

The title of the dreadful was "Tom Wall: Youngest and Best Bounty Hunter This Side of the Pecos River! Becoming a Legend before Thirty! Quick Draw Killer!"

Wall looked at it for a while and then laughed. He handed it back to Veronique.

"Well, I reckon if they ain't put the Ranger part in, they probably got just about everything else wrong too," he said, as Hank dropped off their drinks. Wall pushed the money over the bar, but Hank waved his hand.

"I started you a tab, son. Go get yourself in some trouble there. I got other people need drinks." He winked and left.

He grabbed his beer and she reached for her drink; a glass of wine of some kind. She held it up.

"Cheers, Mr. Wall. Here's to us."

He clinked his beer, as gently as he could, to her wine glass.

"To... us," he said.

The two took a few sips of their drinks and began to talk to each other. He was learning a lot about himself, that was one thing. She must've read that damn penny dreadful a lot more than twenty times. She was quoting entire passages verbatim from the book. Although the stories she was asking him about were pure made up bullshit, it was pretty flattering to hear someone talk to him about him for a change. He watched her as she lit up, talking about his alleged adventures and watching her sink, and then laugh, as he told the real versions.

He also knew when he was being played and he wasn't getting that feeling from Veronique. Maybe it was the beer. Maybe it wasn't, but he was enjoying himself.

Relaxing.

He felt good.

After a few more cold beers and wine, they decided to get something to eat. They asked Hank about the food and he assured them he'd have something nice fixed up for them. In a short while, he brought out two steaming wooden bowls of stew and some

89

crusty bread. Veronique took little bites, but Wall devoured his after the first bite.

"Hank, what kind of meat is this?" Wall asked, with a mouthful of the stew.

"Fresh," Hank replied. "Good ain't it? The wife does a damn good job, don't you think?"

Wall smiled and nodded as he tore back into the bowl. He was finished in five minutes. Veronique giggled as he looked up at her, mouth covered with stew.

"Lordy, excuse me!" he said and laughed a little himself. "Been so long since I had a sit down meal, I forgot my manners."

"I like to see a man eat," Veronique said, grabbing a napkin from the bar and wiping his mouth. She leaned in closer to him and said, "What else has it been a long time for, Mr. Wall?"

CHAPTER 3

Veronique lay sleeping with an arm across Wall's chest. He looked down at her and smiled to himself. They came to his room, took a bath together and spent the next few hours exhausting and pleasing each other. He'd been with his share of whores, but she seemed less like one and more like someone he could be with for a long time. It was a fool's thought to be sure, but he was enjoying all of her, even while she slept.

He had tried to sleep along with her, but he was wide awake. The combination of the beer, food and sex should have knocked him out and he knew this, but he was up and alert. He kept looking at her and stroked her hair. She gave a little smile in her sleep and he felt her snuggle up closer to him.

"I could get used to this," he whispered. Veronique opened her eyes and looked up at him.

"Why Mr. Wall," she said in her own whisper. "You sound a little bit smitten."

Wall had to laugh and she climbed on top of him and kissed his cheek.

"I reckon I ain't alone in it either," he said, kissing her neck.

"No sir, you are not," she said, finding his mouth. They kissed deep and hard for a moment, until she broke off and looked at him.

"You don't always kiss whores like that, do you, Mr. Wall?"

"No, I do not," he said. "But I ain't really thinking of you as a whore. And, it's Tom. Not mister anything to you."

A small tear streamed down her face and she kissed him again. He reached up and grabbed her as they fell into each other again. When they finished this time, he fell asleep, tangled in Veronique's arms, and he slept as well as he ever did.

CHAPTER 4

Wall awoke to find the room dark. Veronique was still sleeping next to him and he carefully got out of the bed. Naked, he walked over to the heavy oak dresser where he'd thrown most of what was in his pockets, and found his matches. He lit the oil lamp on the dresser and looked for his pocket watch. He popped it open and saw through the dim light that the watch had stopped. He frowned, but realized he didn't really care about the time. He had started to think about dragging Clem's body back to Texas.

He looked at Veronique, sleeping peacefully on the bed. What was he going to do about her? It hurt his head to think about leaving her here, but could he haul her and a stinking corpse on a train bound for Texas? He sure as hell couldn't take her on the trail, if he decided to go that way.

He decided he needed some air, so he quietly put on his dungarees, boots, a shirt, and strapped his gun on just in case. He left the room quietly and walked down the dimly lit hallway toward the stairs. As he walked slowly down the carpeted staircase, he heard voices speaking in hushed tones. He resisted the urge to stop and listen, as was ingrained in him from a decade in the Texas

Rangers. It was harder than he thought it would be, and his hand found itself resting on his gun. (That urge, he never resisted.)

When he finished his descent, he saw Bozen and Dooley, the mortician, chatting away quietly. They both regarded him and smiled.

"Nice night for a walk, Mr. Wall?" Bozen asked, smiling.

Wall walked closer to the two men. Dooley looked as pale as milk.

"Feeling a little poorly, Mr. Dooley?" Wall asked.

Dooley swallowed and shook his head.

"I'm... yes. Poorly, that's about right." His voice sounded shaky. "We're gonna prop your bounty in front of the hotel in the morning, Mr. Wall. If you'd like to pose for some of those pictures, that would sure help things along."

Wall shook his head.

"You do what you need to do with him, but I've already done what I needed to do with that bastard. Save for draggin' him back to Texas that is."

Dooley nodded.

"When do you reckon you'll be heading back?" Dooley asked.

"I ain't sure just yet. I'll let you know before the end of tomorrow. Depends on the train schedule."

"Train?" Dooley turned paler, if that were possible. "You gonna put him on a train?"

"If I had wings, I'd fly that crooked son of a bitch back to Texas," Wall said, flatly. "I don't want to have to spend any more time with him than I have to. I spent three months chasing his ass here. I'm done."

Bozen laughed.

"Well, you should take your time to decide, Mr. Wall. Still have a few days on that room after all. Besides, Mr. Dooley can put him on ice, so he doesn't stink up the train when you leave at the end of the week, if that's what you decide to do."

Bozen leaned over the counter.

"And I'm sure your new 'friend' would sure like you to stay a little longer."

Wall nodded.

"I'll think about it" was all he said. He tipped his hat and walked out the hotel door. Dooley followed right behind him.

As he walked along the street, he felt a little chilly, but it also felt good. He still had the lingering smell of Veronique on him and he again thought about getting used to it.

"What do you want, Mr. Dooley?" Wall asked the man behind him. He kept walking and the mortician followed behind him.

"I wanted to talk to you, Mr. Wall. Can you stop for a minute?"

"I can walk and talk at the same time, if it's all the same to you."

Dooley sighed, but walked faster to catch up to Wall's longer stride.

"I was wondering," Dooley began. "If you had thought about leaving a little sooner."

Wall said nothing.

"You know, to get a jump on the trip? Get home earlier? Relax before your next job?"

"This here is my last job," Wall replied. "And I'm relaxing just fine."

Wall stopped and whirled to look at Dooley.

"Some reason I should leave?" he asked a trifle cold.

Dooley stopped dead in his tracks. He looked terrified, but not of Wall.

"Well, sir, I really can't... I'm not at liberty to... oh my..." Dooley was shaking all over. "I can't do this anymore."

"Do what?" Wall was genuinely confused. "What are you going on about, Dooley? You're as white as a sheet."

Dooley grabbed a wooden column and held himself up.

"It's too much," he said, nearly sobbing. "Just too damned much. It's gotta end."

Wall moved toward Dooley and held a hand out to steady the man, but Dooley moved away from him.

"This town is poison, Mr. Wall. The longer you stay, the harder it'll be for you to leave - and leave you must!"

"What do you mean, poison?"

He thought of Veronique and wondered why the hell he got out of bed.

"I mean poison. This place, this damn town, is a trap!" Dooley was tearing up and drooling slightly.

"You're talkin' shit, Dooley. What are you getting at?"

Dooley grabbed Wall's arm and pulled him close.

"Come with me, quickly" he said, and began to drag Wall down the street.

CHAPTER 5

They arrived a few minutes later at a barn that had a sign on the front. "Arthur P. Dooley: Mortician and Undertaker. Do Not Enter!" Although it was dark, the big white lettering was pretty easy to read in the moonlight. Dooley fumbled with a key and unlocked the barn door. He unengaged the lock and looked at Wall, who looked confused.

"Do you have matches?" Dooley asked.

Wall held up his small tinderbox and nodded.

"Come inside, quick." Dooley said, and disappeared into the barn. Wall hesitated a moment and looked around. He had no idea why someone would follow him here, but he'd been a ranger too long to act otherwise. He carefully walked into the barn.

Dooley waited until he was in all the way and closed the door.

"Come here with your matches," Dooley said, and walked quickly over to a large heavy blanket covering up something large. On a small table next to it was an oil lamp. He reached out for the tinderbox and Wall handed it to him. Dooley's hand was shaking so badly, he couldn't strike the match. Wall, not needing to be asked, walked over and took the matches away to light the lamp.

"Thank you," Dooley said quietly.

Wall lit the match and touched it to the wick. He put the glass cover on it and turned the wick up about an inch for maximum light. He was a few feet from the covered object and felt cold.

"This is where I keep the bodies when they aren't on display," Dooley explained. "The blanket slows down the melting a little and it also covers up the box and the smell. You may want to hold your nose or something."

"I've smelled worse," Wall said, but braced himself anyway. Dooley pulled the blanket off and there, between the two ice blocks, was a wooden coffin with the lid off. Inside was Clem, still smiling, and the bullet hole in his forehead, looking like a third eye.

The body was stripped naked to the pants, but there was something not right.

Most of his torso was missing.

Wall moved closer to look and the smell indeed was awful, but it didn't stop him. He turned and carefully grabbed the oil lamp from the small table.

"Careful, Mr. Wall," Dooley said.

"I ain't an idjit," Wall said calmly. "Just want to see what the hell this is all about."

He moved the lamp closer and saw that almost the entire torso was picked damn near clean. There was almost no blood, as if the body had never had any inside.

"So why would you do this, Mr. Dooley? There ain't nothing but a set of ribs left. This some kind of undertaker thing?"

"I didn't do this," Dooley said. "My young associate, Big Pink, did this and he was told to do it. This is why you need to leave."

Wall frowned.

"What the hell do I tell them folks when I go to claim my bounty on this man?" Wall was getting angry.

Dooley shook his head.

"You're missing the point, Mr. Wall."

Wall stepped backward and put the lamp down. He looked at Dooley.

"You're telling me I need to leave right god damn now for no good reason, and then you show me that you desecrated this dumb bastard's corpse, and expect me to haul it back like this?"

"This is what happens to folks who die here, Mr. Wall. This is what always happens to them."

"What, somebody dies and they scoop 'em out like a damn canoe? That don't make no sense at all."

"Do you want to know why he was smiling when you shot him?"

"I just told you, he was a dumb bastard," Wall replied.

"No, no. Think back to before you shot him. What did he say?"

Wall thought about it. He didn't like to think about the act of killing, especially folks he'd killed whether they deserved it or not. It was still taking a life, and although Clem's life wasn't worth shit, it was still a life.

Wall had been walking up the street when Clem had come running out of the bar attached to the hotel.

"Clem Jackson!" Wall had yelled and the stupid son of a bitch stopped dead in his tracks. He looked at Wall for a long time.

"Come all this way to fetch me, Tommy?" Clem asked, snickering. "All this was just for me?"

"I can bring you in one of two ways, Clem," Wall said. "I'd be obliged if you were able to walk to your hanging."

"What's the difference, if I'm already a dead man?"

"A hundred dollars," Wall said flatly, and Clem laughed.

"Well, damn your hundred dollars. You're going to have to kill me now."

"I'd rather not," Wall said. "I'll see you get a fair trial."

"Trust me, Tommy," Clem said, moving toward Wall. "If you kill me now, you'll be doing me a favor."

Wall pulled his gun and aimed it at Clem.

"Not another step," he said.

Clem smiled and kept walking.

"Oh, I'll take all the steps I can get, if you're gonna put me down. And that's what everybody wants."

Wall shook his head.

"Clem? You best stop coming now, I ain't foolin'."

He continued forward.

"Just do it," Clem said, smiling. "I got it comin' and I want it. I want it now!"

Clem pretended to reach for his gun and Wall shot him right between the eyes.

The smile never left his face as he fell. As he fell, Wall had noticed that he wasn't wearing a side holster. He'd shot him unarmed. Normally that would have bothered him, but Clem did, in fact, have it coming after all.

Wall looked at Dooley.

"He said, 'You'd be doing me a favor'," Dooley said, and the words that had been lost on Wall suddenly had some weight.

"How long had Clem been here before I found him?" Wall asked.

"About two days," Dooley said after a pause. "He was living it up the first night. Whores, liquor, the food and the works. All poison." Dooley wiped his palms on his suit. "He didn't want to leave until it was too late. He tried to, but he couldn't. And then you showed up."

Wall sighed.

"Sounds like he was having a good time. Why would he want to leave?"

"Exactly," Dooley said. "That's what you need to ask yourself. Why would he want to leave."

Wall was missing something and he hated missing something. He told this to Dooley. Dooley responded with a question.

"You see any livestock on your way into this town?"

"No I didn't. I figured you had a delivery here and there, what with all this ice to keep it cool."

"Where's all this ice coming from?" Dooley asked. His eyes narrowed. "Where's a dog? Or a horse? Or a god damn fly? For that matter, where's your horse?"

Wall's horse was dead, he knew that much, but that was about it. He couldn't think of a reason for any of the questions, but just because he couldn't think of one, didn't mean there wasn't one.

"Mr. Dooley, I think I'm done here. I'll be leaving in the morning with my claim. I'd appreciate it if you could write something up explaining why his god damn insides are missing."

Wall turned and walked to the barn door.

Dooley hurried after him.

"But you have to leave now!" Dooley cried. "Don't you see? It'll be too late in the morning!"

Wall turned and grabbed Dooley by the jacket.

"I've about had enough of this, Dooley. You talk in circles and you desecrate the dead. If I were still a Texas Ranger, I'd haul you back with Clem and have you strung up."

"This isn't Texas," Dooley said. "You'd have no jurisdiction here."

Wall jerked the man up to his face.

"There's an old saying: 'A Texas Ranger's jurisdiction is wherever he happens to be'." With that, he pushed Dooley back and kicked the barn door open. "Have him ready to travel, Dooley. I'll come for him when I'm ready."

CHAPTER 6

By the time Wall walked back into the hotel, the place was dark and quiet. There was some noise coming from the billiards room next door, but that was to be expected. He had noticed that he couldn't hear a single cricket on his walk back to the hotel and was going to ask Veronique when he got back upstairs.

He climbed the stairs two at a time, and a little faster, as he thought about Veronique. Right now, all he wanted was her. He gave a little distracted laugh and marveled at how often he'd smiled and laughed since he pulled into this town.

It was her.

He decided he was going to ask her to come with him.

Wall reached the top of the stairs and turned right down the hall to his room. He got to the door and pulled his boots off to try and be quiet, in case she was still sleeping. He heard her before opening the door and she was crying. He threw the door open, dropped his boots and drew his gun.

He saw her wide-eyed and sitting on the bed, still naked. She recoiled from Wall as he looked around the room.

"You all right?" he asked sternly. She gave a little yelp and stared at him. "Is somebody in here?"

She shook her head slowly 'no,' and began to cry again. Wall holstered his gun and ran to the bed.

"What's wrong, darlin'? I thought someone was in here with you, hurtin' you or somethin'."

She lunged into his arms.

"I thought you left me," she said through a hail of sobs. She clutched him tightly. "I know it's stupid, because I'm just a whore and all, but..."

He grabbed her back and chuckled.

"I ain't leavin' you," he said. "And you just made askin' you to come with me a hell of a lot easier."

She hugged him tighter and then kissed his neck. She looked up at him.

"Oh Tom, I love you," she said, still crying; a serious look on her face. "But we can't leave."

Wall looked down at her.

"What do you mean, 'can't leave'?"

She sniffed.

"Darlin', we can't ever leave here if we're gonna be together. We just can't."

Wall kissed her head and stood up.

"What are you scared of? Of course, we can leave. Anytime we want."

She pulled a blanket around her and stood up.

"You don't understand. I have to stay here. You can go, but I have to stay."

Wall folded his arms.

"Is it Bozen? You work for him, right? What's it gonna take to get you out of here?"

She shook her head.

"It's more than just that," she said. "A lot more. It's this town, Tom. It's..."

"Poison?"

She looked shocked.

"Who told you that?"

"Dooley. Just showed me a thing or two." He walked over to the dresser and turned the fading oil lamp up a little for more light. He started to gather his things. "Like, Clem Jackson, with a lot of his insides gone. He was trying to get me to leave before sunrise. Said the town was poison."

Veronique walked over to him.

"It is poison, Tom, and it won't matter if it's sunrise or not." She put a hand on his shoulder. "I want you to stay, but only if you love me."

He turned and looked at her. He kissed her forehead.

"I do love you, which is why we're both gettin' the hell out of this place. What do you want to bring with you?"

She gave a sob and a sigh.

"Tom, you don't understand. I can't leave."

Wall took the bedroll and threw it down. He grabbed Veronique and brought her closer to his face.

"I'm getting awful tired of being talked to in circles. Tell me what the problem is!"

As she recoiled from him, the door flew open. Wall snapped his head in the door's direction and saw Bozen, holding a shotgun aimed right at the two of them.

"The lady said she can't leave and she can't, Mr. Wall." Bozen said, smiling a little. "You'd do well to let her loose now."

He looked at her and let her go. She backed away from him slowly, turning to Bozen.

"Don't hurt him, Stanley. He loves me."

Bozen laughed.

"That's because he doesn't know you very well."

Wall frowned.

"Now just a damn minute, Bozen!"

Bozen raised the shotgun and moved closer to Wall.

"You hold on a minute, son," Bozen said. "We were gonna let you ride on out of here, but you're making it awful hard for me to not blow your head off. There's a lot at work here, Mr. Wall."

Wall counted to himself all the way to three before Bozen's shotgun was close enough. He grabbed the barrel, yanked it hard to one side and pulled it right out of Bozen's hands. Wall wrapped both hands around the barrel and drove the wooden handle by the trigger into Bozen's forehead, knocking him down. Wall flipped the gun and cocked it, aiming at Bozen, who was now bleeding from his forehead.

"Why don't you start telling me what's at work here, before I lose my sunny disposition," Wall said coldly. Bozen looked surprised and then he smiled.

"It's all about to become clear, Mr. Wall," Bozen said, holding his head. Wall was about to respond when a sharp blow turned the dark room darker and Wall fell to the floor, unconscious.

101

CHAPTER 7

Wall woke up and couldn't move. He opened his eyes and saw the ceiling of a barn. It hurt his head to move, but he looked from side to side, and saw he'd been tied to a wooden table. His feet and hands were lashed to the table, spread out, and heavy rope was across his chest.

"Hey!" he yelled out. "You best cut me loose!"

A moment later, the barn door opened and he felt a hot rush of air hit him as sunlight poured into the barn.

"Good morning, Mr. Wall!" Bozen said, walking in slowly. Wall strained to see him and the two figures with him. They were Hank the bartender and Veronique. She moved quickly over to Wall and touched his face.

"Tom, I'm so sorry. This is all my fault."

It was Wall's turn to recoil from her.

"Why did you hit me?" he asked.

"I couldn't let you kill Stanley," she said sadly. "He's a no good bastard, but you can't just kill him."

Wall struggled with his bonds to no avail. He looked at Veronique in pure anger.

"I thought you loved me."

She smiled sweetly.

"I do, so very much, my love," she said, and stroked his face. "And I always will."

He struggled again. Veronique looked at him sadly and moved away from him.

Hank leaned closer to Bozen.

"Maybe we shoulda kept Big Pink around a little longer," he said. Bozen shook his head.

"Mr. Wall, do you know where you are?"

Wall stopped struggling.

"I reckon I'm in Dooley's barn with Clem's body cooling off," he said. Bozen clapped his hands.

102

"Yes, poor Mr. Dooley. We had to let him and his charge go earlier this morning," Bozen said.

"That means," Hank chimed in, "we had them destroyed."

"Enough," Bozen said. "Hank, I want to hear something out of you, I'll god damn ask for it."

Wall swallowed hard.

"You have put us in a rather strange position, Mr. Wall. We can't let you leave, but we don't want to kill you either, in spite of your rush to hitting me in the head," Bozen said.

"Cut me loose and I'll do more than hit your head, Bozen," Wall said through his teeth.

Bozen laughed. He walked over to Wall and looked down at him.

"You know what the name Bozen means, Mr. Wall?"

Wall didn't answer.

"It's a German word. It means 'evil.' I don't tell you that to scare you or nothing, but it is my name and there's lots of folks that would say it's appropriate."

Wall looked up at him and said nothing.

"You don't scare easy and I like that, Mr. Wall. So I'm going to make a deal with you for the sake of your lover over there. Are you listening?"

Wall nodded.

"Good. Like I said, I don't want to kill you, but I will. I don't have the burden of feeling bad or guilty about things I have to do, but I don't like to waste things either." He pointed to a different side of the barn. "Your prize, Clem Jackson over there, is a perfect example. Dooley showed what's left of him to you, yes?"

Again, Wall nodded.

"Did he happen to tell you why?"

"No, he did not."

"Food, Mr. Wall. We used him for food."

Wall allowed this to sink in and struggled to get free again. Bozen waited for him to stop, and when he did, he smiled.

"Before you go on and start getting the idea that we're gonna eat you, I want you to consider something. There's a lot of things in this world you don't know or understand. We hate what we don't understand. You hate rattlesnakes, because if you piss them off, they'll bite and kill you. But they have their purpose. Part of God's plan. Just like us."

Wall looked at him with disgust.

"Eating your own kind is part of 'God's plan'? That's bullshit."

Bozen leaned down to Wall's face. He saw that Bozen's eyes weren't any color at all. They were almost all black.

"I never said we ate our own kind," Bozen said.

"What the hell does that mean?" Wall asked.

Veronique carefully walked over to Wall.

"Tom, please listen. We can still be together," she pleaded.

"Yes," Bozen said, still near Wall's face. "You can still be with her, very much alive and probably pretty happy. But I'm only making this deal once."

Wall looked at Veronique, and then back at Bozen, who looked hungry.

"What we are, and by that I mean everyone in this town, isn't as important as what we do." Bozen stood back, becoming aware of his drooling. "We take the unsavory elements of society and dispose of them. Like Mr. Jackson. We lie in wait for brigands, thieves, murderers and the like to come to our town and we kill them. And then, because of what we are, we eat them. So we don't have to go to a big town and kill innocent people. God's plan."

"We aren't really people," Veronique said shyly. "But we're pretty close... and I do love you so."

Wall looked at Bozen in horror.

"You're like god damn spiders," he said.

Bozen looked at Veronique and smiled.

"That's a very good analogy! I quite like that, Mr. Wall."

"You're monsters!"

Bozen's smile faded and he got very close to Wall's face again.

"We are Americans, sir!" Bozen snarled. "This country has been very good and kind to us. The least we can do is not eat those who have done us no harm."

"When I was a little girl," Veronique began. "My family were hunted down and slaughtered for what we are. I am the only one in my family still alive. Here, no one tries to kill me."

Hank stepped forward.

"It works out, Mr. Wall. Sure, what we do seems gruesome to you. But look at what we do. Only the criminals. We're doing regular folks a favor."

Wall remembered what Clem had said before he shot him in the forehead.

You'll be doing me a favor.

"You see, Mr. Wall. We aren't evil. Just like a spider isn't evil for eating bugs and such," Bozen said.

"People ain't bugs," Wall said, his heart pounding.

"Aren't they?" Veronique asked. "You think Clem Jackson wasn't worse than a bug?"

Wall struggled again and he was no closer to getting free than he was before. He looked up and closed his eyes. He was angry and scared; two things he knew were a bad combination in his predicament. He tried to calm himself down, but couldn't.

"Tom, I love you no matter what I am or what you are," Veronique said, moving closer to him. She stroked his face and he didn't bother to move away. He knew he was finished. "What we feel for each other is real. You didn't care that I was a whore. Why should you care now?"

With his eyes still closed, Wall spoke.

"Please tell me this is a nightmare. Please tell me you ain't gonna eat me. I can't believe any of this."

She took both of her hands and grabbed his face.

"Look at me Tom. Look at me!"

Wall opened his eyes and looked into her gray eyes. Son of a bitch, he thought. I do love her.

She smiled at him.

"It's still just me."

Wall began to sob. Bozen stepped closer.

"Here's the deal, Mr. Wall. Stay here with us. Be one of us. Be with Veronique. Help rid this world of truly bad people."

Wall sniffed and opened his eyes. He looked up at Veronique, who was still smiling at him.

"Or?"

"Or, we kill you and put you in the next batch of Hank's wife's stew." Bozen said flatly. "We didn't want it to go like this, I promise you. We don't want to kill you."

"But we'll damn sure eat ya, son. That's for sure," Hank added. Veronique shot him a dirty look and Hank put his hands up. "Hey, I'm just sayin'."

Bozen put a hand on Veronique's shoulder.

"Let's let him think about this," he said to her, but Wall shook his head.

"She can stay," Wall said quietly.

Bozen nodded.

"We'll give you a few minutes," Bozen said, and guided Hank out of the barn.

There was a long time that passed as Wall and Veronique looked at each other. Wall spoke first.

"Can you let me go? I'd never come back here, whatever the name of this town is, I'd leave you all be."

Veronique shook her head and smiled.

"No, you wouldn't, Tom. It isn't in you to leave something be like us... Like me."

Wall sighed.

"I reckon you're right," he said sadly. "Do you... are you... really a monster?"

"I am what I am," she said, and bent down to kiss him. He didn't resist and kissed her back. When she pulled back, he was smiling.

106

"If it's gonna be done, I want you to do it, Veronique," Wall said. "I love you, but I can't live like this, knowing what it is you folks do. I couldn't abide by it."

"No, please Tom!" she cried.

"If you have any love at all for me, you do it. Do it now!" Wall yelled.

Veronique's body began to shake and Wall watched in horror at what was happening. Her beautiful porcelain skin began to darken before his eyes and her lovely gray eyes recessed into her skull. The skin on her face seemed to peel back and displayed an odd, exposed skull, nearly ebony in color. Her mouth, her beautiful smile, became a jagged maw of sharpened fangs, and the thing she was becoming snarled at him. He was terrified beyond belief. He screamed and screamed until everything went black and he felt himself falling.

CHAPTER 8

The sunlight was the first thing Wall saw when he awoke. He covered his eyes with his arms and turned his head away. He blinked several times and realized he wasn't in the barn. He was on the ground. He rolled over to see where he was.

He was in a patch of sand near a river. He heard it trickling in the background. He felt nauseous and retched to one side. After it passed, he sat up and looked around. There was some shade near a tree and his bedroll was underneath the tree.

He kept looking around as he got to his feet. He looked off into the distance and saw a plume of black smoke. He watched it for a while, and walked awkwardly to the tree where his bedroll sat, waiting for him. He sat down and grabbed the roll to open it. Inside were all of his things, the few of them that he had, minus his watch.

Two items were new, however: A canteen full of, probably, water, and a letter. He opened the canteen, sniffed it and drank two large gulps. He held up the envelope that read simply, "Tom."

He knew it was from her.

He tore it open and began to read.

My Dear Tom,

I could not bring myself to kill you. I don't know if you believe me or not, but I do and always will love you. We have burned the town. We have moved on to somewhere you won't find us, and please, do not look for us. We aren't bad or evil. You should know that by now.

If they see you coming for us, they will kill you. I won't be able to stop them next time.

I wish we could have been together, my love.

Veronique

Wall sat and re-read the letter for a good long time, until he began to weep.

He put everything back into the bedroll and stood up. He dusted himself off and found that the rope used to tie him to the table in the barn was still tied around his chest. He grabbed it and untied himself from the thick rope. He held it out in front of him. It was a good five feet of rope. He looked up at the tree where he stood and saw a thick branch.

He started to laugh.

He had just enough rope to hang himself and he laughed.

"I regard myself as a woman
who has seen much of life."
- Belle Starr describing her life
shortly before she was murdered in 1889.

THE WHORE IN THE MIRROR
BY KIMBERLY BENNETT

*Kimberly Bennett grew up in Northeast Ohio and currently resides in Northwestern PA. She has published two short story anthologies, **Twisted Delights** and **A Degree of Wickedness**. Both collections are weird, dark and creepy; her favorite genre. Watch for her third book, a novella, **Evil, Under the Microscope: Unholy Union** in Spring 2013.*

*Kim's short story, **Hades on Ice**, was published in **The Big Book of Bizarro**.*

You can visit Kimberly on the Internet at:
***kimberlybennett.yolasite.com** or drop her an email at:*
authorkimberlybennett@gmail.com.

    The sounds and smells of the saloon wafted up the staircase and down the long hallway to Jessamine's room. The all too familiar odor of cigarettes, sweat and liquor hung heavy in the air. Jessamine could hear men loudly arguing over a poker game gone sour, the player piano pounding out its entertaining tunes for the patrons' enjoyment and glass clinking as the bartender laid down whiskey, bourbon and beer.

Jessamine lay on her bed of silky, pale pink sheets with black pinstripes waiting for her next john to make his way into her boudoir. Jessamine could hear the sound of cowboy boots and spurs on the staircase and eagerly anticipated their arrival. She lay stretched out on her bed with one knee up and her arms thrown above her head. Her raven-colored curls fell seductively in tight ringlets over her sun-kissed shoulders and pillow while her ample breasts threatened to spill over the top of her red corset trimmed with black accents; while her matching black, lace panties did nothing to hide her curvaceous hips.

Jessamine lazily turned her head and gazed at her antique oval mirror that stood in the corner of her room. The rich mahogany tone of the wood lent to its appeal and made it difficult for Jessamine not to run her delicate fingers over its ornately carved frame throughout the day; the surface always felt cool to the touch no matter how balmy the atmosphere.

Jessamine was caught off guard when a young man, barely eighteen, suddenly appeared in her doorway and startled her. She dropped a hand to her chest as her breasts heaved and her heart raced.

"Oh my!" she exclaimed. She secretly kicked herself for being caught unaware.

"Sorry ma'am," the young man replied.

"My name is Jessamine."

The young man nodded at her statement.

Jessamine allowed her eyes to unashamedly gaze at the handsome young man from his gambler hat down to his leather boots. Her panties became wet as she spied a nickel plated six gun holstered on his left side and noticed his hands fidgeting nervously. Jessamine gracefully sat up and swung her legs over the side of the bed and stood. She took the few steps to the doorway as her black granny boots clicked on the wooden floor.

Meanwhile, the young man swallowed hard at the sight of her scantily clad body and fidgeted all the more. Jessamine noticed sweat begin to bead up on his brow and gave him a wicked grin. Once in front of him, she reached up her arms and gently wrapped them around his neck. She drew his face in close to hers and whispered softly, "I'm not gonna hurt you boy. Tell me your name."

"Hank," he stammered as he reached a hand up to politely tip his hat to her.

"Mmmmm, I like that name," Jessamine cooed. "It sounds quite manly." Jessamine loosened her hold and ran her hands down both of his well muscled arms, stopping at his hands. "What's your pleasure today, Hank?" she asked as she broke off physical contact, snatched Hank's hat from his head and placed it on hers. She then turned to make her way across the sparsely decorated room to her vanity; leaving Hank in the doorway to gape at her well-rounded ass.

The young man didn't reply. Hank stood and stared at Jessamine's backside as she reached for her perfume bottle, opened it and dabbed a few drops of the floral scent on her neck and wrists and returned the bottle to its original home. Hank sighed heavily as she then made her way to her overfilled armoire, removed his hat from her head and tossed it on top of her armoire. He watched, as if in a hypnotic state while Jessamine examined several articles of lingerie and after a moment of looking them over individually she would then carelessly toss them on the floor at her feet.

Jessamine knew she could stall the inevitable for only so long; Hank was young, inexperienced and anxious. Once Jessamine was satisfied with her show, she made her way back to Hank with her boots clicking again on the hardwood floor. Jessamine moved close to Hank and tilted her face up to his. She then pushed her tongue between Hanks lips as she expertly used her fingers to unzip his pants. She reached a hand inside and stroked his hardened cock. He leaned more into their kiss as she increased rhythm. Jessamine knew Hank probably wasn't going to last much longer, so she guided Hank over to the mirror in the corner. An amber glow began to grow on the mirror's slick surface the closer they got to it. Once in front of the mirror, Jessamine released her grip and retracted her hand from Hanks pants.

"Is something wrong, ma'am?" Hank breathlessly asked.

Hank wasn't aware of what was about to unfold. Jessamine knew his mind was on one thing only and that was laying her down on the bed and sliding his cock between her legs.

Jessamine placed her hands on Hank's shoulders and gave him an unexpected, hard shove. As he fell, the mirror's surface quickly changed to a liquid form and enveloped his body. Hank disappeared into an inescapable dark death. After the mirror devoured Hank, its glowing ceased and it returned to its reflective form. Jessamine reached out a hand and touched its cool surface while she gazed into the mirror, as her skin became smoother, and noticed her breasts and rear end slightly lift to give her a more youthful appearance.

"Oh my, how am I going to explain this?" Jessamine smiled a wicked smile as she asked the unresponsive mirror.

She backed away and returned to lounge on her bed once again. Satisfied with her conquest, Jessamine relaxed enough to doze off into a blissful sleep.

***

It was almost high noon as Clinton Gregory rode into Abilene with a dust trail swirling behind him. He had been riding hard for nearly five days straight. Sweat and trail-riding filth clung to him as he guided his horse over to the town saloon, slid out of the saddle with expertise, and wrapped the reins around a post near a trough. His horse dipped its head down into the murky water and slurped greedily as Clinton stepped up onto the old plank decking and strode through the weathered swinging doors and into the noisy establishment.

Clinton's boots clunked and his silver spurs clanged as he walked steadily across the worn wooden flooring toward the bar. Several drunken men hovered over the counter and milled about the saloon. The ruckus was unnerving. Clinton paused and then cringed as a brawl let loose in a corner where a cut throat poker game turned into a deadly situation as chairs were flung, the table was overturned, cards went flying into the air, a gun shot rang out and a body slumped to the floor. The room suddenly went silent. Death hung heavy in the air. Cowboys, gamblers and saloon employees stood and stared at the dead man on the floor, Clinton included. A dwarfed man in filthy working man's clothes came out from the kitchen and hobbled over to the dead man, grasped him by his ankles and dragged his body to the rear of the saloon and out a slamming back door.

The room returned to its rowdy state. Beer glasses and booze bottles clanged as the bartender resumed his duties. Men raised their voices at one another as the table was returned to its home along with the chairs. Clinton glanced over at the card table and observed a new game starting, minus one unfortunate gambler.

"What'll you have, mister?" the bartender gruffly asked Clinton; his broad smile stained brown by years of tobacco use.

"A beer," Clinton replied. He watched as the large man turned to retrieve a glass on the shelving behind the bar and pour the alcoholic beverage up to the brim. The contents sloshed about the glass as the bartender slammed it to the counter and held a dirty palm up for payment. Clinton slowly reached into a trouser pocket and pulled out some change and tossed it onto the counter next to the bartender's outstretched hand. He then picked up the beer glass, turned and casually strode over to an empty table, as the man glared in return and slammed his hand over top the coins and slid them across the counter to drop into a coffee can. The bartender then picked the coffee can up and placed it on the shelving where the glasses sat.

Clinton sat down at a table near the poker game. He gingerly sipped at his glass as he observed a young saloon girl, with too much make-up on, glide over to him.

"My name is Isabel," she said as she politely curtsied and then proceeded to sit herself down on Clinton's lap. Her small alabaster breasts threatened to burst from her tight-fitting, cerulean gown as she leaned in closer to Clinton.

"I'm not interested." Clinton smiled at her, set his glass back on the table and politely pushed her off.

The harlot landed on her ass and blushed with rage. She quickly stood up, regained her composure and stormed off to another gentleman over at the poker table. Clinton watched as Isabel planted herself on the man's lap and proceeded to whisper into his ear, while gesturing in Clinton's direction. The man nodded in acknowledgement and returned his attention to his current hand.

Clinton knew he would probably regret his faux pas but never-the-less, he had bigger things to attend to. His main reason for being in this Godforsaken town, and even here at this saloon, was to find out what happened to his younger brother, Hank. Hank had been missing for over a month and Clinton went on the hunt for his sibling, at their mother's request. After several leads pointing in Abilene's direction, here he was at the last place Hank was seen.

Clinton quickly recovered from his thoughts as the dwarfed man returned with a rag and a bucket. He watched the midget set the bucket next to the fresh blood stain on the floor, dip a rag into the soapy water and then slop it on the floor and briefly scrub at the mess. Clinton cleared his throat and watched as the man paused his cleaning and turned his head to glance up at him.

"Where can I find Jessamine?" Clinton asked.

The dwarf just shook his head and looked back down at the floor. "You don't want any of that," he said as he finished scrubbing. The little man then placed the rags in the bucket and rose from the floor. Clinton gestured for him to come to his table.

The man slowly waddled over to Clinton. "Listen mister, some men go up to Jessamine and some men don't come back down."

"What do you mean? Some go up but some don't come down?" Just then, the bartender slammed a beer mug down extra hard on the counter, making the midget jump.

"I told you that you don't want none of that," he whispered. "But if you must know, her room is up the stairs and the last door on the right."

Clinton watched as the man slowly hobbled back to the kitchen with his shoulders slouched while dragging the dirty pail behind him.

***

Clinton stood in front of the last door on the right. He wasn't sure what he would encounter on the other side but he had to find out what happened to his brother. Clinton also didn't understand what the little man meant by his comment, "you don't want none of that," but he was going to find that out too.

Clinton reached a hand out to turn the knob and was surprised when the door flew open. Before him stood the most beautiful woman he had ever seen. Jessamine had wild hair that hung in raven ringlets across her shoulders and halfway down her back while her voluptuous body was adorned with see through lingerie that took the air from Clinton's chest. Her cruel and devilish intentions were hid behind angelic features and an impish grin that bordered on sinister.

"Well, hello!" Jessamine exclaimed as she brushed a locket of hair from her eyes.

Clinton didn't reply right away. He was still entranced by her loveliness. He shook his head to clear his thoughts and quickly regained his composure.

"Hello, ma'am," Clinton replied as he tipped his hat to her.

Clinton watched as Jessamine raked her eyes over his muscular form. She scanned him from head to toe and then finally ended up looking at him suspiciously, square in the eye.

"Come in, please." Jessamine held the door open wide as she gestured for Clinton to step inside.

Clinton uneasily stepped over the threshold and moved out of Jessamine's way so she could shut the door. Jessamine quickly shut the door. Clinton watched mesmerized as Jessamine began to move about the room gracefully. She first walked to her bed, making a point to bend over and expose her ass for his viewing pleasure while she fluffed up her pillows and smoothed her bed sheets. She then made her way over to her vanity and dabbed a few drops of perfume on her neck and wrists. Jessamine paused and glanced at Clinton. She smiled at him and placed the dropper on her breasts and ran it over her silky skin in a figure eight to spread the delicate fragrance.

Clinton waited as Jessamine walked from her vanity over to where he stood. She placed her hands on his chest. She rubbed her palms up and down, causing his nipples and cock to become erect. She then slid her hands down to his waistline and under his waistband. Jessamine was clearly amused by her feminine powers. The evidence of that revelation was prevalent in her glistening dark eyes. Clinton grasped her wrists and forced her to remove her probing fingers from his trousers.

"Did you entertain a young man by the name of Hank a few weeks ago?" Clinton asked Jessamine as she jerked herself free from his grasp and snorted at him in disgust.

"Are you serious?" Jessamine asked sarcastically. "I must see a half a dozen men a day, sometimes more." Jessamine shrugged her shoulders.

Clinton grew angry at her response. He glared at Jessamine as she nervously moved away from him, wringing her hands as she went.

"I know he was here. All you have to do is tell me where he went."

"I haven't seen him," Jessamine growled. Surprisingly, she then leapt at Clinton with her nails outstretched. Clinton slapped her hands away but not before Jessamine scratched him severely on the cheek. Blood trickled down Clinton's face as Jessamine's body collided with his. They both stumbled and fell heavily to the floor with a loud thud. Jessamine landed on top of Clinton. She began to rake her nails across his exposed flesh and tear at his clothing like a rabid animal. Clinton wrestled with Jessamine for several minutes, their bodies entwined and tumbling as they both tried to get the upper hand.

Jessamine was strong and feisty but she was no match for Clinton's strength. He pinned her body beneath his and held her arms above her head with his hands. They both breathed heavy over their exertion. Jessamine resigned herself and relaxed under Clinton's hold.

"Where is my brother?" Clinton asked through clenched jaw.

Jessamine laughed in his face. In a fury, Clinton hopped off of Jessamine and jerked her to a standing position. Her hair was disheveled, lingerie was torn and wrinkled. Clinton wasn't much better. His exposed chest was bleeding profusely from Jessamine's claw marks and his hat had been knocked off at some point during their tussle. Jessamine laughed a second time and Clinton released one of her arms and slapped her hard across the face. The sound of the impact echoed in the tiny room.

Clinton spied his brother's hat lying on the bottom shelf of Jessamine's open armoire.

"Where is he?" Clinton yelled as his anger was brought to a boiling point.

Jessamine replied with more laughter as Clinton's face grew dark and the mirror in the corner began to glow. Clinton paused and quizzically gazed at the mirror. He had never seen anything like it before. He became almost entranced by its presence.

Jessamine took advantage of the distraction and latched onto Clinton's vest. She guided him over to the mirror. Clinton seemed unaware of their movements as he stared at the object. Once they were in front of the mirror, Jessamine turned him with his back to it. Suddenly, Clinton regained his senses and grabbed Jessamine. He whipped her around, placed a booted heel behind her and pushed her roughly toward the glowing mirror. Clinton quickly withdrew a pistol and fired a shot with expert aim.

At that point, everything seemed to move in slow motion. Stricken with surprise and horror, Jessamine shrieked. She then reached out her arms and erratically grasped at the air as she fell backward into the mirror. Clinton watched as the bullet landed in between Jessamine's eyes while she was simultaneously swallowed by the mirror's liquid. Clinton stepped back as the mirror returned to its reflective surface with Jessamine's image etched into it. He then watched as arms, aflame with Hell's Fire, wrapped themselves around her lifeless form and drew her slowly into its darkness.

The mirror suddenly went dark and Jessamine could be seen no more. Large cracks crept across the mirror's surface and blew shards of glass outward toward Clinton as he raised an arm to protect his face. Once the shower of glass ended, Clinton dropped his arm, stepped away from the mirror and turned to walk toward the door. He was stopped mid-turn as the frame burst into flames and devoured the remnants of the mirror, thus incinerating any evidence that it ever existed, except for some inconspicuous ashes on the floor.

Clinton stared down at the pile of ash and instantly felt compelled to touch it. He crouched down and reached out a hand and swirled a finger through the mess. A broad smile spread across his face as he rose.

"Oh, Isabel!" Clinton called out with a renewed exuberance and zest for life.

"Leave me alone and let me go

to hell by my own route."

- Calamity Jane shortly before her death

in Deadwood, South Dakota, in 1903.

SUCCUBI SUNDOWN
BY SCOTT EMERSON

*Perhaps best known for his blog **365 Days of the Dead**, Scott Emerson has appeared in **Weird Tales' "One Minute"** video series, **Everyday Weirdness, Flashshot, Mad Rush, Innsmouth Free Press, Bizarro Central**, and the zombie anthologies **Putrid Poems and Sickening Sketches** and **Poetry from the Grave**.*

*Scott's short story, **Pearl**, was published in **The Big Book of Bizarro**.*

Currently he serves as facilitator for Morgantown Poets, a not-for-profit group that hosts free literary events. He lives in Pennsylvania.

The nameless man rode across the desert in search of his death.

He rode into the sun, shielding its merciless glare with the brim of his midnight-colored hat. Sweat stung his eyes. His mouth was dry as parchment, the skin of his hands and face seared red by the day's heat.

The nameless man carried no rations, no canteen, not even a bedroll. He needed none of them. The pearl-handled Colt .44s strapped to his waist were mostly for show.

He adjusted the belt, tightened around his midsection, moving the ragged strip of rawhide so that it didn't press into his ribs while still keeping his guts contained. The damaged intestines exposed in the fist-sized wound leaked clotted blood and fecal matter. Their smell was almost as unbearable as the pain.

His horse he'd stolen from a livery outside Clovis. The blacksmith and his apprentice chased the nameless man down, less than a mile into the desert, saying nothing as they hauled him off the animal and fitted a noose around his neck. Their eyes wavered as they took notice of the bullet hole oozing in his center, but remained silent. So did the nameless man, even as they strung him from a barren joshua tree.

He put on a good act for them, though, gasping and kicking his dung-stained boots, clawing at the hemp that dug into his throat. He even managed to shift his ruined intestines so that it appeared his bowels evacuated.

After dancing a tuneless jig at the end of their rope he went still. Satisfied that justice had been served, the blacksmith and his apprentice led the stolen horse back to town.

The nameless man waited half an hour, then cut himself down. He went back and stole the horse again.

Nobody came after him a second time.

Again, the nameless man wondered if he was on a fool's errand. Surely the settlement he was headed for couldn't exist; yet the chink who ran the opium den in Talbot Springs had been adamant, swearing to the gods in broken English he was telling the truth. He had even sketched a crude map.

The nameless man accepted it. He had nothing to lose but an endless supply of time. And if gunshot wounds that refused to heal were real, why not the things the Chinaman promised?

The answer to his questions, and perhaps his prayers, arrived less than two hours later, when he came upon two Gila monsters copulating in the sand.

The nameless man brought his horse to a halt, transfixed by how the male pumped into its mate from behind with rapid thrusts. The female writhed into his ministrations, her forked tongue darting in response as she dug her claws into the earth.

The male Gila monster paused in mid-thrust, cocking its head toward the nameless man. "You seek the succubi," he said.

The nameless man swallowed. "Yes. How did you know?"

The Gila monster lowered its gaze to the hole in the nameless man's stomach. A drizzling loop of stray intestine had slipped over the belt, dangling between two flaps of gangrenous flesh. The nameless man grabbed it, inadvertently squeezing out a greasy turd as he stuffed the viscera back inside. He was long past any embarrassment.

"The succubi are not far," said the lizard. "But they require payment for their services."

"I have gold."

"That may be enough. Continue west. By sundown you will find that which you seek."

"Much obliged."

Turning its attention back to its companion, the Gila monster resumed rutting. Before the nameless man could command his horse, the lizard held up a claw. "Wait! Watch this."

Deftly the Gila monster flopped the female on her back and climbed onto her belly. Pumping the stump of its erection, the lizard grinned wickedly. "She loves this shit, man, she fucking lives for it."

The nameless man observed as the Gila monster ejaculated onto the face of its mate. Scrunching its black-bead eyes, the lizard threw back its head, the pink fork of its tongue stabbing triumphantly into the air.

"Yes, yes, you scaly whore, take every drop of it!"

The nameless man rode on.

***

123

Farther across the desert he went, with little to find but sand and rocks and the occasional animal skeleton to break the monotony.

As the sun turned red and dipped toward the horizon he found himself riding through a dune-studded valley. Large rocks jutted from the surrounding hills, casting ragged shadows in the approaching dusk. Slowly the earth swallowed the sun. The sky became a bruised purple.

Deeper into the valley he journeyed. He felt the eyes of unseen creatures hiding in the rocks, following him; whether these desert dwellers were harmless or predators he couldn't tell. He kept one hand on the butt of his .44. An angry blacksmith could be tricked with a little play-acting and spurting bowels, but a starving coyote would keep coming until the walking sack of bone and meat he hunted finally went down.

Shadows drifted across the sand.

The nameless man scanned the hills. He detected movement between the rocks – something scurried up there, low to the ground and agile. Whatever watched him made little noise save for the whispering of sand.

"All right, enough of this Injun-tracking bullshit!" he bellowed. The stillness carried his voice through the valley like a bullhorn. "If somebody's up there, be a man and show yourself!"

No answer. Sand hissed quietly.

The nameless man drew. The pistol had yet to clear its holster when a sudden weight slammed into him from behind, driving the wind from his lungs, as it tumbled him out of the saddle. His right boot got hung up in its stirrup; as he tried to kick himself free, the horse whinnied with fright and reared, hooves swatting at the encroaching dark. He was lifted from the sand, dropped, lifted again, before he got himself loose.

He lunged for the six-shooter he'd dropped as the weight struck him once more, pinning him into the ground. Something with

124

heavy talons grabbed his arms – *mountain lion, been broadsided by a goddamned mountain lion* – and shrieked into his ear. The nameless man craned his neck, exposing the tender hollow of his throat, to see what was upon him.

The creature was a woman. She was nude, the musculature of her desert-filthy body taut and limber, tendons raised on her forearms as she shredded his denim shirt. Her green lizard-like eyes reflected the growing moonlight. A forked, spit-slick tongue squirted obscenely over her lips.

His fingertips grazed the handle of his gun. The she-creature sprang, burying her teeth into his throat.

Oh, you miserable, no-good cunt, look what you've done, bad enough I've got to hold in my rotting innards, you stupid fucking desert freak–

Struggling beneath the she-creature, the nameless man hooked his fingers around the .44's grip and pulled it from the sand, leveling its barrel right between the unholy bitch's glimmering green eyes.

"STOP!"

The thing on top of him froze at the voice puncturing the darkness. The nameless man looked up.

Standing above them was a woman. Fiery red hair spilled over her shoulders to the swell of her bare, upturned breasts, the nipples of which were ghostly pink. Her stomach was flat between delicate hourglass hips. A pale red pubic thatch topped a pair of supple dancer's legs.

The nameless man's cock strained against his zipper.

"Get off him, Malena," she said.

The she-creature perched on his chest hung its head, dejected, like a child denied a toy. Reluctantly she climbed off him, crawling toward the nude redhead on all fours. She sat, obedient, at her feet as the other woman stroked her hair.

"This one's a seeker," said the redhead. Her voice was soothing, a lullaby. She looked down upon him, unabashed in her nudity. "And we mustn't attack a seeker."

The nameless man nodded, easing back the pistol's hammer. Blood trickled down his neck. He dabbed the wound with his fingertips, relieved to feel less damage than expected.

The redhead offered him a hand. "My name is Sabena. Come with me. We'll tend to your wound, and you can tell us that which you seek – oh!"

Had she noticed his erection? Looking down, fearing it was poking out of his trousers like a mischievous prairie dog, he saw the buttons of his shirt torn open. The belt around his midsection had broken during the struggle and his intestines now sat unveiled in a stinking, sodden heap.

Sabena helped him to his feet, equally nonplussed by his injuries. The nameless man stuck a hand against his entrails to hold them in place.

"What happened?" she said.

"Gunshot. I was tracking a bank robber with a taste for rape and murder. Name of Munneke. What the wanted posters failed to mention was that he had powers… spells, I guess you could say. One of them involved enchanted bullets."

Sabena arched her brows.

"I'd followed him to a faro parlor outside San Antonio. Thought I'd gotten the drop on the prick, too, but Munneke was a faster draw than I assumed. Put a round right in my belly. He laughed when I hit the floor, you know that? Sat right there and finished his game while I crawled in the whiskey and tobacco spit and tried to keep in my guts. I blacked out and when I came to, he was gone.

"That was three years ago."

"And it is revenge you desire?"

"No," the nameless man said. "I doubt there's anything I could do to make us even – hell, I don't even think he can be killed – and I damn sure don't want to find out what *else* he's capable of."

Sabena said, "What is it you *do* want?"

"What do you think? I want to die."

Sabena smiled. "Can you walk?"

He nodded.

"Good. Follow me, it's not far." She turned, revealing the rounded beauty of her backside. "You too, Malena, come."

The she-creature remained hunched in the sand. "But I'm *hungry*."

Sabena sighed. "Very well. The steed, then."

The nameless man allowed her to lead him into the night. Against his better judgment he glanced over his shoulder, as Malena leapt upon the horse's flank and sank her teeth into its neck. He averted his gaze when the blood began to flow.

***

How far he followed Sabena into the desert the nameless man could not be sure; he'd been too entranced by the gentle undulations of her perfect ass to pay attention to much else. He had, however, noticed the wet, sloppy noises of Malena's feeding were growing fainter and fainter.

Sabena said nothing as they walked.

Eventually she led him to her village, a cluster of squat adobe huts circling a great phallus-shaped rock. As they got closer the nameless man felt a strange energy humming in the air, as if he were surrounded by one of those new electrified fences. It made the hair on his arms stand erect, his teeth rattle in their sockets. His cock stiffened again.

Even his guts quivered like a vat of rancid gelatin. The sensation was not unpleasant, keeping the pain at bay for the first time since he'd taken that goddamned bullet.

Women lounged in the entrances to the huts, roughly two dozen by his count, most without clothing. Their lithe, muscular bodies were streaked with dirt and sand, several of them sporting patterns of bruises along their hindquarters, their legs. Many shared Malena's bright, feral eyes, others appeared as demure as schoolmarms. Each woman stared at the nameless man with a naked hunger he found both terrifying and arousing.

Sabena led him to the other side of the rock, where he discovered a low, rectangular building crudely constructed of wood and stone. It appeared to be some sort of temple, given the sigil painted over the doorway. The marking meant nothing to him, but its faded, brownish-red color suggested a significance, if not origin.

"Wait here," Sabena said. "Mircalla will be with you soon."

She pushed him across the threshold.

Inside it was dark, cold. The sweat beneath the brim of his hat chilled. Gooseflesh broke out on his arms; his nipples became twin pink pebbles. The nameless man stumbled in the blackness, wondering if he'd step into a sacrificial pit or skewer himself on some ritualistic object. His hands groped shadows.

The electric charge in the air had receded, giving his splattered guts the chance to howl again. His erection, though, had yet to abate.

He heard a single match being struck. The temple ignited with light as dozens of candles illuminated themselves at once, wicks flaring with sudden pockets of flame. In the engulfing, almost overwhelming brilliance, the nameless man took in the temple's interior. A ragged gasp escaped him.

"My God…"

Before him sat a marble altar, the same size and height as a marital bed, its polished surface smooth and unblemished. On either side stood alabaster statues of women possessing an earth mother's full bosom and wide hips, nipples and navel replaced with the same symbol he saw over the temple entrance. From the altar ran two rows of stone pews, a carpet of crushed red velvet running down the center.

"So you're a seeker," purred a voice.

The nameless man turned around.

The woman who greeted him appeared to be sculpted from ivory, her skin so pale he could see the fine purple network of her veins. Yet her features were too striking to ignore – eyes like emerald fire, her lips a rich sensuous red, cheekbones distinct but fragile. Long, raven tresses flowed from her scalp like India ink. The black ceremonial robe she wore clung to the exquisite curvature of her form.

It was worth it all – the ruptured innards, a stubborn death that refused to come, the endless march across the desert – just to be able to stand before this woman and drink in her presence, her being. Even her lizard's eyes were entrancing.

"It is I you've been seeking," she said.

"Mircalla." Her name was like a mouthful of honey.

"Yes, and your name is...?"

"Not important."

"No, I suppose it's not." Mircalla's smile was vulpine. "And you understand what it is you're asking me to do?"

"Yes," he said. "Dear God, yes."

"And why should I?"

"Look at me. My guts are falling out, I'm rotting from the inside. And it hurts like a sumbitch." The nameless man winced; he sounded awfully close to begging. He hoped it wouldn't come to that. "Will you help me?"

"You can pay?"

"I can, I have gol–" The nameless man's eyes widened in sick panic. "My saddlebag! The gold was in my saddlebag! The redheaded broad, Sabena, she had me leave my horse behind, and that other crazy bitch started to eat it – Jesus Christ, I have to go back for it–"

Mircalla shushed him. "Relax. You've traveled too far and difficult a journey to worry about such matters. Yes, the gold would've made it easier, but you will be taken care of."

The succubus led him to the altar. He obeyed without hesitation.

Mircalla embraced him, closing her lips over his. Her mouth was cold, dry, but as their tongues sparred it began to warm, to grow moist. The nameless man caressed her through the ceremonial robe, relishing the tight, firm flesh underneath.

He pulled the succubus closer, unmindful of his drooping innards squishing against her. If the putrid mass offended her, she gave no indication.

Mircalla pulled away from the kiss, slithering to her knees, unbuckling the nameless man's trousers with long, nimble fingers. The head of his erection throbbed painfully as she released it to the cool temple air. Mircalla cooed over its girth, fingertips grazing the underside, before devouring it to the root.

He gasped at the onslaught of pleasure.

Inside the succubus's mouth was like being snared in a warm, wet trap. Mircalla's teeth hovered like wraiths above his cock. He shuddered, eyes gliding back into his skull as her slender, bifurcated tongue scoured his most sensitive membranes. A soggy length of festering intestine uncoiled itself and landed with a smack upon Mircalla's forehead, leaking blood and runny feces down the bridge of her nose. She continued undeterred.

With the head of his cock still pressed against her tonsils, Mircalla gripped the base of his shaft and tugged, triggering as intense an orgasm he'd ever experienced. The nameless man quaked with each shooting wave of ecstasy, clutching his guts as they dribbled through his fingers.

Cupping a palm beneath her chin she spat a tiny pool of pearl-colored discharge, in the middle of which he found a small, flattened oval of tarnished metal.

The bullet.

Discarding the spent slug, Mircalla stood. The robe dropped from her shoulders, puddled at her feet. The nameless man's eyes roamed the flawless expanse of her breasts, her stomach's porcelain sleekness, the shaven cleft between her thighs with its glistening sliver of ruby flesh.

His withering erection grew turgid once more.

Mircalla spread herself upon the altar. Staring at him through her parted legs, the succubus opened the petals of her sex, enticing him with their musky nectar. "Now," she breathed.

The nameless man hurried out of his clothes. Mounted the altar.

Positioning himself between the succubus's thighs, he felt his insides tilt, threatening to pour onto her outstretched belly. Careful not to lean too far, he took her knees in each hand and dragged her toward him, cleaving the sweet slit with his aching hard-on. As he entered Mircalla's sopping canal, the nameless man noticed shadows moving in his peripheral vision.

One by one the women of the village filed into the temple, taking seats in the stone pews. Their nakedness stoked his lust, as did the carnal avarice alight in their eyes. In the front row he saw Sabena, her cinnamon hair and pert, pink-nippled breasts, enough to increase his desire a hundredfold.

He plunged into Mircalla harder. Faster.

The succubi caressed themselves as they watched him fuck, soiled hands gliding over thighs, seizing breasts. Soft mewls of pleasure rose from their ranks. It wasn't long before they were masturbating in concert, fingers piercing vulvas with brisk tempo, the electric charge in the air growing stronger with a cloud of feminine pheromones.

Mircalla's cold hands clawed his back, dug seeping furrows into his skin.

No longer could the nameless man withstand the clenching of her inner muscles. His balls tightened, signaling an orgasm that struck him like lightning.

"NNNGUH, AHH, AHH, FUCK, UHH–"

His back arched, dumping a load of viscera upon Mircalla's prostrate form. Blackish-green excreta sloshed against her stomach in a tide of pus and semi-congealed blood, sluicing off her skin to cascade down the altar; each successive spasm eked out another gobbet of tissue, one more rivulet of shit. Purged along with his bowels was the pain, edged out of his torso by the steadily rippling ecstasy. He felt emptied, cleansed and renewed. Pure.

Withdrawing from Mircalla, the nameless man collapsed into his own offal and smiled, listening as the other succubi climaxed in unison. His hand reached out to touch Mircalla one last time but his fingertips met only marble.

He supposed what came next was a pleasant drift into oblivion with his wilting hard-on cooling on his thigh, the curse and his brains fucked out. Seemed easy enough; he hadn't needed the gold after all. He relaxed upon the altar, eager to meet an eternity without pain, without magic.

Nothing happened.

Had Mircalla lied to him? Was this some sort of trick?

He looked up to see the succubi circling the altar. Mircalla stood among them, as did Sabena. They stared back at him with another lust, the same lust he'd seen in Malena's eyes when she descended upon his horse. Drool gleamed on their chins.

"Thank you," the nameless man said and closed his eyes.

"After being so bad,
I could hear the angels singing."
- Lillie Langtry

A TOWN CALLED RUPTURE
BY RICH BOTTLES JR.

*After an unillustrious print journalism career in southwestern Pennsylvania, **Rich Bottles Jr.** moved to West Virginia at the age of 32 to pursue a career in technical writing. He spends his free time visiting and hiking at the many state parks in the Mountain State, which is also where he develops the concepts for his novels.*

*Rich recently completed a trilogy of WV-themed "humorrorotica," which includes the novels **Lumberjacked**, **Hellhole West Virginia**, and **The Manacled**. In addition to editing and contributing to the Burning Bulb Publishing anthologies **Westward Hoes** and **The Big Book of Bizarro**, he has also written stories for the StrangeHouse Books anthologies **Strange Sex** and **Zombie! Zombie! Brain Bang!***

He is currently working on a horror novel set in West Virginia's Amish Country. His only regret in life is that his out-of-state secondary school education prohibited him from earning West Virginia's prestigious Golden Horseshoe Award.

May no man claim that God is unjust – for no individual now nor ever may stake claim to being the ugliest of God's anthropological manifestations.

134

If Michael and Patrick Sughrue had been born to different mothers, there might have been arguments over which Sughrue was truly more grotesque. But God made sure neither Sughrue would have to wear the unique badge of ultimate repugnancy, because God used Humphrey Sughrue's pestilent seed and Mary Sughrue's vile vessel to cast the Sughrue brothers as twins.

Thus no one studying the features of both Michael and Patrick Sughrue could claim that one brother was uglier than the other. Of course, that didn't stop people from referring to the boys as the ugliest *twins* ever created.

Consequently, Michael and Patrick Sughrue usually traveled at night. It was on one of those nights in 1884 that our Old West story takes place, as the brothers rode into the town of Rupture on horseback under the cover of night.

The main thoroughfare through town, according to a wooden sign at the corner, was called Division Street. As the men rode slowly and silently down the dirt street, they glanced left and right at the weathered, white-washed wood buildings, which were illuminated dismally by hissing gas lanterns.

Michael whispered over to his brother, Patrick, who was riding next to him. "There's something strange about this town, but I can't seem to put my finger on it."

"I know what you mean," answered Patrick.

"Hey, wait a doggone minute," Michael suddenly blurted out, pulling back on the reins to stop beside a barber shop. "Do you see that store on my left?"

Patrick leaned over to peek around Michael. "Yeah, it's a barber shop. So what? It's closed now anyway."

"I know it's closed – it's the middle of the night, dammit!" Michael responded. "I only point it out because there's also a barber shop directly across the street on your side."

Patrick glanced to his right. "It's closed too."

"Don't go there, Pat." Michael threatened. "So, you don't think that it's odd?"

"Odd that they're closed?"

"No, not odd that they're closed, gosh darn-it! Don't you think that it's odd for such a small town to have two barber shops?"

"Maybe it's a his 'n' hers type sit-see-ation, where one barber does just men and the other does wimen 'n' children."

Michael ignored his brother's illogic and turned his head to look backward. "Damn, look it behind you Patrick. Every business we passed had the same type of business on the opposite side of the street. First we passed two identical jailhouses, then two banks, two blacksmiths and now two barbers."

"As long as the town has at least one hotel," added Patrick, "that's all I care about right now."

"I think a hotel is up ahead," concluded Michael, spurring some forward momentum.

After passing a pair of silent saloons, the men came upon two hotels, specifically the East Hotel and the West Hotel, located on opposite sides of the street.

"Which one is we gonna stay at?" Patrick asked. "They both look the same to me."

Michael reached into his vest pocket and pulled out a Carson City silver dollar. He flipped the heavy coin into the air, caught it with one hand as it descended, and then slapped it onto the back of his other hand.

"We'll either *head* west or go east as the eagle flies," Michael announced as he removed his left palm from over the coin. "It looks like we'll be staying at the East Hotel tonight."

While the brothers were dismounting at the hitching post in front of the East Hotel, they witnessed a partially dressed man rush out of the West Hotel carrying a half-open travel satchel, scurry across the dirt street in his bare feet, and run straight into the East Hotel.

"Damn!" exclaimed Michael. "What do you figure is that fellow's problem?"

136

The East Hotel had a wide front porch, connecting directly to the wooden walkway, which connected all the businesses on the east side of the street. The patio-style porch contained a couple of small tables and a few chairs, allowing patrons to sit outside and enjoy the subtleties of small town life in Rupture, Kansas.

Michael and Patrick entered the front door of the lobby just as a sullen desk clerk was asking the partially-dressed man if he had been staying at the West Hotel. "Hell yes," the disheveled man answered. "And I was sound asleep too!"

"Welcome to the East Hotel," grinned the desk clerk as he held out a room key to the man. The man snatched away the key and headed up the lobby stairwell toward his new room on the second floor.

Patrick whispered to Michael, "Pre-haps that West Hotel has them bed-buggers."

"Yeah, maybe we made the right choice of hotel after all."

The clerk looked over to the approaching twins, expressing an expression of shock and disgust as they got closer to the desk. "Um, how may I help you, uh, gentlemen?"

Michael answered, "Now, now, I know my brother and I aren't as *purty* as most of your other boarders, but we still require your hospitable services this evening. My brother and I would like to share a room if you have one which will accommodate us."

"No shit," bluntly replied the clerk. "Would you like a room without a mirror?"

"Without a mirror?" questioned Patrick, glancing toward his brother.

"I believe our friend here was making a funny, Patrick," Michael responded without taking his eyes off the clerk. "Was that indeed an attempt at humor, sir? Perhaps making fun of my appearance?"

"Ah, no," stammered the clerk. "Sometimes there's a surcharge for the couple of rooms which still have a mirror in 'em... Um, the mirrors is always gettin' busted around here – the saloon and all being nearby… people gettin' liquored up and all, you know."

Michael continued to stare down the clerk.

The clerk added, "But we won't charge you gentlemen any sort of surcharge for a looking glass room, since you're from outta town – and we is tryin' tah promote tourism here in Rupture."

"Then one surcharge-free looking glass room it is, my good man," Michael said, breaking his controlled countenance and finally smiling at the man.

The clerk shuddered and reached under the desk to grab a skeleton key with a wooden key tag attached. He placed it on top of the desk in front of Michael. "That'll be a half dollar."

"Room twenty," Michael observed as he picked up the key.

"Well, the key will open any of the rooms, but your room is number twenty," the clerk explained. "Walk up the steps and the room will be on your right."

"Much obliged," added Michael as he handed over a fifty-cent piece.

"Does this town have a bathhouse?" asked Patrick before proceeding to the stairs. "Or should I say two bathhouses?"

"No bathhouses, per se, but our hotel tub is on this floor, in the back room," answered the clerk. "If'n you need a young lady from the saloon to assist you, just let me know and I'll give her a holler."

* * *

Patrick was getting undressed in the first-floor room containing the community bathtub when he heard a light tapping on the door. He finished removing his dusty shirt and hesitantly walked toward the door. Opening the door slowly, he set his eyes on a Rubenesquey blonde, wearing a thin white corset and a frilly petticoat. Her blue eyes scanned Patrick up and down, but she managed not to flinch at the sight of the customer.

138

"Well, at least you didn't run away," he confessed. "Come on in if'n you wanna."

"To be honest," the woman smiled, "the clerk did warn me ahead-a time. But, you know what? Looks ain't ever' thing, like they say."

When she smiled, Patrick noticed her front teeth were a bit gnarled and jagged. She held out her dainty hand and said, "They call me Squirrel Tooth Alice."

If Patrick weren't so ugly himself, he would've kicked the snaggle-toothed bitch out of the room. Shaking her hand, he responded, "My name is Patrick. It's a pleasure to make your acquaintance."

"Well, I hope you'll find my service pleasurable. Why don't you finish undressin' and I'll fetch us some hot water."

"Would you care to join me in the tub?"

Alice looked at Patrick, and then glanced at the small claw-footed cast iron bathtub. "Sorry, but I think that there tub might have some kinda maximum occupancy limit or sumthin', so we might not fit – safely, anyways. But I'll be happy to scrub you down from the outside if'n you want. Just let me go git the water 'n' sponge."

Patrick was naked, shivering in the porcelain lining of the tub, when Alice returned, lugging a large bucket of steaming water. She placed the bucket by the tub and then went back to the door to bolt it closed. "Fer privacy," she explained, purposely pronouncing it as "privy-see."

Patrick watched as she returned to the bucket, turned her back to him, and knelt down. "Would you mind untyin' my corset, so as I don't get it wet while we is splashin' around?"

"Well sure little lady, it looks like it's tied just like mah boots."

"What about my boobs?"

"No, I mean the laces on the corset is tied up, just like…"

"Yeah, my boobs is inside the corset. You'll git to see 'em momentarily, soon as you untie it. Hold yer damn horse, cowboy."

Being rather ticked off at her inability to understand him, Patrick reached inside the laces about halfway down her back and placed his other hand against the middle of her shoulders. Using her upper back as a leverage point, he pulled as hard as he could on the laces.

Alice released a deep groan as her breath was violently forced from her lungs. "Wrong way, wrong way!" she gasped, desperately trying to reach behind her back with both of her hands.

"Now," patiently began Patrick. "As I was a-sayin', yer corset is tied in the same way that I lace up my *boots*. I didn't never say nuthin' about yer boobies."

"Okay, okay," she pleaded breathlessly. "I understand you now. Please let go... I ain't gonna be able to suck you off if my corset is tied too tight."

Patrick loosened his grip and quickly unlaced the corset strings. Alice pulled the constricting garment off as soon as she felt the pressure released. She fell forward on her hands and knees, her breasts heaving underneath, as she desperately tried to catch her breath.

He looked over at her petticoated posterior and pronounced, "Well ain't that a sight fer sore eyes."

From her vantage point on the hardwood floor, she turned her head back to look at him and asked, "What about my sore ass?"

Patrick jumped up inside the tub as he yelled, "Why you little..."

Panicking, Alice rolled over on her back and looked up at the man's towering figure, "I was joking; I was just jokin'. I heard what you said. You said, 'Ain't that a sight for sore *eyes*'."

"Youse about to git a sore ass if'n you keep teasin' me that-a-way."

Alice managed to get back on her feet while Patrick sat back down inside the bathtub. "Well, that would cost you extra, anyways," she concluded.

Upon returning to the side of the bathtub, her bountiful breasts now prominently on display, Alice looked at Patrick's naked body and commented, "Well, I was gonna ask what part of yer body you wanted warshed first, but I see one particular part is volunteerin' all on its own!"

Alice got on her knees, soaped up the sponge in the bucket and began scrubbing down Patrick from head to toe and toe to head, making his man parts presentable for a lady of her stature (i.e., as measured from her knees upward). Besides, she didn't want to spend the next day digging grime out of what was left of her teeth.

When she realized that the darkened waters at the bottom of the tub and in the bucket were threatening to re-pollute Patrick's body, she asked him to get out of the bathtub so that she could towel him off. He was much obliged.

Without changing her position on the floor, she reached up to start drying Patrick's skin-sheening, muscle-rippling, masculinating body. In fact, her hands were trembling inside the towel, especially when she reached her target destination. She immediately dropped the towel to the floor.

"Now you'll learn why they call me Squirrel Tooth Alice," she promised as she cupped Patrick's balls in her hand. Squirrel Tooth Alice began nibbling his nut sack.

"I'm guessing by yer chewin' that you ain't planning to store up any nuts for winter," he quipped, looking down at the hungry face just below his erect cock. His balls ached from the sharp-toothed attack, but his cock ached just as much from the oral neglect it was experiencing.

Soon Alice allowed his dampened balls to plop from her menacing mouth. Using her tongue as a guide along the "Oral-gon Trail," she blazed a northerly path from the hairy roots of his balls, up his rigid bark-like trunk and around the tip of his pink leaf. After a deep breath, she sucked the length of his dick deep into her throat. Her tongue was now exploring his 'hood from within her dark inner sanctum.

Unsatisfied with the pace of the proceedings, Patrick impatiently began fucking her in the mouth, holding the back of her head with both hands and slamming his hips into her face. Alice didn't protest (certainly not verbally), especially since she had long ago learned to control her gag reflex (which also came in handy earlier when she first laid eyes on Patrick).

His pumped up penis used her uvula like an arcade punching bag, sliding in and out over her treacherous teeth with little regard for his own safety. Saliva sloshed out of her suck hole with each stab from his scepter, splashing onto the already dampened floor.

She soon sensed his dick firming up for one last penetrating thrust, but the strong grip he had on her skull prevented Alice from pulling away before her throat was coated by his liquid seed dispenser. The uncontrolled contractions from her gulping gullet massaged and squeezed his organ, taking his pleasure to new heights and/or depths.

After he was certain every last drop of his manna was deposited in her mouth, he pulled away from her skewered face. She immediately looked up at him, displaying an angry demeanor while wiping some sticky spillage from around her lips with the back of her hand.

"I don't believe you just came in my mouth!"

"Believe it baby," he replied. "I was just gettin' my dollar's worth."

"That's not how it's done around here," she explained, eventually rising to her feet.

"Well, I ain't from around here."

"Obviously..."

Alice stomped over to pick up her corset from the floor. She dreaded the thought of having to ask Patrick to lace her up.

"Listen," she said, lowering her voice. "I personally don't mind what we just did, but you gotta promise that you won't tell anyone. 'Cause if'n you do, I could get in a lot of trouble."

"Can I at least tell my brother?"

She rolled her eyes and turned her back to him. "Just lace me up, cowboy."

***

In the morning, Michael and Patrick ordered up some breakfast in the small hotel dining room, but decided to take their grub and coffee outside on the patio. They chose a table that had the best view of the street.

"Brother, you missed some hot action last night," announced Patrick just before he took a sip of coffee.

"Sorry that I chose sleep over debauchery, but I firmly believe in the health benefits of a good night's sleep."

"And I believe in the health benefits of shooting my load in a whore's mouth."

Michael looked over to his brother just as Patrick was chewing a fork full of eggs-over-easy with an open mouth. "You disgust me, brother," Michael added.

The brothers ate in silence, until they saw a man exit the barber shop on their side of street. The man still had an apron tied around his neck and his face was covered with shaving cream. In his haste to cross the street, the man was almost run over by a horse and wagon traveling down Division Street. When the man twisted his body to avoid a collision, the twins noticed that the other side of the man's face was clean-shaven.

"This town is friggin' weird," Patrick observed as the strange man continued his trek to the barber shop on the opposite side of the street.

The horse and wagon pulled up to the front of the West Dry Goods Store, where the farmer jumped off his wagon and disappeared inside the business. He later emerged from the store with a large bag of animal feed, which he tossed into the back of the wagon. The farmer then dutifully drove his horse across the street and purchased an identical bag of feed.

143

"Maybe the first store only had one bag of feed left," Michael commented.

As the men were finishing their breakfast, they noticed a parade of well-dressed couples and families heading to the southern end of town. They also noticed that a well-dressed man emerged from the East Dry Goods Store and took a seat on a rocking chair, probably to also observe the parade of fashionable citizenry.

"What's going on, my friend?" Michael yelled over to the man in the rocker, whose business was adjacent to the East Hotel.

"It's Sunday morning," the man hollered back. "Don't you boys go to church?"

"A-course we do!" shouted Patrick.

Michael whispered to Patrick, "Must I remind you that we don't have any dress clothes?"

"Don't matter," answered Patrick. "We may have work clothes on, but they're clean. Besides, we ain't gonna let some shop keeper belittle us like we is heathens or something."

"Well, something tells me, he doesn't have any plans himself to leave his rocker for church."

"Of course not," Patrick agreed. "The man's a hypno-crit – the worst kind. Just lookin' at his fat ass on that rocker, I know I don't like him. No, sir, I don't like him one bit."

Soon the merchant was yelling at a little girl as she exited the Dry Goods Store across the street. "Hey missy, get your butt over here right now!"

The girl looked to be about seven years old and she was dressed in a very ornate yellow Easter-type dress with clean white shoes and socks. She skipped across the street to where the merchant rocked.

"What you got in the little brown bag there, hon'?" the man asked.

"Momma said I could get some candy a-fore church," she sweetly answered.

"Why didn't you buy any candy at my store?"

"Well, I only had one penny, sir," she innocently explained. "I will buy from you next week."

"Then let me give you a reminder," he sternly said, grabbing the girl's arm with one hand and her waist with the other. The man flipped her belly first onto his lap and lifted up the back of her dress.

"Please no, sir," she begged, allowing her candy sack to drop onto the boardwalk.

The man began viciously slamming the palm of his right hand onto her panty-covered back side, while his left hand held her body firmly on his lap. The girl screamed out in pain, flailing her arms and panicking, as the loud slapping strikes reigned down upon her precious posterior.

"I'll...teach...you...to...spend...all...your...money...on...the ...west...side...of...town...," the man chastised, spanking harder with each word that spat out of his sneering mouth.

The twins raced over to try to provide assistance to the youngster. "Hold on there, fella, you shouldn't be beatin' that little girl that-a way!"

"You need to be mindin' yer own damn business!" cursed the man, who continued battering the little girl's bruised behind. "Strangers don't have no say in what goes on here in Rupture!"

Patrick quickly grabbed the man's arm as it rose up to strike again, and then he managed to push the girl from the man's lap with his other hand. The girl rolled away, shielding her butt with one hand and collecting her spilled candy with the other.

"Why you sons-uv-bitch! I'll make you pay fer what you done!" cussed the merchant, pounding his fists on the wooded arms of the rocker.

Michael reached into his vest pocket and pulled out a small Indian Head one-cent piece. He flipped it toward the seated man. "Here's the fucking penny you wanted. Don't spend it all in one place."

145

The twins quickly walked away from the man as he continued to yell from his chair. The little girl looked up in fear at the freakish faces of the brothers, but eventually asked, "Would you walk me to church? My momma's waiting for me."

Two matching churches stood on opposite sides of the street at the southern end of town. Michael asked the girl which church her family attended.

"My momma should be waitin' fer me at the East Methodist 'piscopal Church, 'stablished in the year of our Lord 1881," she said.

"Do you know the denomination – or name – of the other church?" Michael inquired. "Is it Baptist, Catholic or maybe Mormon?"

"Nah, that's the West 'piscopal Methodist Church, 'stablished in the year of our Lord 1881."

"I see."

As soon as Michael and Patrick entered the half-filled sanctuary of the church, the little girl ran toward her mother's pew, yelling, "Momma, momma, old man Mitchell done tanned mah hide!"

"Hush, Shenandoah, we need to keep our voices down in church," the mother stressed, allowing the child to jump up into the pew beside her.

"But I was saved from the mean ol' Mitchell man, Momma," the girl continued. "A stranger paid Mitchell a penny to make him stop thrashing me, Momma."

"A stranger?"

"Look behind you momma; look behind you!"

The woman slowly turned around. Her face went pale when she saw Patrick walking toward her, waving at her in recognition. "Oh god," she gasped.

"Momma, we is in church!" Shenandoah reminded her.

Patrick and Michael took a seat in the pew directly behind the girl and her mother.

"Michael," Patrick began his introduction, "I'd like to formally introduce you to Squirrel Tooth Alice."

Although she saw no real benefit in the formal introduction, Alice turned around briefly to offer her hand. "Please just call me Alice...If you gentlemen helped my little girl, I greatly 'preciate it," she said while limply shaking hands.

The church service proceeded in the way that other church services normally progress, with some singing, some sermoning and some tithing. The preacher then requested that everyone rise for another hymn. The brothers were glad the selected song was "*Rock of Ages*," because they both were familiar with the lyrics; in fact, Patrick whispered to Michael that "This is mah all time favorite."

> "Rock of Ages, cleft for me,
> Let me hide myself in thee;
> Let the water and the blood,
> From thy wounded side which flowed,
> Be of sin the double cure;
> Save from wrath and make me pure.

> "Not the labors of my hands
> Can fulfill thy law's commands;
> Could my zeal no respite know,
> Could my tears forever flow,
> All for sin could not atone;
> Thou must save, and thou alone."

As the third verse began, Michael and Patrick belted out:

> "Nothing in my hand I bring,
> Simply to the cross I cling..."

Unfortunately, Michael and Patrick were the only ones in the church singing the third verse. Even the piano player stopped playing after the second verse. The brothers looked up to see everyone else in the church glaring at them.

"Naked, come to thee…" Patrick's voice ended in an embarrassing whisper.

Once Michael and Patrick stopped singing, the congregation quickly began filing out of the church. As people rushed past their pew, Michael asked Alice, "What are they all in a hurry for?"

"We gotta go next door to finish the song and hear the sermon from the West Episcopal Methodist Church preacher," Alice explained, grabbing her daughter's hand in the process.

"What?!" exclaimed Michael as Alice started walking past.

"It's… it's," Alice stuttered. "I guess you could call it a tradition. Excuse me now, but we have to go to church. You can do as you please."

Michael and Patrick played along, crossing the street and sitting down in the West Episcopal Methodist Church behind Alice, just in time to sing:

> "Nothing in my hand I bring,
> Simply to the cross I cling;
> Naked, come to thee for dress;
> Helpless, look to thee for grace;
> Foul, I to the fountain fly;
> Wash me, Savior, or I die.

> "While I draw this fleeting breath,
> When mine eyes shall close in death,
> When I soar to worlds unknown,
> See thee on thy judgment throne,
> Rock of Ages, cleft for me,

Let me hide myself in thee."

After the second sermon, tithing and closing hymn, Michael did not let Alice pass without asking, "Could you please explain what's going on in this bizarre town?"

"Shhh!" Alice responded, worried that another parishioner may have overheard his question. "Follow me and I'll try to explain."

"For free, right?" Patrick added.

Alice reluctantly led them behind the West Episcopal Methodist Church, where an old birch tree (Betula nigra) towered over a small cemetery. "Go play on the tombstones," Alice encouraged her youngster, "while I talk to these here fellas."

Alice nervously looked around, making sure no one else was in earshot, before she began her oral dissertation on the history of Rupture. She ignored her daughter as the kid knocked over various gravestones and markers in the cemetery, laughing and giggling as she tore up the solemn ground.

Not long after Rupture was founded, Alice explained, two competing outlaw gangs tried to take over the town, but neither gang was successful enough to gain complete control. One gang was led by patriarch Joe Mitchell, while the other outlaw family was directed by Nels Mathews.

"After a bunch of killins occurred, with no real progress on neither side, the heads of the families met and worked out a truce," Alice continued. "It was decided that the Mitchells would control the east side of town and the Mathews-ez would control the west."

Patrick commented, "Talk about opening up a can of spaghetti!"

"Don't you mean worms?" Michael asked.

"No thanks, I don't eat worms."

"But I heard they're a good source of protein."

"Maybe if yer a damn fish."

"Sometimes you drink like a damned fish."

"And sometimes I feel like beltin' you in the face..."

149

Alice stared impatiently at the arguing brothers. "Can I go on? Or don't you want to hear no more?"

"Excuse us, ma'am," Michael responded. "Please continue."

"Anyways, both gangs still don't trust each other and they get real pissy if they see t' other side of the street makin' more money than themselves, if you know what I mean," she said meaningfully. "In fact, the citizens is afraid to shop either side fer fear that the other will retaliate agin them."

Michael surmised, "So that's why the citizens try so hard to patronize both sides equally when they have business in town?"

"Exactly!" she agreed.

Patrick surmised, "So that's why you wanted me to go across the street last night and shoot my hot load in another whore's mouth?"

***

After Alice and her daughter took their leave, Michael and Patrick remained under the tree to strategize their next move in Rupture and to gather some of the thin river birch branches. They later offered the bundled tree pieces as a peace offering.

"Good afternoon, Mr. Mitchell," Michael extended a warm greeting to the sleeping man.

Upon waking and suddenly seeing the brothers, the man almost fell from his rocking chair in a rage. "You sons-uv-bitch! Why you come back here?! I'll have you killed – I swear!"

"Calm down there, Mr. Mitchell," Michael responded, placing a hand lightly upon the old man's shoulder. "I'm sorry that we had that misunderstanding earlier. You were absolutely right when you said we should mind our own business since we're out-of-towners, so to speak, and not fully aware of the customs and traditions of Rupture. My brother and I had no idea of your stature and standing within this fine community. In fact, as a gesture of goodwill on our part, my brother would like to present you with a gift."

150

"A gift, eh?" Mitchell mumbled.

"Yes, sir," Patrick confirmed, holding out a bundle of birch branches, which was tied together with some twine. "Here's a nice birch rod that you can use on that belligerent brat next time you see her. I'd recommend you soak it in water a-fore you thrash her, if'n you really want to make an impression."

"Why, thankie," smiled the man, imagining the proposed beating as he accepted the gift. "Maybe you boys ain't so bad affer all."

"You're quite welcome," Michael said. "After getting to know the child a bit, we found Shenandoah to be quite annoying actually."

"You got that right," Mitchell agreed. "By the way, what are you boys doin' in Rupture anyways?"

"Just passin' through really," Michael explained. "But to tell you the truth, maybe my brother and I could be of service to the town. We're sort of experts in conflict resolution."

"I can see that," Mitchell observed, looking up at the brothers and then glancing down at the symbolic olive branch in his hands.

"Would you mind if we set up a meeting with you and Mr. Mathews, so that we can describe the plan we developed, which will make Rupture more equitable for both sides and make life a bit easier for the citizens."

"I'm guessin' it wouldn't hurt to hear what youse gots to say," Mitchell admitted.

"Well, we know it won't *hurt* near as much as that birch rod's gonna hurt the ass of the whore's daughter!" added Patrick, causing all three men to break out in a hearty laugh.

***

The brothers ingratiated themselves into Nels Mathews's trust by confiding that one of the whores on the east side was finishing off her clients without sending any compensation to the west.

151

Mathews was upset with the news until Michael explained that he had a plan which would solve the compensation problem once and for all. Mitchell and Mathews agreed to meet in the West Saloon that evening.

"Inner-what-you-airy?" asked Mitchell once the brothers began to explain their proposal at the designated meeting.

"Inner-meaty-airy, you old fool!" corrected Mathews.

Mitchell slammed his new birch rod onto the table in anger, causing the other men to jump back a bit in their chairs. Both Mitchell and Mathews were approximately the same age, looking to be in their early sixties, but Mitchell was significantly heavier than his nemesis while Mathews was taller in stature.

"Now, now, gentlemen, let's try to work together on this," Michael interjected. "Let me try to explain how my brother and I can serve as *intermediaries* between both families, so that each side of town is equally compensated for all business taking place in Rupture."

Michael explained that he would monitor one side of town, while his brother would be responsible for the other side. As business takes place on one side of the street, the brother responsible for that side would collect the money and split it in half between the two identical businesses. Since only the brothers would be handling the money, it would not be possible for one side to hide profit from the other side, plus the citizens would no longer have to split their spending between both sides of the street.

Mathews looked suspiciously at Michael and asked, "And just how in the hell do you expect to cover every transaction that takes place?"

"Yeah," Mitchell repeated. "How the hell can you do that, anyways?"

"Well," began Michael, "I certainly think it's possible to cover all the ground. Let's be honest, Rupture is not exactly a huge city or anything..."

Mathews interrupted: "That still don't explain how you and yer brother are gonna cover both sides of the street – day and night."

Patrick chipped in, "Maybe with cowbells."

"Cowbells?" questioned Mitchell.

"Yeah," Patrick explained. "My brother and I will hang out on the sidewalk and whenever we hear a cowbell ringing at a store, we will attend to it, according to which side of the street it's ringing."

Mathews looked at both brothers simultaneously. "That doesn't even make sense. I don't think yer proposal is gonna work."

"Not a lick-a sense," added Mitchell.

"Well, can you at least allow us a trial run?" asked Michael. "If it doesn't work out, then my brother and I will mosey out of town and you'll never see us again."

"You'd be leavin' all right, but I don't know about the moseyin' part," Mathews warned. "There's a certain amount of trust involved when yer talkin' about handling all our money."

"You can trust us," Michael assured. "We didn't have to tell you about the thieving whore, but we felt it was the right thing to do."

"Okay, so one thing you haven't 'splained is – what's in it for you?"

Michael quickly answered, "Room and board, split evenly between both sides, and occasionally some essentials like clothing and…"

"…whores sometimes," Patrick finished.

Michael failed to tell the two gentlemen about the small stipend that he and his brother planned to surreptitiously remove from some transactions, sort of as a tip for services rendered, whenever odd sums could not be split evenly.

Mathews and Mitchell hesitantly agreed to try the brothers' plan for one week, but warned them again not to cross either family, especially if it involved finances.

"In fact," concluded Mathews as he rose from his chair and began walking across the barroom floor. "Let me show you what happens to people who cheat us…"

He leaned out the stereotypical swinging doors of the saloon and yelled, "Bring 'er in, boys!"

Two hulking men, covered in soot and looking the part of blacksmiths, burst through the doors dragging Squirrel Tooth Alice by the arms. She had a frazzled, panicked, look on her face, which could easily be discerned even though wild strands of blonde hair hung down haphazardly in front of her features.

Her legs and feet scraped effortlessly across the wooden floor, and appeared to be completely limp, as the men dragged her toward an upright piano in the corner of the saloon. They let Alice drop to the floor, so that they could push and turn the piano away from the wall.

Alice, dressed in her usual nightly attire, began crawling toward Mathews and eventually propped herself up on her knees and clasped her hands together.

"Please, Mr. Mathews, I'm sorry fer what I done. It won't happen agin, I swears to you. It won't happen again!" she begged.

Mathews ignored her and looked toward the blacksmiths. "Git 'er outta that corset and strap 'er to the back of the pianner."

"Oh my god, no! Please don't do that, Mr. Mathews! I swear I'll pay you ever'thing yer owed – and more!"

Michael spoke up, "Is this really necessary, Mr. Mathews?"

"Hell yes, it's necessary, dammit!" Mathews yelled. "Don't you agree, Joe?"

"Hell yes, I agree."

The back of the piano had a set of iron wrist cuffs attached near the top, which were likely fabricated at the town blacksmith shops (the left cuff made on one side of town and the right cuff made on the other). Alice, naked now from her head down to the waistline of her skirt, bawled and squalled as the men dragged her to the backside of the piano and locked her wrists in the manacles.

Mathews pulled the piano bench up to the front of the instrument and took a seat. He then looked over to Mitchell and invited, "Would you care to do the honors, this evening, Joseph?"

The twins stayed at their table and felt helpless as they watched Mitchell stand up and grab his bundle of birch rods. "Do we have a bucket o' water to soak these in real quick?" the man asked.

It wasn't long before Mathews began tickling the ivories with the familiar refrain of "*Oh Shenandoah*." Meanwhile, Mitchell did not refrain from tickling Alice's bare back by lightly brushing her skin with the tips of the jagged branches.

Recognizing the introduction, Patrick whispered to Michael that "This is mah all time favorite."

"I thought '*Rock of Ages*' was your favorite?"

"No, no, no, no, '*Rock of Ages*' is my favorite hymn, '*Shenandoah*' is my favorite folk song."

"Folk song? What the hell does that mean?"

"I don't know, it just sounds like the right moniker for this tune, you know, a song that's familiaristical to common *folk* like us."

"What?"

Alice also immediately recognized the song, since she sang it to her daughter at bedtime every night, just before she went out whoring. "Please not this song," she pleaded between sobs.

Mitchell laughed, "After this, ever' time you hear '*Shenandoah*,' it'll remind you not to be a thievin' whore."

Mathews began belting out the opening verse, while Mitchell began belting Alice's back with the birch rod, specifically two hard strikes at the words "Hi Ho."

> "Oh Shenandoah, I hear you calling,
> *Hi Ho*, you rolling river.
> Oh Shenandoah, I long to hear you,
> *Hi Ho*, I'm bound away.
> 'Cross the wide, Miss-ou-ri."

155

Mitchell boisterously sang along during the "Hi-Hos," as he found the lyrical hook gave his old muscles renewed strength while he slashed away at the woman's back. Alice appeared to join in too, although her words sounded more like "Eye-Ow" and seemed to be off meter by a half-beat. Patrick also couldn't resist singing along, quickly noting to Michael that the birching provided an interesting drum-like beat to the arrangement.

True to the lyrics of the song, Alice's cries could easily be heard, even though her wrists were bound directly behind the piano. The long bright welts left by the birch rod crossed the wide expanse of Alice's broad shoulders, causing her Misery. Tiny trickles of blood also formed where the branches nicked her thin skin, rolling in a bead down her spine like a river of sanguine.

> "Miss-ou-ri, she's a mighty river,
> *Hi Ho*, you rolling river.
> When she rolls down, her topsails shiver,
> *Hi Ho*, I'm bound away,
> Cross the wide, Miss-ou-ri."

Alice's body did indeed shiver with each successive blow, which slowly broke her body down until she dangled from the piano like a piece of pulverized meat. Uncontrolled screams streamed from deep within her throat, as the stinging branches enflamed her delicate skin from without. Desperate to escape from the torment, her hands twisted in anguish inside the unforgiving manacles, until the final stroke of the second verse left her vanquished and hanging on the edge of unconsciousness.

> "Farewell my Dearest, I'm bound to leave you,
> *Hi Ho*, you rolling river.
> Oh Shenandoah, I'll not deceive you,
> *Hi Ho*, I'm bound away.
> Cross the wide Miss-ou-ri."

Limp and languid, her body hung in limbo as the final four strikes found their masticated mark. Even though her panicked mind had drifted to another plane, the involuntary reflexes of her ravished body reacted violently to each blow, blood now splashing off her tattered back, while her tortured voice groaned in complete submission.

Mathews, at the piano, closed the song with the familiar ad-lib flourish associated with the comical ending of *"Turkey in the Straw."* Triumphantly slamming the wooden lid over the keys, he sang out: "Two-bit whore!"

Seeing the crestfallen condition of Alice, Patrick and Michael suddenly stood up. Mathews looked over at the twins and bowed slightly from his seated position at the piano. Mitchell dropped the drooping, bloody branches, and performed a slight bow.

Mathews acknowledged the twins' reaction by announcing, "Thank you, gentlemen, for that standing ovation!"

***

The next day, Michael and Patrick were busy installing cowbells throughout the town, developing a system where the bells were attached outside each business and a string was fed through the store to where the cash register was located. Fortunately, the two dry goods stores had plenty of bells on hand, since the area surrounding Rupture was comprised of many large farms and ranches.

Instead of sitting and waiting on the boardwalk for a bell to ring, Michael and Patrick tried to take an active and visible role in their new assignment during the first week of operation. There were times when the men were challenged with simultaneous calls and there were a few burdensome late night calls, but overall they managed to meet the economic needs of the community and there were no complaints from merchants on either side of Division Street.

The doctors on the southern end of town, whose offices were located just before the churches, were especially appreciative of the twins' performance. In Rupture, the doctors served a dual role of both physician and mortician, which was a convenience for some customers but did not provide the level of trust that most people desire when seeking the services of a health care professional.

"Hey, Doc, being both a physician and a mortician is probably quite an *undertaking*," observed Patrick on one of his calls. "Get it? Quite an *undertaking*?"

"Yes, yes," impatiently responded the doctor from the east side of the street as he attempted to treat a patient.

"*Undertaking* as in *undertaker…*" Patrick added, much to the consternation of the patient, who had no desire to be reminded of the doctor's sideline business.

"I told you, I get it, Mr. Sughrue," the doctor reiterated. "I get it already."

The doctor finished sewing up the incision, completing a successful appendectomy, and helped the patient to his feet. "Now, you be careful walking until that alcohol wears off," cautioned the doctor. "You can make payment to this gentleman here."

After the patient paid and stumbled out of the office, Patrick observed, "That was quite impressive, Doc."

"Well, thank you, but if that man had come to me a week ago, I doubt he'd have survived, because I probably would have had to send him next door to get stitched up. Forcing a patient to stagger across the street with an open wound is not ideal."

"I can 'magine," Patrick agreed. "I hope you'll let old man Mitchell know that you're pleased with our service."

"Oh, absolutely, I believe the whole town is appreciative, especially since folks will no longer have to see a pregnant woman waddling across the road with a baby half-hanging out of her cooch because the doctor was only allowed to partially deliver the child."

Patrick laughed, trying to envision the bizarre scene of an upside down baby, swinging from its mother's womb, flailing its arms and bawling, as mom tried to make it to the next doctor.

"Yep, more than one infant ended up dropping out before mom reached her follow-up appointment," the doctor continued, "usually getting dragged along in the dirt by the umbilical cord."

"Ew! That sounds pretty messy, Doc," Patrick snickered. "But if I ever saw sumthin' like that, I believe I'd piss myself."

"Messy? You want to talk messy?" the doctor responded. "Things really got messy when one of us lost a patient or when someone around here died of natural causes."

"Why's that?"

"Look over there in the corner by the medicine cabinet," the doctor answered, pointing to a large six-foot pole with a heavy gray blade attached to the top.

"Holy shit!" Patrick exclaimed. "That looks like one of 'em middy-evil battle axes! The blade's 'bout as big as mah head bone!"

"That it is, Mr. Sughrue, indeed it is. The blacksmiths in town forged one for each doctor."

"Can you even lift that damn thing?"

"Hell, no, I'm not gonna try lifting that weapon," the doctor admitted. "If someone died in town, we would call the blacksmith to take care of the body. But, thankfully, we shouldn't need that service anymore."

"What'd you mean?"

"Well, both churches have a cemetery, so each body needed cut in half."

***

Even though their probationary period was over, the brothers continued to take their new job seriously and continued serving the community into the second week. Every once in awhile, there would be a large purchase at a dry goods store or at a blacksmith shop, resulting in an odd payment amount, which would allow the brothers to skim a penny or two off the top before splitting the rest evenly between the merchants. No one ever questioned the payment amounts, as the business owners began trusting the twins more and more each day.

Michael and Patrick did take advantage of the perks they were offered, but tried to be conservative in their acceptance of gifts from the merchants. However, Patrick didn't hesitate to request a whore from time to time.

Patrick was surprised when Alice knocked on his hotel room door one evening. She managed a forced smile when Patrick opened the door.

"Howdy, Alice," Patrick welcomed. "Or should I jus' say, 'Hi, Ho'?"

"Very funny," she responded as she walked past him.

"Seriously though, I hope there's no hard feelings over what happened the other night in the saloon."

"Now why would I have hard feelings about you sayin' something that got me beat half to death?"

"I don't know. I guess some people can be petty."

She began undressing, hoping that she could fulfill her commitment and leave as soon as possible. She made sure that her injured back was facing him when she removed her top.

"Damn, that still looks tender," Patrick observed as he approached her.

"I even heard a rumor that you were the one who gave Mitchell that wretched bundle o' birches."

"Well…" began Patrick as he started to disrobe. "Let me put it this-a way – I might-a done give him those branches, but I didn't intend for them to be used on you specifically."

Once they were both naked as jaybirds and perched on the side of the bed, Alice squawked, "We're gonna have to find a way to do this without me layin' on mah sore back."

160

"That can be 'ranged, I suppose."

They sat in silence, waitin' for one or the other to make a move in what was fast becoming an uncomfortable situation for all parties. Patrick cautiously draped his arm around Alice's shoulder, but the move caused her to break out in sobs.

"Did I hurt yer sore back?" he asked.

"No, I jus' keep thinkin' of Shenandoah."

"Oh, well, lately I'm not likin' that song as much as I used-tah."

"Not the song, you ignoramus, I'm worried 'bout my daughter," she cried.

"She eat too much candy or sumthin'?"

Alice rolled her tear-drenched eyes and answered, "No, I'm worried 'bout her havin' to grow up in this god-fer-saken town, probably havin' to sell her body jus' like her momma and gettin' abused ever' step o' the way."

"Well, I don't rightly see her runnin' for president or anything like that," Patrick advised. "I mean we all gotta 'cept our lot in life, if you know what I mean, like the cards we is dealt and all."

"I know exactly what you mean, that's why I want to send Shenandoah away from here."

"Send away yer own kin?!"

"It would be for her own good," she explained. "I have a sister in Kansas City that has agreed to look after her. She'd even git some schoolin' and maybe learn to read 'n' write."

"Still though, it's gonna be hard for Shenandoah, bein' away from her momma like that. I mean, personally, I can't imagine being apart from my brother, Michael, if you know what I mean."

"Oh, god," she exclaimed in frustration. "I should-a knowed not to trouble you with my problems." She covered her face with her hands.

"Now, now," Patrick whispered, patting her lightly on the shoulder. "If'n you got yer mind made up 'bout Shenandoah, I'll try to help you anyway ah can."

161

She dropped her hands and looked into Patrick's eyes. "You would? You'd really help us?"

"Well, sure," he stated. "Sure, I'd help ya'll. I mean, I'm not a total monster, if you know what I mean."

Her face brightened up and she wrapped her arms around Patrick, planting a kiss on his forehead. "Oh thank you! Thank you, Patrick."

"Sure, but jus' how you suppose I could help?"

"Well, I checked with the stagecoach and it would cost about ten dollars to send Shenandoah to Kansas City. Unfortunately, I had to give all mah savings to Mathews."

"Well, I sure don't have no sawbuck on me right now, but maybe I could get it together in a couple-a weeks."

"Thank you for yer sincere kindness, Patrick. I now know what happened in the saloon wasn't your fault – it couldn't have been. Your heart is pure and yer kindness knows no bounds."

"Yeah, I guess I am sort-a known fer my kindness – more so than my brother is anyways."

Alice stood up. "Now, how do you want me?"

"How 'bout you jus' lean over the bed with yer ass in the air and I'll git behind ya?"

"Sure, 'nuff, hon'," she agreed, leaning over to place her arms across the bed.

Alice felt Patrick delicately lifting her hair up off her back, which she thought he was doing in order to study the marks that were still present. The next thing she felt was Patrick's heavy leather belt being looped over her head, which he tightened around her neck before she could get her fingers underneath.

"Ugh," she managed to blurt out before the pressure blocked her voice box.

Alice wasn't even able to make a sound when she sensed Patrick's erection violently invading her sphincter. Holding the tail end of the belt securely in his left hand and clutching her hip with his right hand, Patrick pulled back on the belt for leverage as he thrust his spit-covered cock completely into her assailed ass.

Her eyes bulged out their sockets as her face became flushed from the blood trapped inside her skull. She could feel her brain begin to swell within her cranium as she began to lose consciousness, but the burgeoning pain from the merciless thrusts kept her from passing out. She swung her arms around aimlessly in front of her, panicked and unable to prevent the ass assault.

Patrick delighted in the involuntary contractions of her tight anal cavity as her bowels squeezed and squashed his slick shaft. The contractions also caused her bladder to release its musty contents onto Patrick's balls and thighs.

"That-a girl, milk that cock!" he commanded. "There'll be no release for you until I shoot my cream!"

Alice's twisting and twirling torso finally gave out when the lack of oxygen caused her body to go limp, although Patrick kept her head raised by maintaining the tension on the taut leather strap. Seeing her defeated body hanging from the end of his belt, Patrick couldn't help but pull out his pulsating prick and spray his victorious viscidity across her swollen back.

Alice's head and breasts crushed onto the bed as soon as Patrick released her neck from the belt loop. He rubbed his steaming semen into the welts of her back, expecting to produce at least a murmur from his conquest, but Alice remained silent and her chest remained still.

"Dammit, wake up, Alice, you stupid whore!"

Patrick stood back and patiently folded both ends of his belt into his right hand. Taking careful aim, he began thrashing the doubled-up belt onto Alice's defenseless ass cheeks, creating loud thunder cracks which seemed to shake the small bedroom.

After a half dozen or so hard smacks, Alice's hands instinctively reached behind her back to try to protect her body from the searing slashes. Her lungs filled with air as she gasped at the burning barrage from the belt.

Still dizzy and suffering from a debilitating headache, Alice managed to beg, "Please, please, no more…"

But Patrick forcefully pushed her hands away and continued the punishment, ordering, "Keep yer hands off and stay still! This is what happens to whores who abandon their children!"

***

And thusly was begat the man known to history as Patsy the Pimp.

True to his word, Patrick devised a plan to help raise ten dollars for Shenandoah's transport to Kansas City. With four whores in town, split between the east and west side saloons, Patrick would meet each potential customer, negotiate a price for services and collect the fee upfront. This would mean that the opposing saloon, awaiting its share of the profit, would not know exactly how much money was collected.

Patrick also would not have to worry about his brother being aware of his working both sides of the street, since most of the whoring was performed during the time that Michael slept. If Patrick had to *represent* his twin brother at certain times to keep the ruse going, then that would just help his brother get even more rested.

Although the Sughrue brothers were twins, the saloon owners still became suspicious from time to time as Patrick would commonly visit from across the street to deliver "half" of the prostitution profits.

"You sure this is half?" asked Mathews one day.

"Abso-tively," answered Patrick. "The horny feller was only wantin' a blow job."

"And yer brother can confirm this payment?"

"Sure, if'n he was awake to witness it."

"I'm keeping an eye on you. I hope you know that."

164

"Sure do," Patrick concluded. "We wouldn't have it any other way. My brother and I are all about – now how did he say it? Yeah, my brother and I are all about transparency."

"Sometimes I wish *you* were transparent, so I wouldn't have to look at yer extreme ugliness."

"Have a nice day."

Dawn was breaking as Patrick was leaving the west saloon. As he crossed the street, he noticed that a pair of Indians was approaching from afar. Patrick didn't like dealing with Indians. Patrick didn't like Indians at all.

He quickly disappeared inside the east hotel, passing Alice on the boardwalk. "Hey, how's business?" she asked the scurrying man.

"Can't talk right now," Patrick spat. "I got sumthin' to take care of inside."

"Whatever," she said to herself as she strolled toward the east saloon.

She noticed two Indians slowly creeping down Division Street. Each Indian had his own pony, but the older Indian was slumped over slightly in his saddle. Alice figured the older Indian was a Chief, since the man wore an elaborate headdress comprised of many colorful feathers and beads. The younger Indian carried a ceremonial staff.

Mitchell joined Alice on the walkway. "What's goin' on there, whore? Why's them Injuns coming here fer?"

" 'Fraid I don't have a clue, Joe. Maybe they're wanting to buy some firewater or something."

"More likely they wants fire*arms*," Mitchell said. "I don't trust them savages."

The Indians stopped in the middle of the street once they reached the area where Alice and Mitchell were standing. A few other merchants, residents and early-risers also gathered to witness the Native American visitors.

Still mounted on his horse, the younger Indian banged the bottom of the staff onto the ground, causing some hollowed-out gourds, strung from the top, to shake and rattle. "Settlers! Chief White Plume has had a vision!"

"Maybe they already got plenty of firewater," Alice whispered.

"Silence, Settlers! White Plume has had a vision! He wants me to tell you of this vision!"

"Okay, already," mumbled Mitchell.

"Chief White Plume says there is evil in this town. Evil that is not of the Great Spirit. But is an enemy of the Great Spirit. You must seek out this evil and rid your town of it. Otherwise, White Plume sees bad things for this town. Many people will suffer and die unless you take away the evil that lives among you."

The translator stomped the staff to the ground again. "May the Great Spirit protect you!"

The two Indians then turned their horses around and left the way they had come in. Patrick watched them leave from the window of his hotel room.

"Michael, Michael, wake up, Michael," Patrick urged. "Mike, two damn Indians just rode outta town. They was scaring up the townsfolk sumthin' fierce, ramblin' on about evil spirits and such."

Michael tried to wake up, shaking his head and blinking his eyes. "So what?" he responded, rubbing crust from around his eyelids.

"So what?" repeated Patrick. "What if the citizens think we're the evil ones? What if they start treating us with suspicion? What if they start accusing us of wrong-doin'?"

"You're being paranoid."

"No, I ain't paranoidal or paranormal or nuthin' like that. What if somebody finds out we use-tah ride with the Dopples? What if someone comes into town and recognizes us?"

"What if, what if, what if, what if... Let's stop with all the 'what ifs.' Just calm down, Patrick. We're going to continue business as usual until I say otherwise."

"I'm jus' worried is all. Mitchell and Mathews don't play around."

"Neither do we."

***

The twins did continue business as usual, even though Patrick's business was a little unusual, but that was usually none of Michael's business. Michael did notice that the merchants were beginning to treat them differently, especially asking more and more questions concerning the transactions that they handled. Michael also began to wonder why he had not been called to handle as many late night prostitution transactions. He wasn't used to getting so much sleep.

"What's up with the whores lately?" Michael asked Patrick one morning while Alice was sucking him off at the hotel. "Are you the only man in town who wants sex anymore?"

"Watch yer damn mouth!" Patrick exclaimed.

"What?"

"Oh, sorry, Mike, I was talkin' to ol' Squirrel Tooth here," Patrick answered, wondering how Michael could possibly misinterpret his comment to Alice. "Anyways, what was you askin' me?"

"I'm asking if you know why there hasn't been as much prostitution going on in Rupture during the evenings, especially on the damned weekends."

"Oh, well, sometimes I go ahead and – damn, take it easy, Squirrel!"

"Sometimes you go ahead and do what?"

"Handle them."

"Handle what?"

"The whores," Patrick explained. "I handle the whores if you're sleepin'."

"On both sides of the street?!"

167

"Yes, on both sides of the street. Don't worry about it."

"How in the hell do you get away with that? The saloon-keepers expect us to handle the transactions like we originally promised!"

"I don't know how I've been getting away with it. Maybe they think that I'm you sometimes. We are twins you know."

"Bullshit!" Michael answered. "Of course they know who is who. You know that identical twin shit doesn't work for us. Maybe we better have another sit down with Mathews and Mitchell to make sure everything is okay and to assure them that neither of us will try working both sides of the street while one of us is fuckin' asleep."

"All right, already," Patrick conceded. "Set up the meeting if it'll make you feel better. Jeesh, I was just tryin' to let you get some rest. I'm an in-some-maniac anyways, you know that... that...that's it, keep lickin' it right there."

"Okay, then, I'll set up the meeting."

"And I'm coming..."

***

That morning, Patrick gave Alice a ten dollar tip for the blow job she administered. She raced back to her room at the saloon to gather Shenandoah and the luggage, which she had pre-packed, hoping to be able to meet the stagecoach at high noon. Alice tucked a piece of paper with her sister's address on it inside Shenandoah's pocket. She promised Shenandoah that she would follow her to Kansas City as soon as she raised enough money for her own fare. But Shenandoah probably knew better.

Throughout the day, Michael and Patrick continued their due diligence, diligently collecting and distributing the funds which were due for business transactions within the town. They also set up a meeting for late afternoon at the west saloon with the two family leaders of the east and west sides.

The four met at the same round wooden bar table where they originally met – only this time no one was expecting an appearance by Squirrel Tooth Alice. Mitchell and Mathews, who seemed aggravated at the ad hoc meeting, began by directly asking the twins what the hell they wanted.

Before either twin could spin their explanation about the temporary lapse of judgment over the prostitution fees, the four furtive fornicatresses of Rupture sullied their way down the stairway from the second floor.

"Are we gonna be partyin'?" asked Patrick.

"I doubt it," answered Michael, observing the countenance of Alice as she led the other three whores onto the barroom floor.

"Jus' hold yer horse, boys," Alice spoke up, looking directly at the twins. "Before you start spinnin' yer yarn and a-blamin' me for stuff, we girls got something to say to misters Mitchell and Mathews."

"Ladies," Mathews announced. "Let me remind ya'll that this here is a business meeting and you might benefit by learnin' yer place and not speakin' out of turn."

"Yeah, unlessen you want us to put you in yer place," added Mitchell.

"Well," responded Alice. "What we gots to say has to do with *yer* money, but if'n you don't want to hear it…"

"Speak yer piece, woman!" snapped Mathews. "And it better be something worth hearin' or all-a ya's gonna be ridin' the backside of the pianner this evenin'!"

"Gentleman," interrupted Michael. "I'm sure you're familiar with the term 'lying whore'."

"Like lyin' on their backs?" added Patrick.

"Pat, you're not helping here," Michael chastised, glaring at his brother.

Mathews waved off the brothers, indicating that they should keep quiet. "Speak now, wenches, or forever hold yer peace."

169

Alice went on to detail the business *acum*en of Patrick the Pimp and how he was eventually able to tip her ten dollars for a blow job. The other three harlots also confirmed Alice's accusations, describing how Patrick would personally negotiate with clients for all the prostitution services and how they would never know exactly how much money was agreed upon. They tried once or twice to ask a customer how much was paid, but it always resulted in a beating (which Patrick allowed at no additional cost to the consumer).

"If all that's true, Squirrel Tooth," Mathews responded, "why didn't I git a cut of that sawbuck?"

" 'Cause you always allowed us girls to keep our tips, that's why," she answered. "Besides I gave that ten to the stagecoach driver, so he would take Shenandoah to her aunt's house."

"No ten – no evidence," Patrick objected.

"This ain't a court o' law, you fuckin' freak," Mathews ruled, drawing his pistol and pointing it at the twins. "If you two are carryin' any weaponry, I'd suggest you carefully place whatever it is on top of the table."

The twins raised their hands in submission. Michael announced, "Calm down, Mr. Mathews. I assure you, we don't have any firearms. As you can rightly imagine, neither my brother nor I could be considered much of a marksman, considering our poor aim and all."

"Then I say we take our little business meeting outside, so my place ain't damaged none," Mathews suggested. "Git yerself up slowly and start walkin' to the front door."

Mitchell cocked his six-shooter to add emphasis to the command.

"Okay, okay, already," Michael said, rising from his seat. "We're going; we're going. But please remember you haven't exactly heard our side of the story. I think we should get a chance to defend ourselves against the charges that these whores have put forth."

170

"I thought I already told you, that this ain't…"

"I know, I know, this isn't a court of law."

Mathews directed Alice to hurry and round up the blacksmiths and the doctors. He and Mitchell then followed the twins outside to the street, guns being aimed at the Sughrues throughout the short journey. The commotion was already causing a stir within the town and people began gathering around the front of the saloon.

"Git behind the hitchin' post!" Mathews demanded as he reached down to gather some rope, which was conveniently hanging from the horizontal rail. "I wanna git this over with before dusk settles in."

Mathews handed his gun to Mitchell and instructed the man to keep both pistols aimed at the twins. He then ordered Michael to present his left hand. Michael hesitantly held out his left hand and Mathews forcefully grabbed it. Mathews then tied one end of the rope around the wrist and the other end around the vertical post.

Mathews repeated the process using the other vertical post, demanding that Patrick present his right hand. The twins were soon securely tied to the hitching post. Mathews kicked the backs of their knees, forcing them to kneel with their heads just above the horizontal rail.

Once he saw the blacksmiths and doctors arrive, Mathews took Mitchell aside and they talked quietly with each other so that no one else could hear. Soon Mathews walked back to the hitching post, looked down at the twins and announced, "Although this ain't a court o' law, Mr. Mitchell and me have sentenced you both to death by beheadin'."

The blacksmiths, who had retrieved the wide-bladed battle axes from the doctors, quickly moved to opposite sides of the hitching post.

"Wait!" pleaded Patrick. "My brother had nuthin' to do with this. He was asleep when I was sellin' them sluts."

Michael yelled, "Patrick, it doesn't matter! You know that!"

"Who y'all trying to kid?" asked Mathews. "I'm sick of all yer twin bullshit, bitchin' 'bout one bein' awake and one not bein' awake or the other way 'round… So, you wantin' us to just chop off yer head, Patrick, liken that would be okay with yer brother?"

"Whatever," Patrick mumbled. "I'm just tryin' to say it weren't my brother's fault is all."

Mathews stared down at the trembling twins for a moment. The crowd was becoming restless, chanting for blood and gore.

Finally, Mathews declared, "You know what? Maybe we *should* try only cuttin' off Patrick's head."

Michael violently struggled against the rope binding him to the post, and screaming, "Are you crazy? You're the fucking monsters – all of you! You're all fucking monsters!"

Mathews looked over to the blacksmith on Patrick's side and ordered, "Let's divide these conjoined charlatans!"

The crowd began chanting: "No more Siamese; no more Siamese!"

With a final nod from Mathews, the blacksmith raised his battle axe and brought it swiftly down – and through – the back of Patrick's neck.

"No!" shrieked Michael just as a blast of blood sprayed from the torso he no longer shared with Patrick, painting Mathews in red regalia like a drenched demon. Members of the audience also screeched as Patrick's head rolled amongst them toward the center of the street.

Michael quickly passed out from loss of blood and hung lifelessly from the railing, both of his hands still tied to the posts. Mathews shook the dripping blood from his sleeves and pointed to the doctors.

"Don't just stand there! Check his fucking pulse or something!"

Alice and her prostie peers watched from the side in horror, their hands covering their mouths as they gasped. Did anyone really expect it all to end this way? Would it have been better to just keep quiet? Are they going to be reminded of this scene every month when they're on their period? But then Alice remembered the humiliation she felt every time she had to perform some strange sex act on Patrick while his brother pretended to be asleep.

"Good riddance!" she blurted out.

After a few minutes, the deluge of blood drained away and both doctors concurred that the body was deceased. The doctors then untied the wrists and allowed the body to drop down into the dust.

"I guess both of them twins died affer all!" laughed Mitchell, whose comment prompted some giggles and guffaws from the townsfolk.

"Not so fast!" a thunderous voice erupted from above. "You can't kill a doppelganger that easily!"

The hushed crowd looked above, expecting to see someone yelling from a rooftop, but instead they saw Patrick's severed head suspended in the air above the town. The eyes of the head were as red as rubies, the nostrils flared like dual shot gun barrels, and the mouth formed a wide toothless grin.

Someone yelled, "My god! The Injuns was right! Them twins is evil! God help us all!"

Patrick laughed so loud that the earth shook under the people's feet, causing a cloud of dust to rise, but the captivated crowd continued to watch the head. And they continued to watch as the laughing head began to spin, slowly at first and then picking up speed.

Swirling winds captured their hair, their hats, their clothing, eventually becoming so strong that some spectators lost their footing and began falling helplessly to the ground. Soon Patrick's head spun so quickly that all his features became blurred and it looked like a red-streaked planet spinning in its own galaxy. A plume of dust and debris formed on top of the spinning sphere, creating a funnel cloud which fluctuated and breathed like a wild beast trapped in a narrow corridor. Soon the corridor collapsed as

173

buildings imploded, sending shattered glass and broken wood throughout the town. The people who were not killed by the debris were soon swept up into the funnel cloud, their screams and cries muted by the deafening winds. As dusk began to fall across the plains, the monstrous tornado could be viewed from miles away.

***

Old Chief White Plume and his young companion watched from a safe distance as the town of Rupture was being decimated – wiped clean from the barren landscape. "My dream has come true, but they did not heed our warning," the Chief proclaimed in his native language.

The other Indian nodded in agreement, knowing full well that this would not be the last funnel cloud that would wreak havoc in the territory. Evil such as this simply does not just go away.

"I've a feeling I'm not in Kansas anymore," the little girl beside them said.

"Be quiet pale-faced slave child," demanded the younger Indian. "Or we'll kill you just like the stagecoach driver."

The End.

"Each little chapter has its place."

- Lillie Langtry

BIG TROUBLE IN LITTLE ASS
BY WOL-VRIEY

Wol-vriey is Nigerian, and quite tall. He currently resides in a state of uneasy stalemate with his threatening-to-thin-beyond-redemption hair, and believes there actually are things that go bump in the night.

Wol-vriey recycles the ridiculous into reasonable reality for the reader. His WEIRRRD philosophy? WEIRRRD = Warp/Write Everything into Realistic Ridiculous Readable Distorted Dream Dimension Descriptions.

*Wol-vriey is the author of **The Bizarro Story of I**, **Alice's Adventures in Steamland: The Clockwork Goddess**, and **Chainsaw Cop Corpse**. Be watching for his newest novel, **Vegan Zombie Apocalypse**, in Spring 2013.*

*His short story, **Forever Ago Sunshine**, was published in **The Big Book of Bizarro**.*

*Wol-vriey blogs at **http://oddityfarm.wordpress.com**.*

CHAPTER 1

Jude rode into Little Ass late Thursday evening.

The sun was three-quarters set. The sky above it was smeared with red like a goddess had wiped her fanny with it while having her period.

Distorted by shadows, Little Ass looked like a mess of old ships crashed together. The town's name came from the odd shape of the mountains to its south. Instead of being pointed, Mount Ass's twin peaks were rounded.

The Indians said the mountains were a buried goddess's buttocks.

Jude rode through the town, keeping a watchful eye. He had lots of enemies, had no idea where one might turn up.

Little Ass was a mining town fallen on hard times now the gold seams in the mountains were all worked out. A few companies still doggedly drilled shafts and sent men down into the exhausted seams in Mount Ass, but the gold rush had long moved elsewhere. Most of the townsfolk had returned to farming and rustling cattle as professions.

Jude passed Quaker families on their way to evening service, kids playing in the dust, and chattering bosomy matrons coming and going from stores.

He passed a group of black sharecroppers offloading sacks of wheat and beans into a storehouse.

A group of drunks lounged outside a saloon. Beer steins in hand, they were watching two of their number slug it out.

"C'mon Mike, knock that prick's teeth back down his lyin' throat!" a man yelled.

Mike, a blond guy with thick mustaches, flung a punch at his opponent, a redhead. The redhead ducked and tripped him up. Mike grabbed the redhead's shirtfront as he went down. Both men landed heavily in the dust. The brawl continued.

Guzzling their beers, the drinkers exhorted the fighters to greater inebriated violence.

Jude laughed and rode on.

Jude attracted little attention from the townspeople.

He was a tall, thin man in a brown leather jacket and trousers, and a Stetson hanging over his back. He had short black hair, cold gray eyes, a thin merciless mouth, and a nose sharp enough to cut meat with.

A bone-white revolver bounced on his hip as he rode.

Jude had a three days growth of beard. He'd been in the saddle that long.

He'd only stopped once, when his horse, a massive white stallion, had broken down.

On dismounting and inspecting it, Jude discovered the horse was leaking oil from its ass. It had taken him an hour to discover the cause. Nothing serious — he'd been feeding it too much sugar and not enough oatmeal cakes again.

A few spanner twists and the horse was fine again.

Jude had a knack for getting into trouble. He either picked the wrong town to stop in, the wrong bar to drink in, or the wrong woman to bed. Or simply took the wrong job.

But Jude was good with a gun. His gun skills got him out of as many scrapes as his bad luck hex got him into.

***

The town undertaker was loading a coffin onto his funeral wagon when Jude reached his workshop.

Jude reined in his horse and hailed him. "Good evening, Sir. How do I find Zizi's?"

The undertaker smiled. He was a plump, middle-aged, kindly-looking gent. "The brothel? Keep on straight through town, heading for the mountains. Zizi's place is right on the outskirts."

He chortled. "Want a word of advice, son?"

"What's that, Sir?"

"If you want a good woman at Zizi's, ask for Nell."

"Nell?" Jude tasted the name like wine.

"She's the best thing they've got there, son. Take my word for it."

Jude nodded. "I'll do that, Sir. Thanks."

He rode off. The man had confirmed the directions he'd been given.

CHAPTER 2

Zizi's Brothel was a large two-story brick building built by a plantation owner shortly before the start of the Civil War. Why it was situated two thousand miles from the man's plantation was a mystery no one had ever resolved.

Behind it, Mount Ass rose in its dual curves.

An Indian tribe had lived on the mountain. The Indians had occasionally raided wagon trains coming to Little Ass. Now, with the gold boom gone bust, the Indian raiders had also left, seeking greener pastures.

Jude tethered his horse and entered Zizi's.

A Mexican prostitute met him immediately as he stepped through the front door. She was pretty, with a snub nose and full lips. Her big breasts were tightly clasped in a cream-colored bodice. Her tight corset made her waist wasp-like.

He tipped his hat to her. "I'm Jude, Miss. I'm here to see Madam Zizi."

The woman smiled, showing perfect teeth. "Madam, she ees expecting you, Señor! My name ees Rosa. You ees follow me."

Jude followed Rosa. Her hips shook in her skirt like her backbone was congenitally unable to hold her waist stable.

Jude smiled. He knew she was wiggling for his benefit. This was a brothel — her body was a commodity for sale.

Rosa led the way across the large blue sitting room.

To their right was a bar. Three men sat drinking around a table. Prostitutes were on two of the men's laps, obscuring their faces.

Jude had an unobstructed view of the third man. He didn't like what he saw.

The man's dirty blond hair framed a thin, wicked face, with cold eyes and a ruthless mouth.

The man's eyes met Jude's for a moment. In that moment, Jude felt he was looking into a waterless well.

***

Zizi received Jude in her upstairs study.

The brothel owner was an attractive blue-eyed French-Canadian brunette. Her face and figure were just starting to show the signs of old age.

She rose when Rosa introduced Jude. He tipped his hat to her. Her smile was cool, and appraising.

"Welcome to Little Ass, Mr. Jude," she said, "I trust your trip wasn't unpleasant." She indicated the seat opposite hers. "No Indian trouble?"

Jude sat. "The journey could have been better. My horse broke down."

Zizi gave him a queer look, as did Rosa. Both their eyes asked the same question: Could a horse break down?

Zizi waved a hand at the Mexican girl. "Go fetch us some coffee, Rosa."

Rosa left.

Once she'd gone, Zizi stood and paced the room. "Your telegram said you'd be here last Thursday," she said angrily. "What kept you?"

"I told you. My horse —"

She interrupted him, her voice cold as New York snow. "You could have simply taken the railway, Mr. Jude."

"I take my horse everywhere I go, Madam. It is as essential to me as a lady of your profession considers her breasts and vagina."

Zizi's eyes widened at the simile/insult. She stiffened, bristling, and then she relaxed. She was a whore — a prostitute by any other name was still a prostitute. Besides, that wasn't the matter at hand now.

She smiled coolly. "Whatever you say — the length of a journey is never as important as arriving safely at one's destination. What matters is that you are here now."

Jude nodded. He favored her with a confident smile. "Your ranch will shortly be back in your hands."

Zizi frowned. "Don't be cocky, Mr. Jude. I can assure you that this won't be a walk in the park —"

"If it was, you wouldn't have sent for me. I'm expensive, but worth it. I always get the job done." He leaned forward conspiratorially. I've a question. There are three men downstairs, — real roughneck sorts — who are they?"

Zizi's frown deepened. "They're part of my problem, Mr. Jude. The blond's their leader. His name's Ike Dallas. He's Bennett's right hand. Ike's as bad as they come, as ornery a coyote as you'll ever find."

Jude smiled. "I meet loads of coyotes, lady. Their surviving friends generally run the other way on sighting me."

"Just get Edison Bennett off my ranch, Mr. Jude."

Zizi got out a wad of bills from her desk, split it in half, and threw half to Jude.

She sat while he counted the money.

***

Outside the door, Rosa stood eavesdropping.

She'd arrived with the coffee tray a minute earlier. About pushing the door open, she'd heard Edison Bennett's name mentioned.

Rosa was Ike Dallas's main girl at the brothel. She'd initially been impatient to get back downstairs before Ike tired of waiting for her and called some other prostitute to warm his lap.

Now, however, she listened carefully. Ike would be interested in any information that would help Mr. Bennett. He'd likely pay her a bonus for her services if she heard something of value.

***

"It's all here," Jude said. "And my balance?"

"You'll get it, as agreed — immediately once that scoundrel Bennett is off my land."

Jude nodded. He put the money in a pocket.

Zizi scowled. "Where has that tramp gotten to with our coffee? She's most likely letting Ike Dallas feel her —"

Rosa entered. "I ees sorry, Madam. I ees telling Nell zat..." She set the tray down and hastily began pouring.

"No need for haste, Mr. Jude," Zizi said. "I suggest you relax tonight and start work tomorrow. Would you care for some dinner, and afterward..." She cast a sly eye at Rosa's rump, now poised before Jude's face as she poured into Zizi's cup. "... maybe a partner for the night? On the house, of course." She indicated the set of buttocks in his face. "Rosa, for instance, gives fantastic blowjobs."

Rosa grinned broadly. "It ees true, Señor. My mama she ees teach me. Ees a deep throat family secret —"

"I hear you've a girl here called Nell," Jude said. "I'd like her."

Zizi raised an eyebrow. "Nell? Who told you about her?"

"The undertaker, I asked him for directions."

Rosa spat angrily. The gob just missed Jude's coffee. "Zat ees her father, Señor Doc. Can you ees imagine zat, Señor? Zat ze father ees pimping his own daughter?"

182

"Shut up, Rosa!" Zizi snapped. "Just like in your case, prostitution is obviously family business. Organizing funerals doesn't pay if no one's dying."

She nodded at Jude. "She's telling the truth. That was Nell's father you spoke to." Her lips thinned into a cool, enigmatic grin. "But, Nell's a strange one, Mr. Jude. Are you sure you really..."

Jude was curious now. "Send me Nell tonight," he said. He patted his white revolver and laughed. "If the sex isn't up to my expectations, I'll kill her... just like Bennett."

Zizi's eyes widened in alarm. Her gaze darted to Rosa.

Rosa stiffened as she became the center of attention.

Jude realized his slip-up. He pulled out his white pistol and stuck it in Rosa's bent-over ample cleavage. He stirred her breasts with the barrel.

He frowned at the Mexican prostitute. "Did you overhear something, Señorita?"

Rosa shook her head. "I ees hearing nothing, Señor." She was shivering as she spooned sugar into Zizi's coffee.

"Get lost," Zizi told Rosa. "And keep your Hispanic mouth shut." She drew a thumb across her throat. "If you don't..."

Rosa fled.

Zizi regarded Jude coldly. "That was unwise. She's Ike Dallas's moll."

He shrugged. "Maybe. Maybe not." He finished his coffee and stood up. "I'd like to have a bath before dinner."

Zizi stood up. "Of course, Mr. Jude. I'll show you to your room. She smiled lewdly. Do you want Nell to join you in the bathtub?"

Jude shook his head. "She'll be unable to stand the stink of me. But have her join me for dinner. I'll eat her afterwards."

***

Though scared, Rosa didn't immediately head downstairs. She hid in the room opposite Zizi's study and waited.

Her patience paid off. Through the ajar door, she watched Zizi and Jude emerge. The Madam led Jude to a room at the end of the hallway.

A few minutes later, Zizi emerged again.

"I'll send Bess up with hot water for your bath," she said, then shut Jude's door.

Rosa waited till Zizi was out of sight, then she ran downstairs to where Ike Dallas and his companions were drinking.

"I needs to see you upstairs now in ze bedchamber," she whispered to Ike. "Ees life and death important."

When Ike saw she was serious, he got up and followed her to her room.

Once she'd locked the door behind them, Ike began unbuckling his belt.

"No, no, no!" Rosa whispered harshly. "Zat ees not ze why I ees calling you here!"

"Oh no? Get into bed, whore."

"You must listen," Rosa insisted. "Ze new gringo zat is just checking in. Madam ees hiring him to kill Señor Bennett."

Ike paused in removing his boots. His eyes narrowed. "Is that so?"

Rosa nodded. "I ees overhearing zem discuss eet. Madam ees wanting her ranch back —"

Ike resumed removing his boots. "I'll take care of the punk later."

Rosa was dumbfounded. "He ees about having his bath now."

"Rosa, fucking stop yapping and come suck my peter."

"What? You ees not going to kill heem right now?"

Ike rolled his eyes. "So fucking what if some punk wants to kill Bennett? Won't be the first time, or the last either."

"You must kill him now for my honor. He ees stick ees gun in my breasts."

Ike slapped Rosa hard across the face. Her head snapped back, her eyes bugged out.

"You ees loco! What ees you doing zat for?"

"So you know I'm serious here. Now, shut the hell up and take my gringo pecker up your Latino ass, like your mommy taught you to do."

Rosa glared at Ike. The left side of her face was slowly turning as purple as his erection.

"You ees true gringo pig, Señor Ike. Big and bad and smelly and wicked." She examined her face in the mirror. "But still I ees like you. I ees get paid double tonight for my information, yes?"

Ike removed his boots. "Shut the fuck up, Rosa. Get your ass in the bed before I kick you into it."

"You ees ze genuine chauvinistic gringo swine, like ze women's movement ees advertising against. Why I ees love you, I does not know." Rosa began furiously undoing her yellow bodice.

"Forget that," Ike said, fondling his erection. "I'm in a hurry here. Just pull your drawers off."

Rosa dubiously considered Ike's erection. Ike Dallas's penis was short, but was swollen thrice normal size in its middle. It looked like a legless, skinless rat. Or a sweet potato tuber.

Ze ugly gringo rat penis ees nice in ze Mexican vagina, Rosa thought miserably, but in ze Mexican culo, it ees ze very hurtful. Where I ees leave ze lard?

She'd gotten one leg of her underpants off when Ike decided she wasn't fast enough and shoved her down on her belly.

He rucked her skirt up over her back, spit on his malformed penis and forced it into her anus.

"Ah, Señor, you ees not waiting for me to greeze my —"

"Oh, shut your yap, Rosa. Okay, I'll pay you triple tonight. Just stop talking and start fucking!"

Rosa gripped the bed clothes and began whimpering.

Zis pain es good, ees good financial pain, she thought, tears streaming from her eyes. No pain ees no gain. I ees get ze big bonus tonight.

CHAPTER 3

Nell was five feet six inches tall and had corn-colored hair. She was slim, with small buttocks and breasts. She wore a yellow dress trimmed with white.

Nell had full sensual lips and deep blue eyes that twinkled.

Jude thought her good-looking, but not exceptionally so. He'd expected someone as voluptuous as Rosa.

At dinner, she was good company, her conversation witty though occasionally acerbic. She laughed a lot, but Jude deduced that she had a short fuse.

***

Once in Jude's room. Nell's sunny attitude altered. She became all business. Her blue eyes became shimmering pools of avarice.

"Get undressed, Mister." Her smile now was coolly detached and professional. The fun was all gone from her.

Jude wasn't sure what to make of the change. He shrugged. He was getting her services for free. Nothing lost if she was shit in bed.

He sat on the bed and pulled his boots off.

"Hold on a moment," Nell said.

Jude had his pants half off. "Miss, you said get undressed."

She smiled coolly. "I hope Zizi told you I get paid twice as much as the other girls."

Jude shook his head.

"Not in this case, sweetheart. You're on the house. Ask your boss."

Nell shook her head back at him. "Oh no," she said, "I don't do handouts. Get yourself one of the other girls."

Jude glared at her adamant face, then looked down at his erection. He adjudged his penis to be about as hard now as the flinty look on Nell's face.

This queenshit attitude of hers had to go.

He smiled as coldly as she. "I've a better idea," he said. "How about we forget sex altogether, and I just slap the shit out of you instead? How much do you charge for an ass whupping? I've handed out several good ones of recent."

Nell attempted staring Jude down. She saw the ghosts of the men he'd killed in his eyes, and thought better of it.

She rolled her eyes. "Okay, Mr. Cheapskate, I'll do you tonight."

She stripped naked, then lay back in the bed and spread her legs wide.

Jude gasped on seeing her private parts. Maybe he should have let her remove her uppity fanny from his room.

Nell's clitoris was a two-foot-long tentacle. Pink, and pinky-finger thick, it was coiled like a hog's tail.

Nell pulled the meat tendril out to its full length. When she let go, it snapped back down like a spring.

"This is my tentaclit," she said snottily. "It's why I fucking cost more than the other girls — I'm the best pleasure money can buy. You like it?"

The coiled tentacle held Jude's attention like a magnet. He gulped. "I don't know. I've never seen anything like it before."

Below Nell's two-foot-clitoris, her vagina gaped. The opening was normal, pink and moist. Its labia were small and delicate.

Seductress now, Nell licked her lips and squeezed her nipples. She twirled her vaginal tentacle around a thumb. "Well, take your shirt off, Jude, and join me. Your peter ain't gonna pull itself."

Jude smiled. Nell pronounced 'pull' as 'Paul.'

***

They sat facing each other on the bed, propped on quilted pillows. Their legs were parted, with Jude's bent over Nell's. Jude's penis stuck up proud as a Confederate Army flagpole.

Nell lubricated her tentaclit with lard, and then coiled it around Jude's erection.

She looked at him with cryptic eyes. "Just relax. Let me take you to heaven."

Jude relaxed back onto the pillows.

Nell relaxed too. Her face took on a trance-like expression.

Her tentaclit began sliding up and down over Jude's penis.

Shit, Jude thought. The damn thing works. Gripping him tighter than a virgin's vagina, the sexual tentacle milked Jude's penis.

Jude groaned with pleasure. His penis became the center of his universe.

Nell moaned with her own pleasure. Eyes shut, her eyelids fluttered like butterflies. Her breasts gleamed with sweat, her tongue danced over her lips. Her body was taut as a banjo string.

Her eyes popped open. "Jude, it's getting like the Arizona Desert down there. Lard us up again, will you?"

Jude picked up the jar of pig grease and smeared a dollop over their joined sexes.

Nell nodded. "That's better." She shut her eyes again. The tentaclit resumed its up/down motion over Jude's erection.

It squeezed him harder now, stroked him faster and faster.

Nell's sexual tension peaked. Waves of erotic pleasure blew her far out on a sea of sensation. Then her nerves capsized her in orgasm, leaving her stranded on an isle of indescribable experience. She collapsed back, limp on the pillows, feeling wonderfully destroyed.

Her tentaclit continued stroking Jude, but more languidly.

Nell opened her eyes. "Come inside me now," she commanded.

188

Her tentaclit furiously jerked him toward her.

Jude rolled over onto Nell, and slid his penis inside her in one uninterrupted stroke.

She gasped as he filled her. Jude gasped too. The feel of her flesh around him as he entered her was painfully exquisite. She was a well of sensation he was diving into.

Nell's tentaclit curled around between Jude's buttocks and tickled his anus. Then it wrapped itself around his testes and tugged on them, while he pumped into Nell like a steam-powered piston.

Nell spread her legs so wide that Jude imagined this yellow-haired girl was the abyss. He felt her absorbing him into herself.

Jude's pleasure peaked also. With a sexual explosion the like he'd never experienced, his semen poured into her.

Jude went limp on Nell, his mind momentarily wiped clean of all he was here in Little Ass to do.

They fell asleep like that.

CHAPTER 4

Jude's door exploded off its hinges. Jude and Nell both woke up abruptly and spilled apart.

Shotgun in hand, Ike Dallas stepped in through the smashed woodwork.

Behind him entered his two assistants, Claudio and Jonas. Like Ike, both men were tall and thin, and looked wicked. Both wore gray ponchos and held six-shooters at the ready.

Staring at the pair on the bed, Ike wondered how Jude had gotten on with Nell's sexual peculiarity.

He frowned at them both.

"Sorry to disturb y'all lovebirds," he said. "But I been hearing a rumor that our visitor Jude here, ain't a peaceful sort. I heard he's a plannin' to murder Mr. Bennett." He pointed his shotgun at Jude. "Now, Sir, if that's true, I need to kill you."

Nell pulled the bed sheet over herself. She looked aghast at Jude. "You're here to kill Edison Bennett?"

Jude shook his head. "Not true."

Ike laughed. He looked from Claudio to Jonas.

"Unfortunately, Mr. Jude," Jonas said, "even if it ain't true, we's gone kill you just the same — just in case you'se lyin'."

***

Afterward, Ike Dallas was unable to really describe what happened next. Because it was so implausible.

He fired at Jude, but Jude was already in motion. The air filled with feathers from disintegrated pillows.

Nell squealed. Hugging her sheet over her breasts, she made herself as little as possible in the far corner of the bed.

Jude dove off the bed to where his clothes were piled on the floor. His white pistol was in his hand in a flash.

Ike swiveled the shotgun to point at Jude again, but Jude fired first.

The white revolver made no sound at all.

Ike reacted faster than his companions. He ducked to his right. The bullet streaked past him, hitting Claudio.

There was a moment of stasis — a frozen pin-point of eternity when nothing happened — then Claudio jerked stiffly upright.

A mass of bone spikes suddenly punched out of both sides of Claudio's body. Four of these pierced out of the sides of his head.

Ike gaped at Claudio in horror. What the hell was that thing growing out of Claudio's head? A head?

Blood began spurting from Claudio's multitude of punctures.

Ike spun back around to face Jude. Shit! This idiot was dangerous.

Jude was already firing again. Ike let off a shotgun blast just as he squeezed the shot off. The shot caught Jude square in the belly and flung him back against the wall.

Nell screamed. None of the three men paid her any notice.

This time, Jude's strange bullet hit Jonas.

Jonas got Jude with two slugs in the legs before dying, also spiked outward from within by bony spines. He also grew that odd head on top of his own head.

Ike still couldn't believe what the auxiliary head was. Moving with an urgency enhanced by fear, he broke open and reloaded his shotgun.

Jude was pulling himself to his knees. Blood was streaming over his lips and down over his nude body. His belly was a mess of pulped flesh.

Defiance in his eyes, his hand wobbling, he raised his white pistol to point at Ike.

Ike shot Jude twice before the gun sighted on him.

The blasts took Jude's right arm off at the shoulder. Arm and gun-hand clattered to the floor.

Ignoring the strangeness behind him, Ike strode across to Jude.

While he reloaded the shotgun, he and Jude glared at each other with equal hatred.

"Looks to me like you just failed to kill Mr. Bennett, Jude."

Jude, bleeding like a breached dam, spat blood on Ike's boots. "I'm still going to kill Edison Bennett," he said.

"Only when he arrives in Hell," Ike replied. He placed the shotgun against Jude's head.

"Don't kill him, Ike," Nell said.

Ike looked over at her. "And why not? He's good as dead already." He laughed. "He that good in bed, Nell? Okay, I'll leave him for your freak ass — with some modifications."

He waved the shotgun, teasingly over Jude's face. "Or maybe not."

Nell shrieked and launched herself off the bed at Ike. He swatted her aside like she was a fly. Her naked form crashed back down onto the bed. She lay as she fell, on her back and breathing heavily, watching both men.

Ike placed the shotgun against Jude's left shoulder and fired. Jude's shoulder separated in a geyser of blood. Jude screamed like he was in Hell.

Ike kicked the detached arm away. He shot Jude's left leg off just above the knee, then reloaded and shot off Jude's right leg also.

He stood back and admired his work.

Jude twitched in a mess of gore. He was now beyond pain, beyond screaming, beyond all fear of the unknown. He was simply waiting for the blissful oblivion of death.

Ike Dallas understood what Jude's emotionless eyes meant. "Well I guess I must be going, Jude."

Jude's lips formed words. "We'll meet again, you son-of-a-rabid-dog."

Ike smirked. "Only in Hell, Jude, and not anytime soon. You're going early."

Ike looked at Nell. "You'd better hurry up if you want to give him your special before he dies." He reached down between her legs and grabbed her tentaclit. "He enjoy this, freak?"

She raked at his face with clawed fingers. "Don't touch me, you bastard!"

Ike let go of her clitoris and caught her flailing hand in mid-air. He watched her fingers clench and unclench impotently, then let go her wrist.

She glared at him with hatred.

Ike pointed the shotgun at her, and then lowered it with a cold smile.

"Remember this, Nell. The only reason you're still alive is because Valhalla says we can't touch you. But you've pushed your luck too far with me for too long. One day Valhalla won't be around and then..."

Nell was chilled by the frustration boiling in Ike's eyes. She didn't doubt his word that he'd kill her the first chance he got. She utterly detested Ike Dallas, only she knew he hated her a whole lot more.

Her anger fizzled out before his intense loathing. "Why'd you hate me so much, Ike?" she asked.

Ike pointed to her tentaclit. "That." Then he shook his head. "No, it ain't that. I seen lots stranger things in my lifetime."

"Then fucking what?"

Ike shook his head. "I honestly don't know, Nell. Something about you just fucking pisses me off so bad I can smell it in my shit."

***

Ike forgot Nell and Jude. He turned and considered his men's corpses.

Now he couldn't deny what he was seeing.

Both Claudio and Jonas lay in pools of blood with huge fish bones sticking out of them.

Shark bones.

Amidst the mess of their exploded brains, the tops of the shark skeletons — stacked white vertebrae linked by discs of cartilage — jutted from their heads. The shark's tail bones protruded from their crotches like third legs.

A complete shark head topped each skeleton. Each head was as fresh as if the shark had just died.

Ike got over his horror. He thought awhile. Explaining this strange shit to Edison Bennett would be impossible without some evidence.

So he'd fucking take him some.

He walked over to where Jude's severed right arm lay and prized the strange white revolver from its fingers.

He turned, startled by a splashing sound.

Nell was squatting over Jude and urinating on him.

Ike grimaced in disgust. He turned his back on them again.

Ike stuck the white pistol in his pocket, and then he hefted Claudio's corpse over his shoulder. With the shark skeleton embedded in his body, Claudio seemed to weigh as much as a horse.

Grunting, Ike staggered downstairs. None of Zizi's prostitutes showed their faces as he passed their rooms. Downstairs, the parlor was similarly deserted.

Outside, Ike lugged his burden over to where his wagon was parked. He and the dead men had been in town purchasing supplies.

Rosa was waiting. "He ees dead, Señor Ike?" she asked urgently. "You ees keel Señor Jude? And where ees Jonas?"

Then she saw his odd burden. The massive gaping jaws of the head on top of Claudio's head unnerved her. "Sheeeit, Señor Ike, what ees zis you ees bringing here?"

Ike didn't reply. He hefted Claudio's corpse into the rear of the wagon and went back inside for Jonas's body.

Claudio landed on top of Zizi. Zizi was trussed up and gagged in the wagon rear, en route to the Bennett ranch. Already scared, Zizi squirmed in redoubled horror when she saw what had happened to Claudio.

Rosa was still gaping at Claudio when Ike returned with the second corpse. Her confusion doubled. "What ees zis? What ees happen inside?"

Ike heaved Jonas's body on top of Claudio's and turned to her. "Rosa, stop gawping like you've never seen a man with a fish skeleton stuck through him before."

Rosa was about to retort, but thought better of it.

She thought: Though ees true Señor Ike ees paying me thrice as much tonight, he ees likely to put ze ugly gringo rat prick into ze tight Mexicano culo again if I ess annoys heem. And ze Mexicano ass cannot endure it again tonight. And likely, he ees not even paying for ze usages afterward.

She climbed up beside Ike in the driver's seat and they set off.

In the wagon rear, Zizi lay still as a corpse below the weight of the two odd corpses.

CHAPTER 5

Jude woke to an acrid smell so thick it seemed to be dissolving his lungs. It stank like an unwashed stable. It punched up into his brain like smelling salts.

He became aware of warm liquid falling on his head and trickling down over his face. The liquid stank too. It took Jude a moment to work out what it was.

What the hell? He forced his eyes open.

He was staring up at Nell's vagina, pig-tailed clitoris coiled above the pretty pink opening.

Nell was urinating on Jude's head. Her dress was pulled up around her waist and she was squatting over him.

"Nell, what the hell are you doing?" Urine streamed down over Jude's eyes and cheeks and into his mouth.

Nell saw that Jude was awake and got down.

Jude spat the pee out then raised a hand and wiped his face clean.

What in the...?

Violent images flashed before Jude's eyes, reminding him of what had happened. His four limbs had been shot off his body. So how was he currently holding a hand in front of his face?

Also, as Jude understood the nature of body injuries, he should be dead, planted six feet under. So what?

He calmed himself and took stock of where he was.

He was in a laboratory of some sort. There were tables by the room's walls, with bubbling glass cauldrons on them. There were test tubes in racks and several microscopes.

Jude lay in a metal bathtub full of urine.

He had four limbs again. Two arms and two legs, like before.

Only these limbs weren't his, he was certain of that. His new arms and legs were joined to his body by a yellow transparent substance that nonetheless felt like skin. In addition, the gaping hole where Ike Dallas had blown out his gut was now plugged with the same see-thru substance.

The smell of urine hung heavy as rain clouds in the lab.

Jude sat up in the bathtub. "Nell, please tell me what the hell is going on."

"I'll get father," Nell said, and vanished out the lab door.

***

"Nell's urine has special healing properties," Doc said. She urinated on you at Zizi's to keep you alive, then brought you here, where I've patched you up again."

Jude was more than intrigued. "How?"

Doc waved a dismissive hand. "A research secret. Can't divulge how I repaired your body. Suffice it to say that my daughter's urine is essential to your current well-being, Mr. Jude."

"Just 'Jude' is fine."

Doc nodded. "The transparent substance attaching your new limbs to your body is pee-flesh... urine-flesh..."

"It's meat made from urine," Nell said.

Jude looked at Doc. "How can human tissue be formed from urine?"

"You're not a scientist," Doc said, "so I won't bother you with the explanation. It's complicated. All you need to care about is that it works." He scratched his forehead ruminatively. "Now, you need to realize, Jude, that —"

"Why did you fit me with these limbs? Why not simply reattach mine back to me?"

Doc smiled kindly. "I couldn't. There was extensive trauma... tissue damage... to your body at the points you were shot, and not enough undamaged limb flesh to work with."

196

"Whose arms and legs are these then?"

Doc pointed to a limbless torso lying on a table Jude hadn't previously noticed. "His."

Jude studied the corpse. The dead man was blond with thick mustaches. He looked to be about thirty-five. The cause of his death was instantly clear: a deep fracture in his left temple.

Jude thought he recognized the man's face from somewhere. "Who's he?"

"A miner called Mike Scofield. He was killed an hour ago outside the saloon just down the road. Got kicked in the head by a horse while trying to pour beer down its ass."

Jude now remembered the man. He'd been one of the drunken pair slugging it out outside the saloon when Jude had ridden past it on his way to Zizi's.

Jude nodded. He studied the muscles of his new arms and legs. Mike Scofield had clearly been in tiptop physical condition.

He flexed his new fingers several times, and then shook his head.

"These hands are wrong for me," he said grimly.

Nell stared at him in surprise. "But why? Mike was strong as a bull."

Jude climbed out of the bathtub. Urine streamed off him like he was a waterfall. "Because I'm not going to wield a pickaxe and dig for gold with them, that's why. I'm a gunfighter — I can already tell I can't shoot with these hands."

"You won't be shooting anyone," Doc said. "Not here anyway."

Nell spat into the bathtub. Her spit became a worm that slithered over her pee. "Ike Dallas kidnapped Zizi last night, before he even came to your room. She's likely dead by now."

She spat some more into the tub, then added: "The girls say it was Rosa that betrayed Zizi." Her expression became enraged. "I'm going to find and kill her."

Jude winced. Zizi had been right — he'd been dumb to run his mouth off. Or to assume the Latino whore could be scared silent.

He smiled grimly. "Thanks for fixing me up, Doc, but I am going to be shooting."

Nell winced. "No need to kill Edison anymore like Madam paid you to. She's dead. Your business deal is over. Walk away. Take the money. Go."

"Take Nell with you, when you go," Doc said. "She's a good girl."

Jude coldly stared them down. "This business just got personal. Ike Dallas tried to kill me. I'll settle that score if it's the last thing I do."

Nell rolled her eyes. "And I suppose you expect us to help you?"

Jude shook his head. "No point getting you both killed. Stay out of this."

"She can't," Doc said. "Wherever you go, she goes. No, it's actually the other way around: Where she goes... you go."

Jude stared hard at him. "You got us married while I was unconscious?"

Doc shook his head. "Nell's urine is what's currently keeping you alive. You need to have her with you at all times, for regular infusions of it."

Nell dipped a cup into the bath of urine. She raised it to her lips, pretended to sip from it. "Regular infusions," she mouthed at Jude.

Jude gaped at Doc incredulously. "What the hell?"

(He was also amazed because he'd just realized that Nell had somehow peed a bathtub full of urine. And in how many hours? What did she have for a bladder? A herd of horses?)

Doc nodded. "If she doesn't infuse you regularly, you'll die. It's that simple." He smiled reassuringly. "You don't have to drink it. You can soak in it like just now, or even pour it over yourself;

that will work for short spells. But drinking her water will restore you fastest, particularly if you get injured."

"And since you're planning to go get shot up —" Nell interjected.

Jude just stared at Doc.

"One more thing," Doc said. "The fresher her fluid is, the faster you'll heal."

Jude stared at Nell in dismay. The liquid gravity of his fate slowly weighed down on him.

He looked at Doc like a dog begging not to be whipped. "You mean I'm stuck with this... to her... for as long as I live?"

Doc nodded. "Sorry Jude, only thing you don't get is the wedding ring."

Nell glared angrily at Jude. Then she walked over to him and whispered in his ear. "Stop acting like you don't like me, you ungrateful prick. I fucking saved your life. The sex last night wasn't that bad, either, was it?"

Jude forced a grin. "I guess I'm screwed then. But Doc, I at least need my right hand back, and I need my gun."

"I can reattach your hand," Doc said. "I'll simply remove this new one at the wrist."

Jude nodded. He turned to Nell. "Did you bring my gun here?"

"The white pistol? Ike took it."

Jude's expression turned black as a moonless night sky. "Another reason to visit Bennett's ranch," he said. "I need my damn gun back." He scratched his chin. "Only problem is how to get to the ranch house unseen."

Doc thought a moment. "Don't worry about that. I'm Little Ass's undertaker. Edison's sure to order a pair of coffins from me for his men's funerals. You'll be in a third one when I make the delivery."

CHAPTER 6

Like everyone else on the EVB Ranch who'd so far seen it, Edison and Valhalla Swede Bennett both gaped at Claudio's corpse when Ike Dallas dumped it on their parlor floor.

"Jonas is the same way, boss," Ike informed them. "He's outside in the wagon with the groceries."

"How'd a shark get inside him?" Edison asked. He was a tall thin man with slick black hair and a pencil-line moustache. Claudio's abominable fusion of man and fish threatened to make Edison spew his dinner everywhere. He walked over to the bar and mixed himself a stiff whiskey.

Ike explained in detail. "With this," he concluded, handing Jude's white pistol to Valhalla. Edison's wife was a svelte blonde wearing a floor-length evening gown that entirely covered her feet.

Edison returned with his drink. He and Valhalla studied Jude's gun.

"It's made of bone, Edison," Valhalla said. "Smells like fish bone."

Edison raised a startled eyebrow. He finished his whiskey, then broke the weapon open to check its ammo.

There were three shells in the cylinder, and no spent casings. Edison thought the three empty chambers odd. Even odder, the ends of the unfired shells looked like frayed meat.

He shook the bullets out into his hand.

Frowning, he held one up so Valhalla and Ike could see it. Lamplight glinted off the bullet's fingernail.

"What sort of a weapon fires severed human fingers?" he asked.

***

"A Comanche medicine woman gave me the gun, along with my horse," Jude told Nell and Doc. "I don't know where she got

200

them. I rescued her husband from being killed by Union Army soldiers and she was grateful."

He flexed his reattached right hand. The surgery had been crude. Doc had hacked the miner's hand off at the wrist, stitched Jude's original hand on in its place, and asked Nell to urinate on it. Jude had watched the join knit together with the transparent urine-flesh.

He dried his hand off with a towel.

"Thanks, Doc. This is much better. I can fight now." He frowned. "I need to get my gun back, before Edison Bennett starts using it on people. Who knows, I may even be in time to rescue Zizi."

***

Ike dumped Zizi down on the parlor floor.

Rather than being cowed now, Zizi was furious. Her eyes glared knives at Edison and Valhalla. She'd worked herself into a rage during the trip out to the ranch. How dare Edison treat her this way, over what was rightfully hers?

"Ungag her," Edison said, stroking his moustache. "Sit her up."

"You evil son-of-a-drunk-skunk," Zizi shrilled once her mouth was free. "How dare you — ?"

"Shut up, Zizi," Valhalla snapped. "Ike's already told us what you were planning." She pointed to where Rosa sat by the fire. "Your whore here confirmed it, so don't try playing innocent."

Zizi turned to Rosa in a rage. "You stupid slut! I'll tan your butt so hard you'll need to wear a sombrero over it!"

She turned back to Edison. "Let me go!"

Edison regarded her with interest. "I don't think so. You'll most likely only try to have me killed again. Thank God, that Jude punk you hired couldn't keep his mouth shut." He grinned mirthlessly. "I really think it's time you died, Zizi."

He looked to Valhalla. "What do you say, darling? Should we show her mercy?"

Valhalla snorted. "Don't ask silly questions, Edison. I warned you to kill her back when you took the ranch over, remember?"

Edison's face tightened at the retort, his lips compressed to thin lines. His eyes smoldered. He said nothing.

"How about testing Jude's gun on her?" Ike asked. "Then you'll see for yourself how it works."

Edison's simmering anger found an outlet. He smiled. He suddenly felt much better. "Yes, let's do just that."

He reloaded the finger bullets back into Jude's white pistol.

"Let me go this moment," Zizi shrieked. "I'll have the sheriff on you!"

Edison snapped the gun's breech shut and offered it to Valhalla. "You were right dear, we should have killed her. Would you like to — "

She sniffed. "You do it, Edison. You know I don't like dirtying my hands with garbage."

Edison nodded. He turned and pointed the white revolver at Zizi. "Just an experiment, Zizi."

She stared at him, adamant. "Don't you dare shoot me, you yellow prick!"

"Shut up, Zizi," Valhalla said nonchalantly. Her eyes narrowed. They glittered with anticipation.

Edison shot Zizi. There was the odd moment when the finger projectile visibly streaked through the air at her, and then it punctured her belly and disappeared.

Zizi's eyes bugged out. She jerked convulsively as the spikes of shark bone punched out of her sides. With a sound like someone taking a watery shit, a rotting shark head erupted like lava out of her brain.

Chunks of brunette scalp splattered everywhere. Zizi's eyes rolled back in her head. She slumped back, dead.

Edison gaped at her like he was seeing a ghost.

"See that, boss?" Ike asked.

Edison remained speechless.

Valhalla winced. "We should have killed her outside," she said. "All that blood she's spilling will be the devil itself to clean up."

Ike motioned to Rosa. "Go call some maids, tell them to bring mops and buckets."

Later Same Night

"I'm worried by this evening's events," Valhalla Swede Bennett told her husband when they were alone in their bedroom.

Edison kicked off his boots, and then undid his jacket. "Why, dear? With these latest developments, everything's going wonderful for us. Zizi and her hired gun, Jude, are both dead — there's no one to contest ownership of the ranch with us anymore. And now we can take over Zizi's brothel as well."

Valhalla turned her back to him.

"Unbutton me," she said.

Edison did so. He loved the way her white skin appeared out of the dress like magic as the fabric separated.

Edison finished undoing Valhalla's buttons. He sat on the four-poster bed and watched her undress.

He felt the same sick, evil thrill as always when his wife dropped her skirts to her ankles, revealing her lower body.

Valhalla Bennett's buttocks and legs were those of a wolf. They were covered with white hair, and her legs were jointed in three places. Her feet were lupine paws, which was why she always wore floor-length dresses.

She'd had her tail docked. It had made the backside of her dresses look funny.

Both Valhalla's sex and sexuality were lupine. As primal as that of a wolf in the wild. Her violent, aggressive eroticism occasionally overwhelmed Edison.

He however didn't regret stealing her away from her previous husband: Doc, Nell's father.

Valhalla Swede Bennett was Nell's mother.

***

"We'll have a summoning," Valhalla said. Naked, she padded over to a wardrobe and took out a wooden disc.

The disc was two feet wide and covered with runic writing. Its middle was depressed into a shallow bowl in which a red hexagram was inscribed.

Wearing only his nightshirt, Edison watched her. "Is this utterly necessary, Val?"

"It is. I sense danger."

Edison nodded. "Okay then." He began removing his nightshirt.

***

They fucked doggy-style on the floor. While Valhalla occasionally appreciated the missionary position, her lower anatomy meant canine-style penetration suited her best.

"Don't wait for me," she insisted. "What I want from you now is your seed, not your love. Empty yourself into me quickly. This is urgent."

Edison gripped her hairy haunches hard and stabbed himself deep into her wolf-vagina. He pulled out, stabbed inside again. Pulled out, stabbed again. He rode her down into the plush blue carpet, till her breasts spread out like saddlebags from her chest.

He reached under her and grabbed her bristly belly hair then stabbed into her again and again.

Valhalla squealed in pain. Edison was hurting her.

Edison Bennett never fucked his wife gently. He rode her hips like she was a horse and he a bandit fleeing a posse. Hard and fast and desperate, always on the verge of falling out of the saddle.

Valhalla never objected — she liked it hard and fast. Only now she was dry. The unmoist friction felt to her like skin rubbing on skin.

Edison came. Then he pulled out of Valhalla's bruised sex and flopped onto the bed, exhausted. His body trembled with overwhelming sensation.

Squeezing her thighs tight together to prevent spillage, Valhalla quickly repositioned herself over the wooden disc on the floor. She squatted and relaxed, letting Edison's semen drip out of her.

She'd aimed it perfectly. The cum plopped into the shallow depression forming the disc's middle.

Valhalla now crouched by the side of the disc. Stirring the gelatinous pool with a finger, she recanted abominable incantations over it.

The lines forming the bowl's red hexagram glimmered like fire.

The semen became more than it was.

It transmogrified into the future as presented by the millions of children who would never be born because the sperm cells — the keys to their existence — lay in the bowl dying, a negation rendering every possibility of their ever existing a pathetic lie.

The never-born opened the door to the future they would never experience to Valhalla.

Valhalla Swede Bennett looked and saw.

The future she saw in Edison's semen was as murky as the liquid revealing it. Indistinct display of days unborn.

Valhalla however clearly saw carnage and destruction. And bloody violent death. Possibly even hers and Edison's.

She saw all there was to see. The visions dissolved like rape fading into repressed memory.

Valhalla crouched beside the disc, drained by the summoning experience.

"Edison," she whispered, her voice like yesterday's ghost. "Edison, we've a big problem. Edison...?"

There was no reply. Valhalla looked at the bed and rolled her eyes. Edison was sound asleep. His chest was rising and falling as rhythmically as his buttocks had been when he'd been fucking her.

CHAPTER 7

"This sure is some weird horse," Nell said. "Never seen one with a crank up its ass before."

It was noon of the next day. Nell and Jude were hitching Jude's horse to Doc's funeral wagon. Doc's regular horse, a threadbare gray mare, cropped grass and looked placidly on, pleased to be relieved of work.

Jude cranked the white stallion's ass-screw several more times. Once he was satisfied the horse wouldn't break down on their way to the EVB Ranch, he dropped its tail back down over the lever.

He walked over to stand by the animal's head, running his fingers through its mane and feeding it sugar cubes.

Nell stroked the horse's flank. She liked its rough feel on her palm.

Jude pulled a rifle from a saddle holster. "The old squaw gave me this also," he said. "It's good too, only not as deadly as the pistol."

Doc took the firearm from Jude. "It's made completely of wood!"

"Looks like a carving," Nell added. She scowled at Jude. "You're going into a gunfight carrying a carved rifle? And taking me along?"

Jude nodded. "The bullets are even stranger." He got out a leather pouch from the horse's saddlebags and opened it so they could see.

Nell gasped at the white objects filling the pouch. She looked at Jude in confusion. "It fires human teeth?"

"How is that even possible?" Doc asked.

Jude shrugged. "You're the scientist, Doc. All I ever ask of a weapon is that it works."

Doc handed the wooden rifle back to Jude. "Time to deliver Edison's coffins," he said.

"Two won't be enough," Jude said, climbing into the back of the hearse wagon. Once seated on one of the pinewood boxes, he slid back the wooden rifle's breech cover and poured teeth into it. He slid the cover shut again. "We need a couple more coffins to bury Ike Dallas and Edison Bennett in."

***

Doc's hearse wagon rolled up to the EVB Ranch at half past two in the afternoon.

Nell was sitting in the driver's seat with her father. Jude lay in one of the coffins in the rear.

Jude stank like a dirty toilet now — the urine smell evaporated off him like cheap perfume off a whore.

He also felt much less sensation than he had before.

Shut in the coffin, he attempted coming to terms with this new version of himself. And also with the fact that he was chained to Nell from now on.

Well at least she's pretty, he thought. It could have been a lot worse — she could have been a dog.

Jude's desire for revenge smoldered in him like coals in a blacksmith's furnace. He kept seeing the sadistic grin on Ike Dallas's face when the man had been shooting his limbs off.

Oh yes, he thought, judgment day's coming for you, you ugly sack of Apache excrement.

***

They were passed through at the ranch gate without so much as a peep into the wagon's rear.

"Yeah, Señor Doc," a Mexican guard said. "Two people ees shot up last night. We ees gotta bury zem quick."

***

They delivered the coffins to the rear of the ranch house.

"Those two on the left are yours," Doc told the cowboy who came to unload the coffins. "Best pinewood I got."

"We need three boxes," the cowboy replied. "Someone else caught a bullet last night. Some mad prostitute first attacks Mr. Bennett, and then she puts a gun in her mouth and blows her insane brains out. It took the maids hours afterwards to clean up the parlor."

Doc and Nell looked at each other with grim expressions.

"I'm sorry about that," Doc said, "but you can't have this third coffin. There's already someone in it." He made a helpless gesture. "Not my fault at all, Mr. Bennett's messenger only said two."

"It was an oversight," the cowboy said. "Ike was thinking only of Claudio and Jonas."

"Still —"

The cowboy hefted the first coffin out and stood it by the wall. "No problem," he said, returning for the second. "You're going back to town from here, Doc. Give us this box, and get another for your stiff. The boss has no problem with paying."

"It's impossible," Nell said. She tried desperately to think of a good explanation as to why it was impossible.

The cowboy frowned. He peered suspiciously at Jude's coffin. "What's so special about this stiff anyway? Why can't they ride in the open for a few minutes? Who've you got in there?"

"No one special," Doc replied quickly.

Too quickly.

The cowboy's eyes hardened. He slipped his gun from his holster and pointed it at the coffin. "Open up that third box, Doc, I want to see who's in there."

Doc blanched. The cowboy shoved him out of the way, now certain something was amiss. "Open it," he told Nell. "On the count of three, I'm gonna start shooting. One... two..."

The coffin lid burst open before Nell could pull it off. Jude sat up, pushed her out of the way, and plugged the cowboy between the eyes with a tooth-bullet.

The cowboy's ten-gallon-hat toppled off his head. Next, a mass of short spines exploded out of his face. A head poked out of his right ear, a spiky tail out of his left ear. Four furry legs waved below the upper jaw of the man's open mouth.

The cowboy toppled backward dead, blood mixed with erupted vitreous humor dribbling down his pin-cushioned cheeks. The porcupine implanted in his head started shrieking piteously, wrenching itself violently to break free of its skull prison.

Doc and Nell gaped at the dead cowboy, then at Jude.

Jude nodded grimly. "Like I said, it's not as effective as the white pistol. Porcupines only kill if properly placed, and the critters ain't silent either."

Neither Doc nor Nell replied.

The porcupine's squealing got on Jude's nerves. He kicked the cowboy's head. The porcupine's head shattered. It went silent and limp.

"I heard what he said about needing a third coffin," Jude said. "That's a real loss. With Zizi dead, I don't collect my balance if I kill Bennett." He frowned. "Being shortchanged pisses me off." Then he smiled. "Not that it matters. Revenge is its own pleasure."

"What the hell!!?"

They spun around. A cowboy stood behind them gaping at the dead man.

"What the hell you done to Jackson?"

He looked about to sound the alarm, so Jude shot him.

The cowboy dodged sideways — the porcupine implanted in his neck. He began screaming. Jude quickly put another tooth-bullet through his head. The cowboy stopped screaming when a porcupine exploded through his face.

Jude decided it would waste too much time kicking both squealing animals to death. He turned to his companions.

"All hell's about breaking loose here," Nell said angrily. "So much for sneaking in unnoticed."

"Don't lose your cool," Jude said. "We still have the element of surprise on our side." He gestured to Doc. "Time to shoot our way inside. You any good with a gun?"

"Wait," Nell said. "Let me first go in the house alone. I'll see if I can find your pistol. I'll be safe."

Jude was unconvinced.

"I'm serious," she insisted. "None of the cowboys will dare touch me."

Jude looked at Doc.

"She's right," Doc said bitterly. "The lady of the house has given strict orders that no one is to bother her in any way, on pain of death."

Jude nodded.

Nell got a water bottle from the wagon. She emptied it, then squatted over it and peed in it. When it was full, she stoppered it again and handed it to Jude. "In case you get shot up before I return."

She kissed him on the nose, and then ran off around the corner of the house.

Right after she vanished from sight, three ranch hands armed with rifles charged around the opposite corner of the building.

On sighting the two dead men, they began firing. Bullets zinged through the air around Jude and Doc and ripped holes in the wagon canvas.

Jude yanked Doc into safety behind the wagon, and then returned fire with his wooden rifle.

He immediately hit one of the cowboys. The man began screaming as a mass of quills erupted out of his belly.

The other cowboys became more cautious and changed their attack tactics. They took cover behind a stack of hay bales. From this place of concealment, they popped their heads out, fired, then ducked back into hiding again.

The cowboys also started yelling for backup.

Jude stopped shooting. Waste of teeth.

He began worrying that the cowboys would shoot up and kill his horse.

CHAPTER 8

In their bedroom, Edison and Valhalla Bennett heard the gunfire and shouting.

"It's started," Valhalla said.

"Yes," Edison agreed. "You were right, as always."

"Not me, Edison. The never-born never lie."

Edison nodded. "Of course, dear."

Edison Bennett was not a superstitious man. He feigned agreement with Valhalla's claims that she could read the future in his semen primarily just to keep her happy. His secondary reason was because assisting Valhalla in her semen-witching afforded him additional opportunities for sex with her.

(For Edison, sex with Valhalla Swede — owing to her canine distortions — was always heavenly.)

Though his wife's cum-predictions came true with disturbing accuracy, Edison attributed her correctness to canny foresight, not mumbo jumbo. He was currently trying to reason out last night's strange experience. To Edison, there had to be a scientific explanation for sharks exploding out of Zizi when he'd shot her.

Now, Edison buckled on his Colt Peace Maker and picked up a Winchester rifle.

"You'll be much safer here, Edison," Valhalla said. "Trust me."

"Safer? I can't just sit here and wait for people trying to kill me while the ranch hands fight, darling. That's no better than cowardice."

"Pride has nothing to do with this, Edison."

"Pride has everything to do with this, darling."

"Be reasonable, Edison."

"No, you be reasonable, darling."

Valhalla dropped her bathrobe, and squeezed her breasts. "For heaven's sake, Edison, You're in danger, don't you understand? Please stay here and let's do another summoning. Maybe there's an easy way out of this."

Looking at her, Edison was sorely tempted to remain in their bedroom. He got an immediate erection. His stiffened member bent agonizingly in his breeches. Valhalla's beautiful human upper body, her sleek wolf hips framing that matchless continental carmine canine cunt…

Then his resolve hardened. "No," he said. "I will fight to defend my property."

He stomped off out of the bedroom. His footfalls as he descended the stairs floated back up to his wife through the ajar door.

CHAPTER 9

Ike Dallas and Rosa were the only two people in the Bennett ranch house not to hear the shooting outside.

They were having sex in the windowless, soundproof, wine cellar.

"Oh I ees really love you, Ike," Rosa moaned as she came. "You are ze perfect man for me."

Rosa had been happy since last night. After Zizi's death, she'd been appointed new brothel manager. Valhalla had convinced

212

Edison that it would look suspicious if they took the brothel over now Zizi had 'gone missing.'

Rosa was rewarding Ike for his contribution to her professional ascension by letting him insert 'ugly gringo rat-shaped penis' into her 'tight Mexican culo' for free.

CHAPTER 10

A reinforcement of cowboys had Jude and Doc pegged behind the wagon.

Doc was unharmed but gibbering with fear. Jude wondered how the man did an undertaker's work if he was so afraid of death.

Most of the gunfire directed at them was hitting the wagon. Wood splinters were flying everywhere.

Jude was concerned about a ricochet hitting his horse. The horse was also a gift from the grateful Comanche squaw. It was even more special than his guns.

The white stallion was nervously clopping the flagstones. It could smell danger in the air. It wanted to be away from there.

Then Jude realized that his horse was only in danger if he was near it.

"Run into the house," he whispered to Doc, "see if you can find Nell."

Doc's reply was a blank stare. "Huh?"

Jude repeated the instruction. Doc nodded. He handed Jude the water bottle of Nell's urine he'd been holding for him. Then he scampered away between wagon and wall, going like hell was after him.

Doc disappeared around the corner of the building.

Rifle held high and firing; Jude stepped out from behind the wagon, and advanced on the cowboys.

"Hey there he is! Kill the bastard!"

Slugs whizzed through the air at Jude. Teeth-bullets whizzed back at the cowboys.

The salvo of bullets hit Jude and blew holes in and through him. He gritted his teeth against the pain. Hiding behind the wagon, he'd suddenly realized that with his present constitution, he was close to invulnerable.

The cowboys gaped in amazement as shot after shot hit Jude, but he didn't go down. They also saw that the liquid pouring from his wounds wasn't blood. It was transparent yellow.

Jude was bleeding urine.

Okay, Jude thought, I've seen everything now.

He remembered Doc's instructions and raised the flask to his lips. He took a long draught of Nell's 'waters.' Almost immediately he felt his body knit together again. He stopped leaking urine. His wounds plugged up with gleaming transparent pee-flesh.

Jude kept advancing on the cowboys. Kept firing.

Half a dozen cowboys already lay dead, all with porcupines stuck in their bodies. Some had several of the quilled mammals embedded in their flesh.

One cowboy had a porcupine in his crotch. He was having a screaming fit to wake the dead. Jude regretted hitting the cowboy that low. He rectified his mistake by shooting the hapless man in the head to put him out of his agony.

Terrified, the surviving cowboys turned and fled. They'd never seen shit like this before, and didn't want any more of it.

Jude shot one of them in the buttocks. The man was yowling at the top of his voice as he turned the corner out of sight.

Jude frowned grimly. He reloaded teeth into the wooden rifle, stuck a toothpick in his mouth, balanced his Stetson just right, and went after the fleeing cowboys.

"Come back here and die, you damn cowpokes!"

CHAPTER 11

Nell stormed into the Bennetts' bedroom.

Startled, Valhalla spun around. She relaxed on seeing who it was, though her expression was tight with displeasure.

"What do you want, Nell?"

"Hello to you too, mother."

"Cut the wisecracks, what do you want here?" She smirked. "Don't tell me you're part of the plan to assassinate Edison."

"Assassinate? Is that what you call it? Mother, Edison is a worthless, slimy piece of Apache shit!"

Valhalla slapped her daughter. A hard crack that flung her head back. "I won't have you talk about my husband like that in my house, you little whore."

Nell's face clouded with rage. "It takes one to know one mother. Didn't you fuck your way into Edison Bennett's heart?"

Valhalla slapped Nell again. Harder than before. "I won't have you talk like this to me either, you hussy!" She spat in her face. "Now run on home to that impotent, corpse-loving father of yours!"

Nell's rage spilled over. She grabbed a hunting knife lying on a drawer and leapt at Valhalla. "You've gone too far now mother!"

Valhalla was stunned when her daughter stabbed her in her left breast. "You little shit," she gasped, sinking to the floor as blood began staining her sky-blue bodice. "You disgusting piece of Sioux squaw afterbirth…"

Nell's rage cleared from her eyes as she watched her mother bleed. Horror filled her. She regarded the bloody knife she was clutching with awe.

"You stabbed me in the heart, Nell — you Judas bitch!"

"I'm sorry, mother —"

"I don't want your damned sympathy," Valhalla yelled. "Disgusting slut!"

Nell's rage returned magnified, fueled by a decade's frustration over her strained relationship with her mother. It was all she could do to not leap on Valhalla Swede Bennett and stab her forever. "Fine, mother," she yelled back, "have it your fucking way, as always. As usual, you're always right!"

Nell rushed across to a table where she'd espied Jude's white pistol. She stuck the revolver deep into her cleavage.

Still clutching the bloody knife, she ran out of the room without a backward glance.

"Yes, go on, prostitute!" her mother sputtered behind her, blood spilling over her lips with each word. "Run away like the excrement you are!"

CHAPTER 12

Thirty seconds after Nell exited it, Doc ran into the Bennetts' bedroom.

He froze in shock on seeing Valhalla. He stood, framed in the doorway, catching his breath and staring at her in horror.

Doc still loved Valhalla Swede. Despite her having ditched him ten years ago.

Seeing her dying broke his heart. His eyes misted.

Valhalla opened her eyes. "Moses? Mo, is it really you?"

Doc rushed and knelt by her side. "Who did this to you?"

"Our daughter."

Doc winced at the hatred in her voice. "Nell?"

"That little pig-tail-clitorised freak stabbed me."

Doc considered. It was most likely true. Nell had a temper to her. Also, her hatred of her mother ran deeper than a Mount Ass mine shaft.

"That ungrateful tramp. And to think that she's still alive today only because I warned Edison's cowboys never to lay a hand on her…"

"Calm down, my dearest," Doc said.

216

"I hate that little cocksucker. I wish we'd never conceived her."

Doc sighed. This was the problem. Nell had simply inherited her mother's temper. He was certain the girl hated herself now for stabbing her mother. Only thing was, she'd also be too proud to admit it. She'd keep claiming that Valhalla deserved what she'd done to her.

"Calm down. You need to conserve your strength," Doc told Valhalla.

"Kiss me, Mo," Valhalla whispered.

Doc was caught totally unawares by the sudden change in her attitude. "Huh? Val, what did you just say?"

She stared him deep in the eye. "Kiss me, Mo. I want to die in your arms."

His body trembling with deSire for her, Doc bent down to oblige her.

Their lips pressed together like mating snails. Their tongues entwined. Valhalla's regurgitated blood seeped into Doc's mouth. It flowed over his tongue, down his throat . . .

Doc suddenly felt odd. He felt paralyzed. He felt himself stuck to Valhalla.

He pulled his mouth off hers. His eyes probed hers for an explanation.

Her eyes were no longer fearful of dying. They were now cold calculating ovals. He realized she'd tricked him.

Hell no, he thought. How the hell can I be so dumb?

"Let me go, Val. You can go to hell, for all I care now."

Valhalla laughed coolly. Her teeth were shimmering ridges of blood.

She shook her head. "You always said you loved me to death, Mo. Here's your chance to prove it."

Sensing disaster looming close on his near horizon, Doc fought to pull away. He was unable to.

In horror, he discovered their flesh was melting together.

All their clothes were gone, stripped away as if by magic. His belly was attached to hers.

With a wolf growl, Valhalla grabbed Doc's head and forced his mouth back down on hers. An irresistible force opened Doc's mouth to admit her tongue and blood.

Doc's mind dissolved with his flesh.

Blood streamed from Valhalla Swede's mouth into Doc's and back again, to and fro, to and fro, to and fro. On each return it brought part of Doc back with it.

Doc shrunk like he was being whittled away.

When Doc was completely vanished inside her, Valhalla stood up. The treatment was a success. Her chest still hurt but...

She examined her wound in a mirror. Her stabbed breast looked... ugh.

Then she smiled with cool amusement. Edison was always saying he loved her for herself, not her body. As though there was any difference. Well, he'd have to love her and her disfigurement for a while.

Not that she'd show it to him immediately.

She got dressed.

CHAPTER 13

Winchester rifle held ready, Edison Bennett stalked his way around his ranch house, looking for the attacker.

Damn, he thought, I hate this.

Turning the side of the building, Edison found Doc's funeral hearse. He studied the white stallion harnessed to it with a practiced eye. Excellent horse. Maybe he'd talk Doc into selling it to him. And where the hell was Doc anyway?

Then he saw Jackson's porcupine-faced corpse. And that of the other cowboy, which still had live porcupines squirming in it.

What the hell? That punk Jude's dead, so who...

A queasy feeling stirred in Edison's gut. Maybe Valhalla was right. Maybe he should have remained upstairs.

Edison shrugged off the cowardly thought. Never would he hide behind his wife's skirts. He'd protect his property. Hell would be welcoming anyone who tried taking this ranch away from him.

Controlling his fear of the appalling death that had befallen his ranch hands, Edison resumed his search.

***

Edison Bennett was a vet by profession. It was because Valhalla Swede Jones had gotten mange on her doggy buttocks that they'd met.

Valhalla had been so embarrassed during that first visit, it had taken her an hour to explain what the problem was. Then it took another half-hour for her to show Little Ass's skeptical new veterinary surgeon that no, she wasn't a nut job, and yes, she actually was half animal from the waist down.

For Edison, it had been love at first sight — of Valhalla's wolf-lower-body.

His love of dogs was what had prompted him to study veterinary medicine in the first place. He had however never dreamed of taking his love of canines as far as a liaison with Valhalla would permit. Edison thought bestiality sickening. But when the dog's best parts were attached to a breathtaking woman, what could he do?

Edison was unmarried at the time. He'd turned the charm on and seduced Mrs. Jones. Valhalla Swede Jones, realizing the benefits of having her own personal vet, soon left her husband's side for her lover's.

Edison Bennett had always wanted to own a ranch — acres of land with horses and cows and cowboys and the intoxicating smell of hay. When Zizi's holding caught his eye, his new bride provided him with an astonishing, if abominable, means of driving the

219

French-Canadian heiress off her inheritance and into a life of prostitution.

***

Edison heard someone coming. He ducked out of sight behind the outside stairway leading to the roof.

Jude walked into view, and then walked past Edison.

Edison disliked Jude on sight. The man looked to him like a serial rapist. Worse still, he obviously lacked class and social graces. Valhalla would be incensed if he ever made friends with such an uncouth person.

Immediately Jude passed him, and Edison stepped out of concealment. He padded quickly after him, placed his Peace Maker against the back of Jude's head, and fired. The bullet blew a chunk of Jude's brain out through his left eye.

Jude knelt forward, and then collapsed to the ground.

Edison hadn't witnessed Jude's gunfire exchange with the cowboys and so believed him finished. He didn't bother turning Jude over to examine him, or shooting him again to make certain. No one survived a head wound like this — not from a Colt .45. He put Jude's twitching down to his brain's futile attempts to keep him alive.

And why the hell was he bleeding water?

Edison picked up Jude's rifle and examined it. He also found the bag of teeth ammo.

Musing on the weapon's oddness, he walked around the house to tell the cowboys that the fight was over.

***

Once Edison was gone, Jude sat up again.

220

He took a DEEP draught from his water bottle. A yellow pee-eye immediately replaced his destroyed orb. Urine-meat repaired his damaged brain. His confused thought processes re-equalized.

Jude got to his feet. Now this is REALLY personal, he thought angrily. Edison Bennett, I'm REALLY going to kill you.

It was after thinking this that Jude discovered his wooden rifle was missing.

He spat. Sheeeiiiiit!

CHAPTER 14

Running down the stairs, dripping knife in hand, Nell wasn't bothered about her mother dying. In her experience, Valhalla appeared to have a cat's number of lives.

Mother deserved to be stabbed, she felt. Nell was only surprised she'd waited this long to do it.

How dare the daughter-abandoning old witch insult daddy like that?

Reaching the bottom of the stairs, Nell heard voices coming toward her from the rear of the house. She darted across the parlor, running toward the kitchen.

"¡Hola!, Señorita Nellie." Nell froze in the kitchen doorway.

She relaxed on seeing it was the cook, Consuela Gomes, who'd hailed her.

Consuela was a jolly, middle-aged woman. Nell liked her. Keeping the bloody knife out of sight behind the doorjamb, she leaned into the kitchen. "Hi, Connie."

Consuela beamed back. The smell of baking bread accompanied her sunshine smile out of the kitchen. "You ees here to see your mama, Nellie? She ees upstairs in ze bedroom. She ees just sending down to me to make her some lunch."

"I've just seen her, Connie." She faked confusion. "Connie, I'm scared. Why all the shooting and shouting?"

Consuela shrugged disinterestedly. "Ah, don't be scared, Señorita. You know how it ees with ze cowboys. Zey ees always getting ze drunk, then zey ess acting ze crazy — ellos actúan loco. I ees see Mr. Bennett going outside just now. Hopefully he ees making zem shut up."

Her expression became serious. "Ah, ees good you ees come, Señorita. Your ma, she ess looking underneath ze weather. She ees not eating like ees good for her. Ees like — "

Nell remembered Consuela liked to talk. She could keep her here for an hour. A suitable escape lie came readily to mind.

"I've gotta run, Connie. Ma sent me to find Ike Dallas."

Consuela snorted. "Señor Ike, he ees now tiring of Italiano prostitutas and ees chasing Mexicanos. Ten minutes ago, I ees spying him eating Rosa's chocha in ze wine store like she's buttocks ees a tortilla." She spat. "Ees too much ze gringo ees abusing ze proud Mexican pepita like zis — Ees eating la chocha very sloppily! Zis time I ees tell your mama, Señorita. Zis Señor Ike, he ees a bad gringo —"

"Bye, Connie," Nell said and fled down the corridor.

Running, Nell felt a return of the anger that had prompted her to stab her mother.

She was mad at Rosa. At the moment she wished she could see her and kill her betraying ass. She'd not forgotten how Ike Dallas had humiliated her yesterday, either.

She intended getting even with both of them.

***

Nell reached the rear of the house. All that remained now was for her to exit. She could see the daylight outside. Then she saw Edison step up onto the rear porch.

Damn, she thought. Once he discovers I've stabbed mother, I'm deader than Zizi.

It didn't occur to her to simply abandon her bloody knife and try to bluff her way past Edison.

Edison however, hadn't seen her. He was still looking outside, addressing a hand. Nell turned around and rushed back through the house again, finally hiding in a bedroom.

Hell, she thought, pulling Jude's white pistol out of her cleavage and staring at it, I need to get out of here.

CHAPTER 15

With both his guns taken from him, Jude was forced to hide.

The water bottle was now empty. He'd used the last of Nell's urine to repair the head wound Edison had given him. He hooked the container in his belt and forgot about it.

He swore in frustration. Unless Nell got his Comanche guns back for him, this attack was done. He couldn't storm the ranch house with normal weapons. There were simply too many cowboys.

Then he remembered his horse and ran to where the wagon was parked. Along the way, he salvaged a Colt and a belt of shells from one of the dead cowboys. From another corpse, he took a rifle and more ammo.

He unharnessed his horse and swung up into its saddle. The white stallion reared high, pleased to be freed from its restraints.

Jude smiled grimly and trotted slowly around the house.

He'd decided to kill the time waiting for Nell by killing Edison's cowboys.

The cowboys soon spotted him, and the gun fighting resumed.

Jude was careful this time, however, both for his horse's safety and his own.

CHAPTER 16

Edison gave up on defending his property and honor. With this particular assassin, it seemed a bridge too far.

He didn't understand how one man could be so hard to kill. He'd been congratulating himself on his resourcefulness, and berating his cowboys on their ineffectiveness, when Jude had ridden up behind them and begun shooting.

Edison had gotten a good look at Jude's new left eye — transparent as a marble, cold as a snowball. That oddity, combined with the hellspawn smirk on Jude's face, had put the fear of death into him.

Valhalla was right — in this case discretion was the better part of valor. At least until he thought up a counterattack strategy that would work.

He fled back into the house.

He'd not seen Ike Dallas, nor had any of the other hands. One of the cowboys claimed his ranch manager was dead, killed by this demonic Jude invader.

***

Rushing into his bedroom, Edison collided in the doorway with a maid departing with a lunch tray. Woman and tray both upended and ended up on the floor. The remnants of Valhalla's lunch spilled everywhere.

Valhalla stared in disgust at the mess the maid had made.

Edison winced at the mess. Then, with Jude's wooden rifle, he shot the maid once in each breast.

"It works," he told Valhalla. "Simple as eating pie to use."

He tipped the hapless maid — now screaming horribly from the agony ripping her porcupined mammary glands — out of the bedroom window.

She stopped screaming when her neck shattered on the courtyard flagstones.

Fanning herself, Valhalla walked to the window and peered down. She nodded with satisfaction at the dead woman. "I hate it when people make a mess of my house," she said.

***

"Where's the white pistol?" Edison asked suddenly. "I don't see it anywhere."

Valhalla's face distorted with rage. "My stupid daughter stole it. She's in league with the assassin."

Edison said nothing. He was taken aback by Valhalla's outraged glare. He'd never seen her so angry. She looked mad enough to murder Nell.

"I have his rifle," he said. "It fires teeth." He held it out for her inspection. "What I don't understand is why this Jude won't die. I've killed him, Ike's killed him... Which reminds me, we can't find Ike."

Valhalla wasn't listening. Her facial expression suddenly transformed from rage to a stolid purposeful gaze. Her turbulent emotions became similarly calm. Her thoughts settled to stream-surface placidity. So her daughter had sided with the enemy? She would show the little hussy who was boss — who was mother, and who daughter.

She turned to Edison.

"Take your clothes off. I want to perform a summoning."

She got out the wooden disc with the runes from the wardrobe and spread it out on the floor. Then she removed her skirt.

(She kept her bodice on so he couldn't see her breasts. She had work to do, not answer questions.)

Seeing her naked doggy buttocks, Edison got an instant erection.

But still... he thought.

225

"I don't think this is the time for that," he said.

"I do," Valhalla retorted with ominous finality. "Hurry up and get undressed. Come and give me your semen quickly. I want to summon Rattackus."

A thrill of horror went through Edison at her mention of Rattackus. Rattackus wasn't one of Valhalla's mumbo jumbo imaginations. Valhalla's summoning of the abominable mutant creature allowed him to drive Zizi off her ranch in the first place.

Edison remembered Rattackus squeezing its pale, slimy way from the surface opening of a Mount Ass mineshaft. It had looked disgusting, like the world's biggest maggot.

But was it necessary in this case? Surely this was overkill? Even if Jude was proving abominably hard to dispatch to the afterlife.

"Edison, what are you waiting for? Come here and fuck me right now!" She sounded to Edison like Miss Montgomery, his dreaded teacher from elementary school.

"Coming dear," he replied, rushing to stab his erection deep into the waiting viciously-violet velvety wolf vagina.

***

Once Edison had spurted into her and withdrawn his member, Valhalla squatted over the summoning board again. The semen plopped into the seer-space excavation like living rain.

She concentrated and muttered incantations. Guttural words which filled Edison with fear.

"Rattackus naemnoyus, Rattackus shymys, Rattackus pyus pyaen yaeyks... Rattackus..."

The red hexagon framing Edison's cum turned black as night.

CHAPTER 17

Nell's next abortive attempt to flee the ranch house wound her up in the wine cellar. More oncoming voices meant she needed to hide quickly again.

She shut the door before realizing she wasn't alone.

On seeing who was in the room with her, Nell quickly pushed Jude's white pistol deep into her bodice — well out of sight.

"Oooh, Señor Ike, you ees so very good in ze fucking. I ees enjoy zis pussy-fuck, ees like ze sugar, not like in ze ass, oooo —"

The stone walls amplified the noise of the door clicking shut, reverberating it like a gunshot in the crowded space.

Rosa and Nell stared at each other.

Ike Dallas lay on a row of wine casks. Rosa squatted on him like she was shitting in his groin.

Ike was drunk, his eyes red with wine. He waved at Nell. "Hi, freak."

Rosa wasn't drunk. Her face distorted with rage.

"You ees spying on us? How dare you ees come in here!"

"Rosa, this is my mother's house. I can go wherever the hell I like in it."

"Talk to me with respect!" Rosa growled. "I ees Madam Rosa now. You ees now working for me." She resumed gliding up and down Ike's erection. "If you not show ze proper respect, I ees whipping you till ze bones ees showing on your backside."

"Work for you? I don't work for you!" The coin dropped. "You're in charge of the brothel now?"

(Both women were prostitutes. Neither saw anything odd in carrying out a conversation whilst having sex. For them, such was as normal as day following night.)

"Ah, Señor Ike, ze cock is so good, so hard..." The lust cleared from her eyes. "Yes, I ees ze new Madam. Zizi ees die of ze beeg fish." Rosa managed to preen herself while fucking. Her gaze hardened. "From now on, gringo puta, you will call me ze Madam Rosa."

Nell smirked. "Not in a million years will that happen. If Zizi is dead, that brothel's as much mine now as if it's my inheritance. You? Wait till I speak to mother about this! She'll —" Nell shut up. She'd remembered she'd left 'mother' possibly dying in a pool of blood.

"What?" Rosa mocked. "You ees not ask mama to sack me anymore? Wassa matter, puta? Oh, I ees knowing: you ees just remembering zat mama ees hating you. Ees zat it?"

Nell utterly hated Rosa then. The woman's last statement had sliced her too close to the bone. It took all her willpower to refrain from dashing across to bury her knife in her heaving bosom. But...

"Listen you —" she stopped. Rosa wasn't paying attention to her.

Ike, who'd been listening to the angry exchange with boozy amusement, reached his point of no return.

"Shit," he groaned, grabbing Rosa's hips and spurting into her sex.

Rosa ground dutifully on him till he'd finished. Then she got off him and glared at him with reproach.

"Ah, Señor Ike, you ees not wait for Rosa before you ees coming." She pointed. "And now ze cock, it ees soft."

"Sorry darling. You were so busy talking; I thought you weren't interested in making it."

Rosa wheeled angrily on Nell. "Zees ees all your fault!"

"In what fucking way?" Nell's mind was only half on the couple. She needed to get Jude's gun to him. He could come kill Ike Dallas himself. She had no desire to do so anymore. The revelation that her mother had put Rosa rather than herself in charge of the brothel had emotionally flattened her.

Rosa, however, was far from done with Nell. "Ees your fault because you ees interrupt your Madam's orgasm. Now it ees your responsibility to make me come."

Nell decided it was time she left. "Oh no, I ain't eating your pussy, Rosa. Use your hand. A big girl like you should know masturbation doesn't make you go blind, or give you hairy palms."

"Slut! Dirty puta!"

"Stop pointing fingers, Rosa," Nell said wearily, "We're both dirty putas." She opened the door and peered out into the corridor. The corridor was clear.

Rosa was incensed. She pulled Ike's revolver from its holster, cocked it, and then rushed after Nell.

Nell was about to step outside when she felt herself violently yanked back by her hair. She fell on her buttocks onto the floor. Her head slammed against a beer cask, stunning her.

Rosa slammed the cellar door shut. The gunshot sound woke up Ike, who'd drifted into post-coital slumber.

"What are you doing, Rosa?"

"I ees teach zis piece of shit to be respecting her Madam."

"Give me back my gun. Her mother says not to harm her."

Rosa spat. "She ees tell you zat, not me. I ees shoot zis gringa and say I ees not know her mother ees loving her a tiny bit."

Rosa waved the gun at Nell. Nell was still groggy from hitting her head on the beer keg. She held her knife in front of her to keep her adversary away. Rosa kicked her wrist. The knife flew out of Nell's hand and clattered down by the door.

Rosa dragged Nell across the floor by her hair, over to Ike Dallas.

Ike was sitting up. Rosa pushed him back down. "Not yet, Señor. I ees still having my interrupted orgasm. Debo tener mi orgasmo!"

Ike shook his head. "I can't make it again right now, Rosa."

"Don't worry — she ees help you." Rosa pushed Nell's head between Ike's legs. "All right, prostituta; begin sucking ze gringo cock immediately!"

Nell shook her head. Not from modesty — she was after all a prostitute and penises were her business — but from confusion.

229

Despite his being a regular at Zizi's, Ike disliked Nell so much that he'd never bought her services before. This was Nell's first sight of Ike Dallas's oddly shaped member.

In confusion, she wondered why it looked so much like a legless rat — tapered at both ends and massively swollen in the middle, like the missing parts from the ends had been squeezed into its center.

"Zis ees ze sweet potato cock," Rosa interjected into Nell's thoughts before she made the association herself. "You ees lick it sweetly, puta."

Nell stared at the weird penis in horror. "I'm not licking this," she said.

Ike was getting bothered. He tapped Rosa's shoulder. "Let her go, Rosa. If the freak tells her mother — "

Rosa shrugged his hand off. She shoved the gun barrel into Nell's right ear. "You ees lick, puta, or your brains ees exiting your other ear. I ees impatient to have ze orgasm, so I ees only counting to four. Ze one... ze two..."

Nell was scared now. This crazy Latino bitch was loco enough to shoot her and damn the consequences.

She shut her eyes and took the head of the tuber-like penis between her lips.

CHAPTER 18

The white stallion's hooves spat sand up behind them like a quartet of shovels.

Pistol in right hand, reins in left, Jude rode at the cowboys. He and they fired simultaneously on one another. Relentless as approaching death. Bullets flew both ways like birds.

One nicked Jude's ear. The acrid smell of stale urine reached his nostrils from the wound. Jude smiled despite himself.

A cowboy twirling a lasso rode at Jude. He was galloping furiously, his mocha horse frothing at the lips. The cowboy rode closer. His lasso whirled above him like a plaited halo.

Jude popped him between the eyes. His lasso flew away backwards. The cowboy toppled sideways off his horse. Another horse trampled his body into the grass.

A bullet hit Jude's arm. Urine spilled out of him onto his jacket sleeve. Jude winced. Getting shot wasn't in itself a problem. If however, a bullet shattered an arm bone, he'd be unable to fight back.

His bottle of urine was empty — he couldn't repair himself.

He sighted the gunman who'd hit him on the roof of the ranch house. Jude reined in his horse. In a smooth motion, he let go of its reins, raised the rifle, and fired. The man toppled off the roof.

Jude resumed his horse's reins. His gun barked in his hand. More cowboys toppled off their mounts.

He reloaded the six-shooter. The gunfight raged on.

Jude now started worrying that something had happened to Nell.

CHAPTER 19

As Rosa had instructed Nell, she licked and sucked on Ike Dallas's member like it was a sweet.

Nell was revolted. She could taste both Ike's semen and Rosa's vagina on it, and also some shit. In addition, because of the organ's odd shape, she had a nightmare anticipation of it biting her. Its pee hole looked too much like a mouth for comfort.

Rosa finally yanked Nell's head back.

She opened her eyes. The spindle-shaped cock now stood erect, flagpole proud.

Rosa shooed her with the pistol. "Back, back. Zis cock ees for me alone." She climbed up on Ike Dallas and once again squatted over him.

Nell began dreading life as a prostitute with Rosa running the brothel. The woman was an absolute monster.

"Ah yess, Señor Ike, you ees so good. Yes! Be grinding it slowly like zat." She reached back for his left hand and placed it on her chest. "Now, Señor, squeeze zis —"

Then Rosa froze. From pre-orgasm bliss, a look of confusion overtook her features. She looked back at Ike.

"What you ees doing to me, Señor?"

Rosa's look of confusion altered to one of pain. Her lips twisted in agony, her face became a mask of horror. She fought to separate from Ike, but couldn't, they'd somehow become fused together.

Nell looked at Ike. His eyes were glassy, focused on sights inside his head. Idiot drool dribbled from his mouth.

Rosa began screaming. Her belly swelled like she was having a baby, then it swelled more than that. Rosa's chest swelled too.

Her eyes became pools of terror. Blood began bubbling from her lips.

Nell backed away to the wall, her eyes riveted on the screaming Mexican prostitute. She felt her way along the wall till she reached the door. Still not taking her eyes off Rosa, Nell crouched and felt the floor by the door till she found her knife.

She held it in front of her the way Father Francisco, the Catholic priest, brandished the cross to ward off evil.

Nell was terrified by what was happening to Rosa. She nonetheless remained in the room, transfixed to the spot by her deSire to witness the conclusion of this erotic horror.

Proportionate to the distortions ravaging her body, Rosa was stretching between the legs also. First her vagina widened like she was birthing a child, then it ripped open completely.

Nell was horrified. Wriggling at the base of the now torso-sized penis were a pair of scaly legs ending in black claws.

With a loud shriek, Rosa died. She'd clung onto life this long by sheer force of habit.

The front of Rosa's corpse now opened up like it was being unbuttoned. Starting at her ripped vagina, her torso separated into two like she was being prepared for autopsy.

Nell whimpered with fright when she saw the huge rat head peering from the wreckage of Rosa's chest. Still firmly attached to Ike at his groin, the rat was ugly beyond belief. It was hairless, with pale varicose-vein-laden skin covered in mucus and slime like a newborn human baby.

Worse still, it was still growing. Expanding out of Rosa and into the wine cellar.

By stages, Rosa's corpse first looked like a cloak the rat-attachment was wearing, then a hood, then a rapidly shrinking hat.

Then, using a forepaw that looked like a grotesquely distorted human hand, Rattackus swiped Rosa's corpse off its head.

It ate her in three bites.

Muzzle stained with blood, the rat god now polished its whiskers and regarded Nell with its beady eyes.

Below the monster rat, Ike Dallas now lay lifeless. His eyes were leeched of humanity and emotion. His intelligence had transferred into the creature growing from him.

Nell unfroze. In gibbering horror, she turned and fled the room and the house. She had no real memory afterward of what route she'd taken to exit the building, nor of whom she'd encountered along its corridors. She just kept running, her terror of what was growing in the wine store was of a magnitude greater than her fear of violent, angry cowboys.

***

Inside the house, Rattackus continued growing. The rat god expanded till it filled the cellar, then the pressure of its expansion crumbled the cellar walls outward like the bricks were loaves of bread.

In the pandemonium that ensued, as the rat god burgeoned out of the west wing of the ranch house, many people died. Some, when portions of the house fell on them. Others were trampled by Rattackus. Yet others were eaten by the god.

***

Nell collected her wits about her again. She felt no pity for Rosa. The Mexican woman being dead simply meant Zizi's brothel was now Nell's.

Amidst the ensuing confusion Nell searched for Jude.

CHAPTER 20

A shot hit Jude in the heart.

He peered down and grimaced. It was worse than undignified to watch urine spewing from one's chest.

Cruelly ironic, he felt this pseudo-emotional proof of his being chained for life to Nell. Jude didn't love her — but with the way his heart was leaking her excretory waters, the pump apparently didn't share his lack of deep feeling for the woman.

Pissed-off by piss, Jude looked around for who'd shot him. He'd give the shithead what for.

There were rider-less horses all around now. Bloodied bodies lay in grass and dust. Most were dead. The few wounded clutched where they'd been shot and tried to crawl to the safety of the house.

A group of mounted ranch hands was clustered to Jude's left, near the stacked bales of hay. Another group was riding around the right side of the house toward him.

Jude decided whoever had shot him was among the group by the stacked bales.

He yanked his horse's reins hard left and galloped toward them.

234

He'd decided Nell was either dead, or — figuratively or literally — tied up. Either way, he couldn't hang around waiting for her.

He was now fighting for his life. He couldn't flee: if he rode away, the cowboys would pursue him and shoot him in the back.

Jude winced. The cowboys would just keep filling him with slugs till the sheer weight of the metal in his body dragged him to the ground.

Two things happened simultaneously then.

The side of the house Jude was riding toward began crumbling, and... his pistol jammed.

Jude flung the gun away and grabbed up the rifle. Gripping the horse's flanks with his thighs, he fired on the cowboys.

Then a third group of cowboys rode around the bales of hay.

Shit, Jude thought, I'm in TROUBLE.

He was seriously outgunned now.

"I ain't going down without a fight though." He gritted his teeth. "And I'm taking as many of you sons-of-bitches with me as I can."

Bullets slammed into him from front and back, till he was riddled with them. Bullets shattered his arms and legs. Jude bled endless streams of urine from his multiple punctures, till it seemed to him that his entire body was simply an extension of Nell's extraordinary bladder.

Jude collapsed forward on his horse.

With a whoop of victory the cowboys rode forward to claim Jude's body.

Then the west wing of ranch house exploded outward and Rattackus emerged into the light of day. Bricks, timber and house pillars flew through the air as though flung by God Almighty.

The victorious cowboys stared at the rat god in confusion. They began shooting at it.

Rattackus grabbed a horse and rider in a prehensile forepaw and stuffed both into its immense maw. Its whiskers snapped the

235

air like immense whips as it crunched the pair into mush, their blood streaming out through its teeth.

It swallowed, then grabbed another cowboy and horse.

The cowboys abandoned all intent of fighting Rattackus and scattered in terror.

Jude's white stallion sped through the confused cowboys toward the rear of the house, where it had just spied Nell emerge.

***

The horse halted beside Nell.

"Fix me, I've work to do," Jude said, and fell out of the saddle.

Nell quickly hitched up her skirts and began urinating on him.

Jude's horse watched her awhile, and then it began eating the flowers by the wall under the balcony.

***

Three minutes later, Jude was himself again.

The ground where he'd healed was now covered with bullets extruded from his body. His wounds were all patched up with the pee-flesh.

Jude contemplated a moment, wondering if it was possible for him to become so shot up that fixing him would make his entire body into urine-flesh. Humans were about seventy-five percent water — Jude was sure he was already about forty percent pee now.

Nell handed him his white pistol. She pointed over at Rattackus, now reared up on its rear legs and grabbing and eating the milling rider-less horses. It was growling loudly. "We've got a bigger problem than we came here to fix," she said.

Jude nodded grimly. "For sure. Do you know what it is?"

Nell's face blanched as she remembered her ordeal in the wine cellar. "It's Ike Dallas's penis. While he was fucking Rosa it started getting bigger and bigger and then it ate her."

She thought, and then added, "I've seen one like it before. That one emerged ten years ago from Mount Ass. That was the reason Zizi fled the ranch — it attacked the house and killed half her cowboys. Then it turned on the townsfolk of Little Ass. It killed a fifth of the people, including the sheriff. Then Edison got rid of it. He killed it. He said he'd used some veterinary poison.

"After that, Zizi didn't stand a chance of getting her ranch back. The ranchers and townspeople all turned a deaf ear when she protested. There was a suspicion... still is... that she'd been responsible for the monster's appearance."

"I can just imagine that," Jude said. Looking over at Rattackus, he could see a man-sized shape where the monster's genitals should be. "You're saying that's Ike dangling between the rat's legs?"

Nell nodded. "Yep." She grinned evilly. "I always knew Ike Dallas was a prick, but not that big a prick."

"Give me your knife," Jude told Nell.

She handed it over.

Jude ran out from the cover of the house to where a cowboy's corpse laid, his head full of a still-living porcupine.

He stomped the porcupine's head in to stop its squealing. Then he pulled both the cowboy's gloves off and hacked off all his fingers, excluding the thumbs.

He ran to another corpse and chopped off that dead man's fingers also.

Then he ran back to Nell's side. He broke open his white pistol and loaded fingers into it. He clicked the cylinder back into place in the gun and spun it once.

He whistled his horse over. When the horse came, he lifted its tail and gave its ass-lever a few cranks so it wouldn't break down on him.

237

He swung himself up into the saddle.

"Best you wait here," he told Nell. "This is real dangerous."

She shook her head emphatically. "Not me. I'm coming with you. Are you kidding, Jude? There is no way I'm leaving your side with that thing around."

She grinned. "Besides, you seem to need repairing a lot. You'll get nowhere without me."

Jude winced. This was much worse than marriage.

Then he nodded. He reached down and pulled Nell up into the saddle.

CHAPTER 21

When the ranch house began shaking, Edison forgot about buttoning up his fly and ran to the bedroom window to peer out.

He surveyed the ensuing carnage angrily.

"Your rat god is destroying our house," he told Valhalla testily. "I thought you had ways of containing the blasted rodent."

Valhalla rushed to the window also.

Together they watched the hairless monster emerge from the west wing of their home amidst building rubble.

Its head was the size of a wagon. Its twitching ears looked like brown sails fluttering in sea breeze. The varicose veins covering Rattackus's fat-laden form twitched as though each possessed an individual heart.

"Hell and damnation!" Valhalla swore. "I've made a mistake."

"What are talking about?"

Her facial expression was as earnest as her voice. "I thought you said Ike Dallas was outside the building."

"I never saw him downstairs. I'd assumed he was coordinating the cowboys, but they'd not seen him either. One of them even suggested he was dead." Edison squinted at the monster rat. Panic began building in him. Over the intervening years he'd forgotten how big the thing was — almost as large as the ranch house. "That,

238

however, is neither here nor there. What does Rattackus have to do with Ike Dallas?"

"Ike Dallas is its familiar. After we scared off Zizi, I had to store the rat god somewhere. Ike was the somewhere."

It took a moment for Edison to understand what she meant. The cowboys had found a dazed Ike wandering out on the range the week after Rattackus had driven Zizi off her ranch. Ike had had amnesia. He'd seemingly survived an Apache raid on a stagecoach headed north, and trekked his way onto their land.

Edison shook his head. "So that's why you didn't allow me to sack the drunken bum all this while?"

"Calm down, Edison," Valhalla said softly. "We can rebuild this house. All it will take is money, and we've an excess of that." She smiled thinly. "I overreacted just now — I was bothered about the antiques in the parlor — those we bought on our trip to France."

Edison nodded wearily. He looked out of the window. As though on cue, at that moment Jude rode into view.

"There he is," Valhalla said. Her expression turned icy when she saw Nell was riding pillion to Jude. "What is most important now is to kill this assassin."

"Yes," Edison agreed. "But so far he's proven atrociously hard to kill. And now the bastard has his pistol back."

"It will be little help against Rattackus. Though a mindless brute, Rattackus is a god after all."

She pointed. "And you have his rifle, Edison. He can't use it anymore."

Edison smiled wickedly. "But I can, mon Cherie."

Valhalla nodded. "It's my experience that most supernatural assassins are susceptible to being killed by their own weapons. Likely this one too."

"But your daughter — she's with him?"

She shrugged. "There's nothing I can do if Nell's so intent on committing suicide, is there? All she ever does is cause trouble."

Edison pulled a chair up to the window. He raised the carved wooden firearm to his shoulder and sighted along its barrel. "Order us up some coffee, will you, darling? I feel like having some target practice."

"I'm afraid you'll have to wait, Edison," came the reply. "Judging from where Rattackus emerged from, I'd say the kitchen is destroyed. Which means Consuela is dead for certain. Eaten maybe…"

Edison grunted in disgust. He hated missing his afternoon coffee. He leaned on the windowsill and aimed the wooden rifle at his galloping enemy.

***

Valhalla put herself into a trance. She concentrated, focused. Across a psychic bridge, she made connection with Rattackus's minute mind.

The connection was momentary, but she made the most of that moment.

Valhalla forced an image of Jude into Rattackus's mind, along with the knowledge that the man riding the white stallion was its hated enemy.

CHAPTER 22

Rattackus faced Jude across bloodstained grass. Either dead or fled, the EVB Ranch cowboys were nowhere in sight.

Jude spurred his horse and sped toward Rattackus.

"Are you sure this sort of direct attack is wise?" Nell asked. This close to the humongous rat, she questioned the wisdom of her accompanying Jude. It now seemed wiser to have agreed to watch their fight from safety.

"I need to find out how powerful this monster is," Jude replied.

Once in pistol range of the creature, he reined in his horse. The stallion reared up, hooves kicking the air.

Only by gripping Jude's waist with all her strength did Nell keep from being sent flying backward.

Jude emptied the white pistol's full cylinder at Rattackus.

They retreated a short distance and watched.

Five shark skeletons sprouted out of the rat god's left forelimb, the sixth out of its left flank. Because the creature was so huge, however, the effect that the embedded bones in its flesh had was similar to that of sticking a penknife in a human arm — painful, but with little actual damage done.

Rattackus ripped the skeletons out of its limb. It tossed them out of sight over the house.

"We'll need something MUCH more powerful to kill it," Nell said. "Even using up every dead cowboy finger we can find won't do more than slow it down."

Jude smiled as he noticed that Rattackus was now hobbling, favoring its pierced limb.

"I have something MUCH more powerful to hit it with," he said. "But first I need to slow it down more."

Jude reloaded his gun with fingers.

They rode hard at Rattackus again.

The creature reared up again, awaiting them.

***

"This should slow you down a little," Edison said, firing the wooden rifle.

***

Jude spurred his horse faster at Rattackus. Then, almost in range of the monster, he felt a hard impact to his left knee followed by a sharp sting. He yowled and looked down.

He winced on seeing the porcupine embedded in his knee.

He looked beyond Rattackus, quickly scanning the ranch house to see who had his gun. Edison waved back at him from an upstairs window.

Jude spat in anger. He shook his fist at Edison. Too bad the white revolver wouldn't shoot that far.

He reached down and broke the porcupine's neck to stop its squealing.

The offensive whine silenced, Jude returned his attention to his monstrous opponent. The momentary distraction of his attending to his porcupine wound however proved crucial.

"Watch out!" Nell screamed.

Jude, instinctively firing at Rattackus once he'd turned to face it again, saw the danger too late to avoid it.

Jude noted that all six finger-bullets had scored hits on Rattackus's slimy belly.

The rat god squealed its horrendous pain and lashed out in a defensive reflex.

Jude watched the huge paw sail closer and closer to him, its horny nails slicing the air like monster scythes. He swerved the horse to avoid the impending contact, and then ducked as the tips of Rattackus's flailing nails cleared the white stallion's head.

He didn't duck far enough.

The rat god's index claw ploughed a furrow through Jude's head, deep as a farmer preparing a field for sowing crops.

Jude's brains were ripped out of his head.

Nell had ducked lower than Jude. She hung so far over the horse's side that she was looking through its legs.

She looked up. Jude's brains were smeared on the rising rat-paw like semen on a whore's tongue. She vomited at the obscene sight.

Jude's eyes went dead. With his body jerking spasmodically, his horse skewed away from the huge rat, and charged toward the ranch house.

Rattackus licked Jude's brains off its paw.

Nell hauled herself back into her pillion position. Then she stood up on the running horse. Holding Jude's shoulders tight, she urinated into his shattered skull. Her pee was thick — an amber flow like she had a heavy fever.

Damn, she thought, I'm becoming dehydrated.

Jude's brain immediately reformed as a transparent yellow mass. His skull knit together over it. He took a moment to get his bearings, then wheeled his horse around and headed away from Rattackus.

"Damn I'm getting tired of this nonsense," he told Nell as they rode away. "I stink like a urinal."

"Just be thankful I'm riding along with you," she retorted. "I like the way you smell."

Jude didn't reply. He rode to a point two hundred meters from Rattackus and halted the horse. He helped Nell down.

"Time for our alternative approach," he said. "Consider that last attack our appetizer. It should keep big monster rat over there preoccupied long enough for me to get our entrée ready for it."

Nell looked at Rattackus and saw what he meant. The rat god sat on its haunches, licking its wounded forelimb and pondering the problem of how to remove the shark skeletons embedded in its belly without flooding itself with pain.

Nell was very amused by the sight of Ike Dallas flattened like a pancake under the creature's ass.

CHAPTER 23

Jude pushed his horse's tail aside. While simultaneously pressing hard on its last left rib, he furiously wound up its anal crank.

The most obvious result of Jude's cranking was that the horse got an erection.

"What are you doing?"

Jude didn't slow the circular motion. "You'll see shortly."

Rattackus growled in pain as it ripped a shark out of its belly. Its anger and pain rippled in waves to the nearby hills and back again.

Nell stole a nervous glance at it. She turned back to Jude. "I hope you're right about this, Jude," she said.

He saw she was looking embarrassed. "What's the matter?"

She pointed to her crotch. "I'm all out of pee. I can't fix you up again if you're wrong."

He nodded. "I also hope I'm not wrong."

Jude stopped winding up the horse.

Nell glanced between the horse's rear legs. The white stallion's erection throbbed angrily. Nell decided she'd hate to be the first mare the horse encountered now. It would likely ride her to death.

Jude had meanwhile walked around to the white stallion's head.

Nell watched him twisting its ears for a few moments. Then she heard a click inside the horse's head.

Gripping the horse's mane and pulling in opposite directions, Jude split the horse's neck open.

Rotating it on a bone hinge in its lower half, Jude swung the horse's head downward till it hung facing rear.

"This sure is one weird horse," Nell said. "I've never seen a horse you could open up before."

Rattackus screamed again. Nell looked over at it again. "That's the second skeleton ripped out," she told Jude. "Four to go."

"We're on schedule." He released a catch inside the horse's neck. With another click, a pitted metal tube slid up out of the horse's neck."

"That looks like a cannon muzzle," Nell said.

"It is. Now all we need is ammo." He latched the cannon securely into place between the horse's shoulders. The horse's dangling head neighed nervously at its erection.

Jude fed the horse's head an oatmeal cake. He patted its flanks to calm it.

Nell pointed to the neck-cannon. "What does it fire?"

"Legs."

"Legs?"

"Human legs."

Rattackus screamed twice in quick succession then, preventing Nell's confused question. Instead she said, "It just ripped out two skeletons at once. Only two left."

"We've a bit of a problem," Jude said. "No legs to fire."

Nell stared at him incredulously. "A bit of a problem. You fucking call that a bit of a problem?"

Rattackus screamed again. They both looked at the monster. Black goo poured out of the holes in its belly where it had torn the embedded fish bones out of its flesh. The gashes looked like vaginas with semen slurping out of them after copious ejaculation.

Rattackus stared back at them. Rage glittered in its beady black eyes. Nell shuddered. The creature's eyes were horizontal wells from which evil dripped.

"Only one more to go," Nell said. "How many legs do we need?"

"One," Jude said. "But it's eaten all the cowboys and their horses."

He noticed she was staring pointedly at him. "What?"

"Your legs. Take one of them off."

Jude looked over to where Rattackus sat. The creature was bracing itself for the final pain of removing the last shark skeleton. This one was embedded deep in its groin, just above its Ike Dallas genitals.

"Take one of your new legs off," Nell insisted. "I'll fit you with another later."

"How do I do that?"

She pulled her knife out of her girdle. "Don't worry. I'll do it for you."

Without waiting to see if he agreed or not, she sliced Jude's left trouser open at the hip and began sawing through the urine-flesh forming his left hip joint.

Despite forming a stronger bond than normal flesh, the pee-meat was easy to cut. Jude let her do it. He steeled himself against the pain. His thoughts were resolute.

Desperate moments demand desperate measures, he thought grimly.

CHAPTER 24

Your daughter's cutting off his leg dear," Edison said. "Strangest thing I've ever seen."

The combat field lay at a slight angle to the ranch house. Edison and Valhalla had an oblique view of the combatants. Rattackus's front parts were, however, hidden from them.

Valhalla stared at the surreal sight of Jude's horse with the cannon in its head and its head swinging between its legs watching its erection. Rattackus clearly had the upper hand in this scenario.

But still — she was filled with unease.

This was the disaster she'd seen occurring in the semen. But its nature remained as vague to her now as when the never-born — the testicle children — had shown her their transcribed version of the future.

Valhalla knew something was about to go wrong. She had no idea what it was.

"We must leave here, Edison," she said worriedly.

He looked at her in surprise. "Leave? But we've won. Once Rattackus attacks them — it's over."

"We haven't won, Edison. I saw this in the summoning. Something will go wrong."

"I don't see what possibly can go wrong, Val," Edison retorted with considerable warmth. Look — now that she's sliced his leg off, she's stuffing it into the weird tube in the horse's neck."

Valhalla glared at her daughter forcing Jude's leg into his horse's neck-cannon. Nell was having trouble getting the foot in past the ankle.

"Not a day goes by that I don't regret giving birth to her," she growled. She pulled on Edison's arm. "Let's go! I mean it, we're in danger!"

Edison shrugged her off. "Go yourself if you're frightened, darling. Wait downstairs for me. The view is excellent from here. Absolutely ringside." He was surprised by the terror in Valhalla's eyes. "Go on, Val. I'll be fine. You honestly don't think I'll flee the house with triumph so imminent, do you?"

Valhalla gave it one last try. "Edison, I know you think I'm being overly superstitious, but this is serious, you're in — "

Edison chortled with mirth. "Nonsense dear. Now I'm certain you're just trying to scare me."

A momentary warning flickered through Edison's mind — Valhalla's predictions did have that invariable trick of coming true. What if...

He shrugged off his worries. What could possibly go wrong? Nothing, he could see, except if the divine rodent turned on them. But he knew from experience that Valhalla was able to control Rattackus.

Across from them, Nell, after a hurried discussion with Jude, stopped forcing his foot into the horse's open neck. She left it hanging out of the cannon, sole facing toward the rat god.

Then she walked back over to Jude, and she and he began arguing over something.

Watching her daughter's heated argument with Jude, Valhalla suddenly felt ill. An overwhelming sense of urgency filled her. Her every psychic nerve screamed at her to flee.

Rattackus screamed loudly then. The sound hardened Valhalla's resolve to reach the safety of somewhere else. Anywhere else.

"Edison," she said calmly. "We really must go — "

His condescending smile infuriated her. "Edison, this is no time to be pigheaded."

Edison gave her a tight, controlled smile. "I intend watching this duel to the finish, dear. I'll meet you downstairs in five minutes. Rattackus must have dealt with this fool by then." He tapped the wood rifle meaningfully. "And if it hasn't, I'll see how our Jude holds up to an overdose of his own medicine."

Valhalla gave up trying to convince her husband. She quickly packed up her summoning disc, and then fled both the bedroom and the house.

CHAPTER 25

Nell looked at Jude. "Okay it's loaded, where's the trigger?"

Jude pointed to the horse's erection. "Yank back on that."

Nell looked at the horse's penis. Its glans now dribbled mucoid pre-cum.

She looked back at Jude and shook her head. "Oh no, not me. It's your horse."

"True, it is my horse," Jude replied, "but handling erections is your professional area of expertise."

"Human erections."

"A prick's a prick, and you're a prostitute."

Nell looked at him coolly, "Are you insinuating that I do bestiality, you son-of-a — "

"Nothing like that," he interrupted smoothly. "Handling penises is against my principles. It's why I've never used this weapon before."

Nell goggled at him. "Never?"

He nodded.

"Never? And you're gambling our lives on it?"

Jude sighed. "The woman who gave it to me assured me on her life that it would work." He smiled. "Darling, I suggest you yank that penis right now."

Jude's self-assured smile infuriated Nell. "What the hell?"

"Nell dearest, I'm looking at the rat monster over your shoulder, while you're looking angrily at me. Pull the fucking penis back."

"No, I will fuc —"

Rattackus screamed, louder than it had before. Nell felt a fear so primal at the sound that she almost pooped herself.

"Last set of shark bones out of it," Jude said coolly. "Certain death is now headed our way."

Nell turned. It was true. Rattackus was now back on all four limbs and bounding toward them. Its mouth gaped open, its horrible gleaming eyes reflected its clear intent of eating the two humans and their horse.

"It's very stupid, endlessly coming back for more," Jude said. "What if I simply give it another dose of fish bones?"

Rattackus was now close enough for Nell to see down its throat. And it was fast closing the intervening distance.

She looked back at Jude.

He shook his head. "I assure you — I would rather die than handle that horse's member."

Nell decided 'what the hell?' She wasn't about to die just because Jude was scared of being thought of as queer. She grabbed the horse's penis and yanked it back.

The immediate result was anti-climactic after the emotive build up. With a soft 'pop,' Jude's leg ejected from the horse-neck cannon and sailed through the air at the approaching rat god.

Rattackus seemed unstoppable. The projectile speeding toward it appeared pathetically inadequate to halt its murderous intent.

Jude's leg hit Rattackus flush in the chest. There was a moment of silence — as when angels walk through a room — then Rattackus began screaming.

It screamed so loud that both Jude and Nell covered their ears.

Huge bones were forcing their bloody way out of the rat god's body. Bones the size of a ship's framework.

Rattackus lurched right and left desperately as the strange skeleton inside its body punctured a multitude of pathways out of its flesh, ripping it apart.

It turned and ran toward the ranch house. Half way there it stopped running. By now, two row of bones dwarfing even its own immensity for humongousness projected from its sides. Viscid black blood streamed down its body, bubbling in tar-like pools wherever it plopped on the ground.

"It's almost dead," Jude said, hopping in front of his horse for an uninterrupted view. "Just one more thing."

The 'thing' occurred.

Rattackus's head exploded and twenty feet of vertebral bone ejected from it. Topping this spinal column was a fish-like head.

The biggest head either Jude or Nell had ever seen in their lives.

CHAPTER 26

Edison Bennett stared in disbelief at the monster head that had just erupted from Rattackus's head.

He was a vet, so he only had to see the festering blowhole on top of the rotting skull and its baleen-grimace of a mouth to recognize it as a blue whale's head.

Edison momentarily forgot that the whale's appearance was the culmination of a life and death struggle with himself as the star prize. He wondered how what he was witnessing was even possible.

Then Edison noted that Rattackus's body — impaled by whale ribs and deceased — was tottering.

For a seemingly endless moment, the rat god's headless form stood outlined against the afternoon sky, supported on a tripod of its rear legs and the whale's tail skeleton. Then the sea dweller's tail bones separated under the burden they were never designed to bear and Rattackus toppled over.

It fell slow as a landing balloon.

In horror, Edison realized that it was falling onto the ranch house's front. It was falling directly at him.

Edison flung Jude's rifle out of the window and turned to flee. He'd only taken two steps when the rat god's whale pierced carcass crashed into the bedroom.

The crash totally demolished the house frontage. Edison Bennett was crushed to a pulp of meat so mangled between whale bone and rubble that it was unrecognizable as once having been a human being.

Valhalla Swede's semen witching had proven right once again.

CHAPTER 27

Jude and Nell made their way around the ranch house wreckage. Jude, unable to walk with a missing leg, sat on his once-again-normal horse. He fed the animal sugar cubes to keep it happy.

(He was certain it had found being opened up [and used as a weapon] a distressing experience.)

"I need to find father," Nell told Jude.

Jude too, wondered what had become of Doc after he'd entered the ranch house.

"I need to find my rifle," he said. He reloaded his white pistol and kept it in his lap in case of trouble.

Rattackus's bulk lay through the middle of the house. "With all these bones sticking out, it looks like a rotting ship," Nell said. She mused. "What is it, Jude?"

"A whale's skeleton," he replied. "These Comanche weapons sure are effective."

He pointed. "There's my rifle."

Nell dug the weapon out of the rubble. She also found the bag of teeth bullets. She handed both up to him.

251

"Thanks." He dusted the rifle off and stuck it into its saddle holster.

***

Nell pointed. "There's Ike."

Jude and Nell went over to look at him.

Between Rattackus's rear legs, Ike Dallas lay bloodied. Rattackus had crashed down onto its front, so Ike was positioned looking up at them.

Ike's head was pillowed on a monster green turd. The turd had bones in it.

Nell found the sheer immenseness of Rattackus's backside staggering. The huge veins on its buttocks looked like a network of plumbing and ladders. "It's like a meat house," she told Jude. "Its anus looks like a door to somewhere."

Nell worried that the huge rear opening would inundate them in excrement at any moment.

Ike Dallas was still alive, but fading fast. Even attached to Rattackus like he was, with his fused legs forming its penis and the rest of him its scrotum, Jude and Nell didn't think Ike should be bent double like now, with his feet right behind his head.

"His back's broken," Nell whispered to Jude. "Serves the prick right."

Ike nodded at them. His face was stony. His eyes asked for no sympathy.

Jude nodded back. He felt a grudging respect for the man. Ike Dallas was hard as a chisel to the end.

"Hey, freak," Ike said to Nell. "You and your new boyfriend won."

"Ike," Nell said patiently. "Stop calling me a freak. Show some fucking solidarity. We're both freaks."

Ike spat angrily. "Yeah, that we are." He spat again. "I hate being in the same category as you, Nell."

252

He looked at Jude. "See you in Hell, Jude. You're all shot up. Looks like you'll be joining me there shortly."

Jude shook his head. "That'll be a long, long, time from now, Ike." He nodded at Nell. "You see, Ike, Nell here is my longevity assurance policy. It's sort of like life insurance, only it works while you're still alive, not after."

"What the hell you talking about?"

"Her pee's magic — fixes you up."

Nell grinned nastily at Ike. "Too bad you weren't nicer to me, you prick."

Now he was dying, Ike's memory was foggy. Still, he remembered Nell peeing on Jude after he'd shot him up back at Zizi's.

He scowled. "She wets the bed too? I guess even bladder incontinence has its uses."

"Just admit he's smarter than you," Nell said angrily. "I'll fix you too if you ask me nicely."

Ike Dallas scowled. "Screw you, Nell, there's no way under God's blue sky I'm ever begging you or anyone else to pee on me." He suppressed a groan of pain. "Okay, fucking get lost, both of you," he said. "I want to die in peace."

"Want a cigar?" Jude asked.

Ike nodded.

Jude got one from the horse's saddle. He lit it and gave it to Nell. She handed it to Ike.

Ike took a puff. "Thanks."

Jude turned the horse away.

"Did you see my father?" Nell asked Ike.

"Doc? Nah, I didn't even know he was on the ranch. You have any idea what happened to Rosa?"

Nell gaped at him. "You don't remember?"

Ike shook his head. He thought awhile, and then gave up. "Waste of time trying to recall things anyway when you're dying."

He waved Nell away. "Now get after Jude. Go on, Nell, git — leave me alone. I've got me maybe ten more minutes of living, and I want to enjoy this cigar."

He resumed smoking, cold eyes focused somewhere in the sky.

Nell left Ike Dallas to die in peace. She ran to catch up with Jude.

***

Jude was looking over the demolished building when Nell reached him. "I sure hope Doc didn't get buried in this mess."

Nell looked horrified. "You're not suggesting —"

"I'm just hoping. He went in, but doesn't appear to have come out again."

"Neither did mother, either," Nell said, pleased.

Valhalla Swede walked into view just then.

Jude noticed her first. "That's your mother, I presume. She's quite good-looking — looks like you."

Nell looked over at Valhalla and spat. "Speak of the devil's sister." She calmed, her worry for Doc overriding her dislike. "Have you seen father, mother?"

"You tried to kill me, you little tramp," Valhalla replied, her expression aloft and cold.

Jude turned to stare at Nell. "You did?"

She shrugged. "I obviously didn't succeed. I need more practice — I've never tried to murder anyone before."

Valhalla looked coldly at Jude. "You killed my darling Edison, you dumb prick."

Jude couldn't think of a reply. Now the deed was done, everything seemed to have been for nothing.

Nell rescued the moment from becoming more awkward than it already was. "Is father dead, mother?"

Valhalla turned from glaring at Jude to look at her daughter.

"He isn't dead, Nell," she said. "He's here with me.

Nell looked suspiciously at her. That didn't sound right. "Mother, what are you talking about?"

"He's with me," Valhalla repeated. "Forever."

She ripped open her bodice, so the pair could see what she meant.

Nell was horrified. Jude was stupefied.

Valhalla's entire left breast was now Doc's head.

The breast-head clearly lacked intelligence. Its eyes rolled idiotically, its mouth blabbered silently, and its lolling tongue slobbered spittle everywhere.

Nell froze in shock. Horror rolled over her like shower water. Urine filled her empty bladder and forced its way out.

Jude quickly got out his water bottle and stuck it under her. No point wasting my life's blood, he thought.

"What the hell did you do to him?" Nell screamed. Echoes of her horror ricocheted back at them.

"He sacrificed himself so I could live, daughter."

"You killed him? Wasn't abandoning us both enough?"

Valhalla's eyes narrowed to slits. "Don't get melodramatic, Nell."

Nell grabbed Jude's white pistol from his lap and pointed it at Valhalla.

"You're going to die too, mother," she said. "For good, this time."

Valhalla's eyes became unsure. "You wouldn't dare."

For a moment Nell was herself unsure. But then she stared at Doc's face gaping idiotically in Valhalla's breast, his eyes staring in different directions, his dribbling mouth muttering garbled nonsenses. The horrid sight crystallized her resolve.

"Try me, mother," she said.

She shot Valhalla.

There was that moment when nothing happened. Then a mass of shark spikes exploded out through Valhalla Swede Bennett's body.

Valhalla gurgled and collapsed.

Nell's eyes were expressionless pools, their surfaces reflecting neither pleasure nor distress at the act of murder she'd just carried out. She looked down at her mother.

Amazingly, Valhalla was still alive. Blood burbled over her lips and her body twitched like an epileptic's. Her eyes spoke horrors unspeakable.

Doc was finally dead. A shark quill had exited directly through the center of his eyes.

Nell finally smiled. "Goodbye daddy," she whispered to the breast-head.

Valhalla's lips moved. "Ple... ple... ple..."

Nell shook her head.

"Not this time, mother. You're slipperier than an eel. I'd like to see you wriggle your way out of this." She extended a hand to Jude. "Your rifle. Fucking load it."

He got the wooden rifle from its holster, loaded it with teeth and handed it to her.

Nell shot Valhalla in the face. Then after the porcupine had exploded into her head, she shot her in what remained of her face again. Then she shot her all over her body, leaving untouched only the left breast housing Doc's dead head.

She fired and fired.

"For heaven's sake — stop shooting!" Jude finally growled at her. "She's been dead since you shot her in the head that first time. I can't stand the squealing of those damn porcupines."

Nell surfaced from the trance state she'd lapsed into. She gazed at Valhalla's spike body in awe.

"Now you're really dead, mother," she said dully.

Her tension broke. Relief flooded her. The enormity of what she'd done settled on her and she began sobbing. She ran to Jude and wrapped her arms around his waist.

***

"We need to bury them," Jude said. "The buzzards will get them if we leave them like this."

"Let them rot together," Nell said. She was once again seated behind Jude. "Let the vultures eat both of them. I don't want mother pulling another of her escape acts."

She rested her chin on Jude's shoulder and giggled. "C'mon darlin', let's get back to town. I got me a fuckin' brothel to run."

Jude turned the white stallion toward Little Ass, and they galloped off.

Coda

The buzzards descended on the EVB Ranch to feed. They were hungry and came in their droves. When night fell, the birds departed and the coyotes took over eating.

There was a lot of food. The scavenging animals paid most attention to Rattackus's immense carcass, but several of the smaller ones, unable to get bites of the main prize, foraged and ate the dead cowboys lying around the house.

A pack of juvenile coyotes faced the task of disposing of Valhalla Swede Bennett's remains.

The creatures didn't enjoy eating her. The porcupines punctuating Valhalla's flesh couldn't be bitten through. The coyotes had to settle for what little unpunctured meat existed between the spiky mammals.

The only part of Valhalla's destroyed corpse that the young prairie wolves did enjoy eating was Doc's head — her left breast. The head was tasty and meaty and despite its appearance of solidity, boneless, lacking even teeth.

The coyotes quickly ate it off her body, leaving a gaping hole in her chest. Then it occurred to them that they could gain access to Valhalla's innards by pulling her body apart limb from limb.

While they worked at separating her flesh, transparent goo seeped out of Valhalla's corpse. The goo had been slowly exiting her body since she'd dropped dead. The last of the goo seeped out when the coyotes ripped her porcupine-studded corpse apart.

This goo, Valhalla Swede Bennett's essence, slid out from beneath the corpse's torso. It slithered snakelike amongst the feeding coyotes till it found what it sought — a young female just on the brink of adulthood.

The girl-wolf was oblivious to the strange substance pooling beneath her rear region.

Valhalla's goo coiled like a snake, then it struck upward, piercing straight into the coyote's vagina. The coyote stood paralyzed while all of the goo disappeared into her sex.

Then, she began transforming.

She stood up on her rear legs like a human, and began growing taller. As she grew, so did her upper body alter also, becoming that of a human woman.

Finally, Valhalla Swede Bennett was herself again.

She smiled down at the prairie wolves ripping her erstwhile body to shreds. She tickled one or two behind the ears, while they rubbed themselves happily against her legs.

Of course, the coyotes made no attempts to attack her. She was one of them.

The End.

OTHER GREAT TITLES FROM

www.BurningBulbPublishing.com

THE
BIG
BOOK
OF
BIZARRO

JAM PACKED
OVER
50
WEIRD TALES

EDITED BY
RICH BOTTLES JR. AND GARY LEE VINCENT

WARNING:
The Big Book of Bizarro may be one
of the most controversial and dangerous books you'll
ever read.

The Big Book of Bizarro brings together the
peculiar prose of an international cast of
the most grotesquely-gonzo, genre-grinding
modern writers who ever put pen to paper
(or mouse to pad), including:

NIGHT OF THE LIVING DEAD horror writers
John Russo & George Kosana

HUSTLER MAGAZINE erotica contributors
Eva Hore & Andrée Lachapelle, and

Established Bizarro genre authors
D. Harlan Wilson, William Pauley III,
Laird Long, Richard Godwin and
so many more!

From Alien abductions to Zombie sex,
The Big Book of Bizarro contains
OVER FIFTY STORIES of the

most outrélandish transgressive fiction

that you'll ever lay your capricious

and curious hands upon!

www.BigBookofBizarro.com
www.BurningBulbPublishing.com

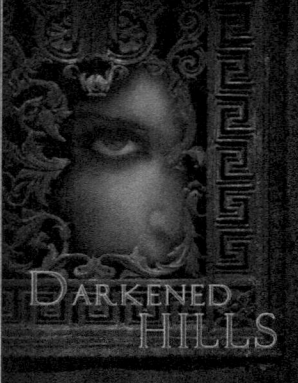
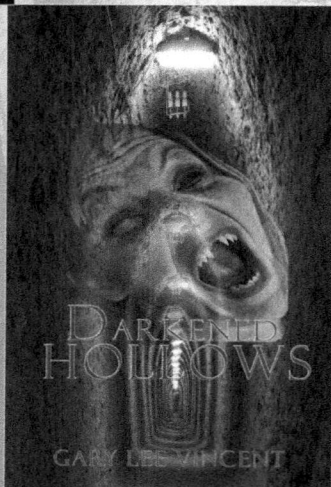

DARKENED HILLS

When evil descends on a small West Virginia town, who will survive? Jonathan did not start out his life to become a rambler, it just worked out that way. William was a troubled youth with something to hide. Both were from Melas, a small town tucked away in the West Virginia hills... a town where disappearances are happening more and more frequently.

After the suicide of a wanted serial killer, the townsfolk thought the nightmare was over. But when a centuries-old vampire is discovered they find out the hard way it's just getting started. Dark secrets can only stay hidden for so long and when the devil comes to collect, there will be hell to pay. Can Jonathan and William find a way to stop the vampire before it's too late? Find out in *Darkened Hills!*

DARKENED HOLLOWS

In the heart-stopping sequel to the award-winning *Darkened Hills*, Jonathan and William must return to West Virginia to face possible criminal charges stemming from their last visit to the damned town of Melas, where both had narrowly escaped the clutches of a vampire seethe.

And as livestock start mysteriously getting murdered with all of their blood drained, worried farmers are searching for answers - leaving the local Sheriff and his deputy racing against time to learn the cause before a more violent crime is committed.

DARKENED WATERS

When the world goes to hell, the chosen must arise!
As Talman Cane orchestrates a flood of epic proportions in this third installment of the *Darkened* series the towns of Melas and Tarklin are caught completely off guard by the deluge. Hell-bent on finishing what they started, the evil brothers return to the lunatic asylum to take care of the witnesses and add to the ever-growing army of the undead.

Aided by Lucifer himself and the insane vampire demon Legion, the stage is set to channel all of the forces of hell to come forth. In an all-out race to survive, Jonathan, William, and Amanda soon discover they are up against impossible odds as Lucifer opens the Gateway to Hell, ushering in the zombie apocalypse and the End Times.

Find out who will survive this cosmic battle of the ages in Darkened Waters!

COMING SOON: DARKEND SOULS!

Available at
amazon.com

Burning Bulb

RICH BOTTLES JR.

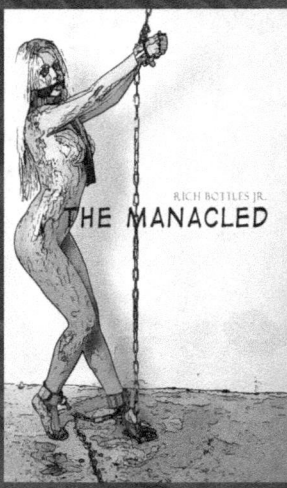

WEST VIRGINIA HUMORROROTICA

LUMBERJACKED

If you are easily offended or do not possess a truly depraved sense of humor, this story may not be the light summer reading fare you desire.

As for the four feisty female freshmen stranded on top of West Virginia's third highest mountain, they have no choice but to experience the sick, twisted debauchery and perverted mayhem described deep inside the tight unbroken bindings of this horrific missive. *Lumberjacked* takes the reader to a nightmarish world where character development and aesthetic integrity are prematurely cut short by the swinging axes of maniacal lumberjacks, who are hell bent on death and destruction in the remote forests of Appalachia. And at the climax, when paranoia crosses over to the paranormal, Lumberjacked makes Deliverance look like a family raft trip down the Lower Gauley.

HELLHOLE WEST VIRGINIA

From the heights of Mothman's perch high atop the Silver Bridge in Point Pleasant to the depths of Hellhole Cavern in Pendleton County, evil lurks within the shadows as the sun sets upon the haunted hills and hollows of West Virginia. Bizarro author Rich Bottles Jr. blows the coffin lid off horror genre clichés with this tour de force cast of Eco-friendly vampires, beach-yearning zombies and sex-starved she-devils.

THE MANACLED

What happens when twin brothers lease out the former West Virginia State Penitentiary with the false purpose of filming a documentary on supernatural phenomena, but their true intention is to make a pornographic movie? Chaos ensues as the disturbed spirits of murdered convicts, along with the reanimated dead from the neighboring Indian Burial Mound, take their vengeance on the unwary and undressed trespassers. Zombies, ghosts, mobsters and porn collide in this bizarro tale from horror author Rich Bottles Jr.

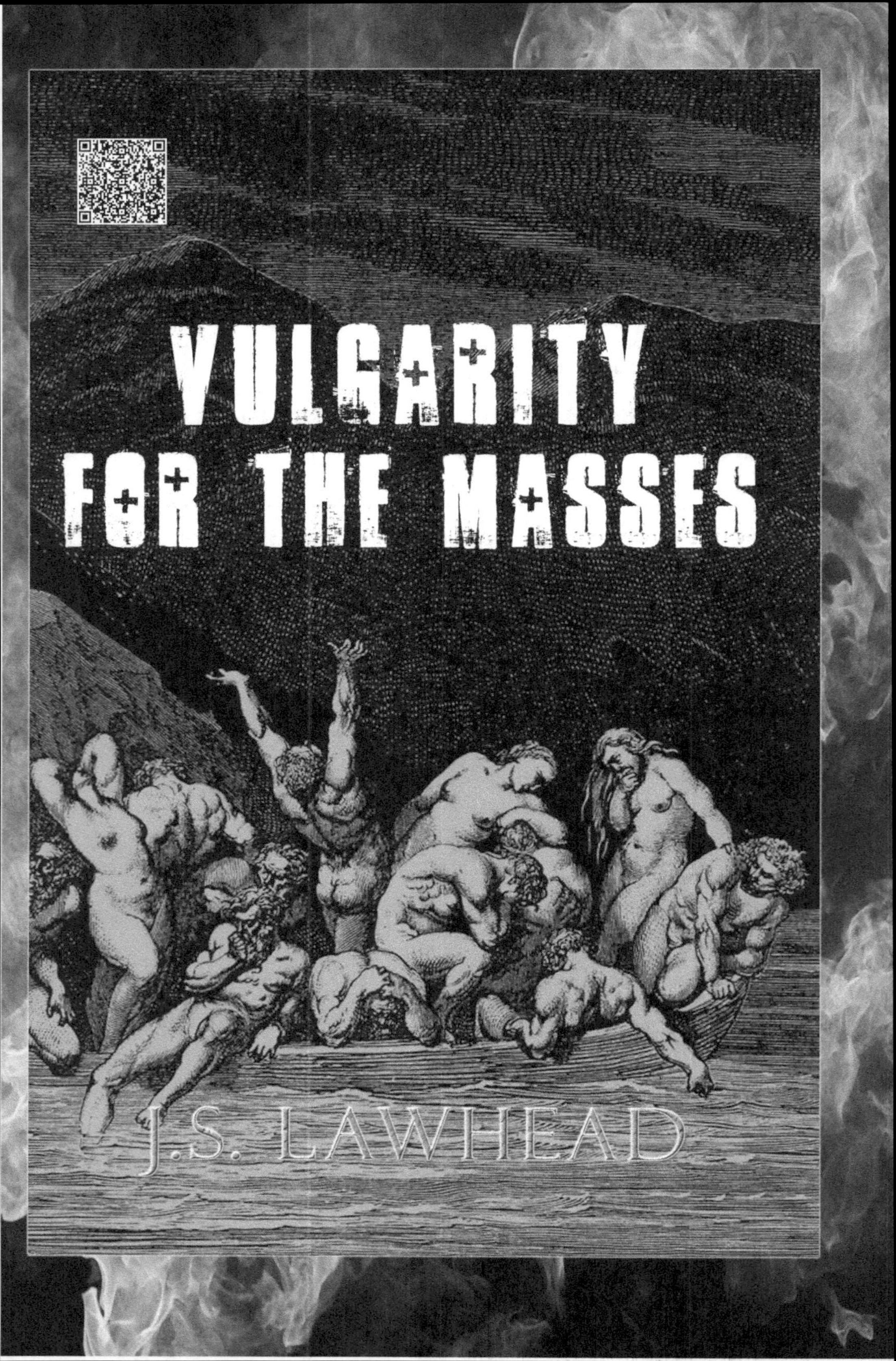

VULGARITY
FOR THE MASSES

J.S. LAWHEAD

Minor Confessions
of an Angel Falling Upward

Planner Forthright
As Edited By Joey Madia

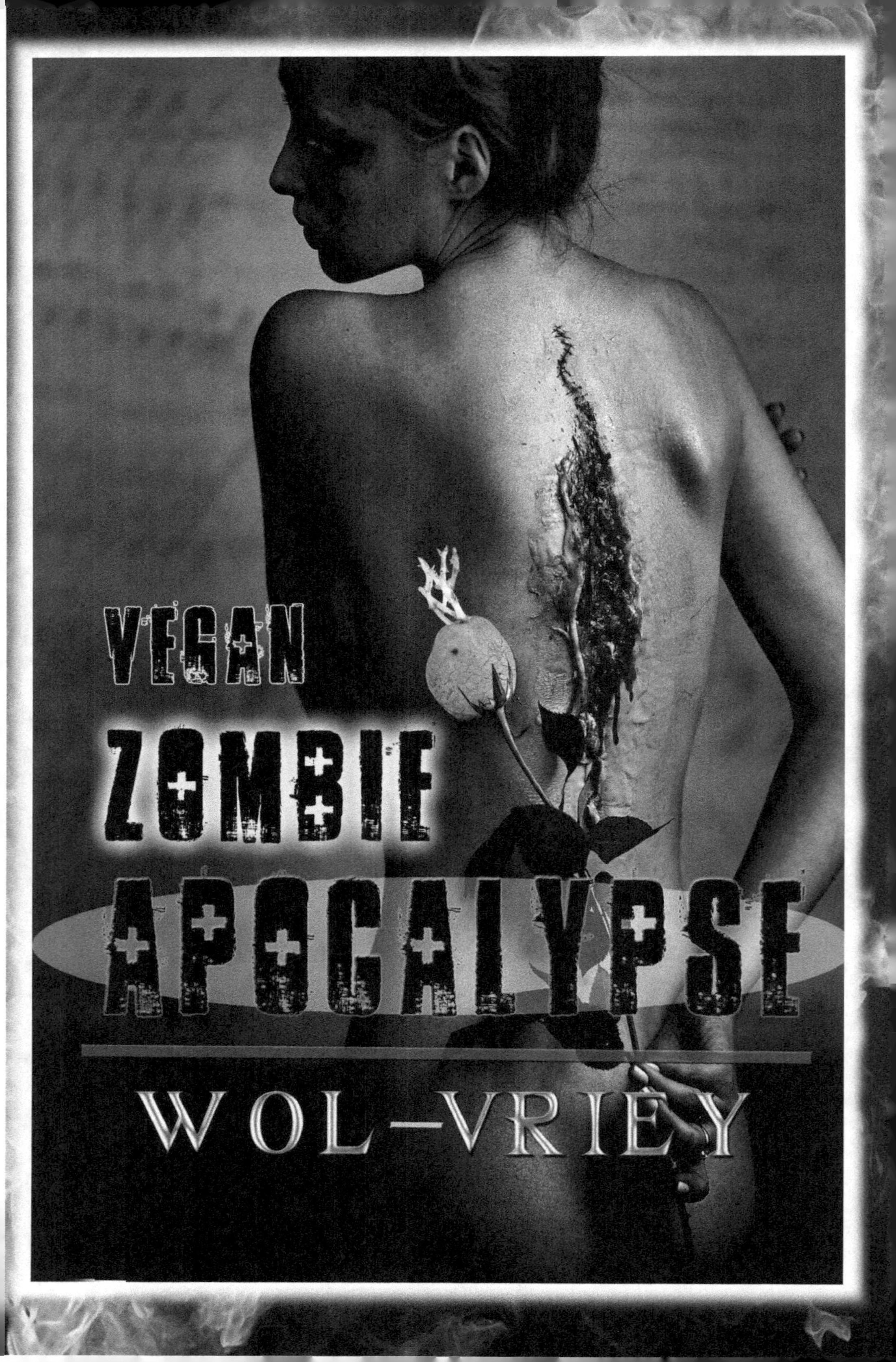
VEGAN
ZOMBIE
APOCALYPSE
WOL-VRIEY